DUTCH TREATS

CRIME FICTION BY DUTCH AND FLEMISH AUTHORS

Edited by

JOSH PACHTER

Genius
Book Publishing

Dutch Treats: Crime Fiction by Dutch and Flemish Authors
Copyright © 2025 Josh Pachter

Published by:
Genius Book Publishing
PO Box 250380
Milwaukee Wisconsin 53225 USA
GeniusBookPublishing.com

ISBN: 978-1-958727-13-3

250901 Trade

CONTENTS

INTRODUCTION

BY JOSH PACHTER

In 2003, *Ellery Queen's Mystery Magazine* editor Janet Hutchings asked me to find a story by a Dutch author for EQMM's new "Passport to Crime" department, which featured a translated tale in every monthly issue. I'd been writing my own fiction for the magazine since the late 1960s, and after living in Amsterdam in the early '80s and learning the language, I'd been translating comic books and nonfiction and occasionally fiction for some time, so I was happy to oblige.

Over the next eight years, I contributed several more translations of stories by Dutch authors to "Passport," and in 2011 Janet asked if I might be able to provide her with something by a writer who came from a country *other* than Holland. I'd learned by then that about forty percent of the population of Belgium, The Netherlands' next-door neighbor, speak French, while sixty percent speak Flemish, which is similar to but not the same as Dutch. And since sixty percent of Belgium's population amounts to a mere six million people, while there are some *sixteen* million people in The Netherlands (plus another million or so Dutch speakers in North and South America and the Caribbean), most Flemish writers *write* in Dutch, which significantly increases the potential market for their work. So I began translating stories by Flemish crime writers for "Passport," too.

Since Janet's original invitation in 2003, I've translated several dozen stories by Dutch and Flemish authors for EQMM—and along the way I've also translated two for its sister publication *Alfred Hitchcock's Mystery Magazine*, three for Martin Edwards' anthology *Foreign Bodies*, two for Maxim Jakubowski's anthology *The World's Best Crime Stories*, one for my own *Friend of the Devil: Crime Fiction Inspired by the Songs of the Grateful Dead* anthology, one each for *Black Cat Mystery Magazine* and the Canadian *Mystery Magazine*, and an even dozen for Akashic Books' *Amsterdam Noir*, which I co-edited with my good friend René Appel.

I've been reading crime fiction in translation for decades and, for whatever it's worth, I think that the stuff coming out of The Netherlands and Flanders (the Flemish part of Belgium) is as good as anything being produced anywhere in the world, so it's my pleasure to collect for you in this book a sampling of the stories I've translated.

Most of what you'll find here originally appeared in EQMM, although I've also included three stories from *Amsterdam Noir*, the two from AHMM, and the ones from BCMM and *Friend of the Devil*.

If you like them and want to read more by Dutch and Flemish authors—and I think and hope you will!—some of the authors represented here have novels available in English, some translated by me and some by other translators. I particularly recommend René Appel's *The Amsterdam Lawyer* (Genius Book Publishing), Bavo Dhooge's *Styx* (Simon & Schuster) and *Santa Monica* (independently published as by "Bo Dodge"), Hilde Vandermeeren's

The Scorpion's Head (Pushkin Press), and Bram Dehouck's *Sleepless Summer* (World Editions). For a taste of Dutch short stories translated by me and by authors *not* included here, I encourage you to try *Amsterdam Noir*. And if you aren't already familiar with the works of Janwillem van de Wetering, Nicolas Freeling, and Robert van Gulik, you should be! Van de Wetering's Grijpstra and De Gier series, Freeling's Van der Valk series, and Van Gulik's Judge Dee series have all been well known for many years—and all are deserving of the acclaim they've earned.

One brief note about capitalization: The Dutch don't capitalize "van" when it's part of a last name, as in Mensje van Keulen, while the Flemish do, as in Bob Van Laerhoven. Even the Dutch capitalize the v, though, when the first name is omitted, as in "Van Keulen's work has won many literary prizes." Now you know!

In America, a "Dutch treat" is a date or other outing where all participants pay their own way. (Ironically, the closest equivalent in the Dutch language would be an *Amerikaanse feestje*, which translates literally as "American party." We'd call it a potluck supper, where each guest brings something for everyone to share.)

If you'll forgive the linguistically mixed metaphor, what follows is a smorgasbord of Dutch treats, some written by Dutch writers, some by Belgians, but all of them originally written in the Dutch *language* and each of them a treat for lovers of quality crime fiction.

Eet smakelijk! Or, to translate that into English, *bon appétit!*

No, wait, that isn't English.

Ah, you know what I mean....

Josh Pachter
Midlothian, Virginia
August 2025

1

JOYRIDE

BY RENÉ APPEL

Hans glances quickly to his right. Angela sits slumped beside him. She's pulled the seatbelt across her breasts but hasn't buckled it. It's pointless to insist. *What difference does it make?* She'd say something like that. *You planning to have an accident?* She does things her own way, he's known that for some time. "An independent woman," they said. Some substituted the word "bitch." Whatever they called her, they all agreed that, since her election as mayor, things have gone lots better than under Vermalen, the stuffy old Christian Democratic Appeal hack who occupied the mayoral throne for the previous several decades. He was lily-white and pure, Vermalen, but also bland and boring. Angela's party was the Liberal Democrats, and her gender causes many to mistrust her. They say she's all show and no substance—and she certainly does put on a good show. But within six months of her election she's made herself so popular that even the CDA's chairman seems eager to get in her good graces, instead of playing his usual opposition-party games.

And now, just like that, she's sitting in his car. She kicks off her stylish heels and raises her feet to the dash, showing off her long, shapely legs to their best advantage. It's hard for Hans to resist running his palm along the sprinkling of freckles that make her tanned flesh even more attractive.

My God, what a gorgeous woman! The top button of her blouse is undone. The reception at City Hall lasted longer than he'd expected, and they'd bumped into each other in the parking lot as if by pre-arrangement. They'd chatted briefly. Ordinary, innocuous chitchat, you know? The new sports fields, the office complex his company is building, the expansion plan for Stavingerveld. Maybe there'd be gossip about the two of them, but his business recently landed a couple of major contracts with the city, and naturally they have to talk them over from time to time.

He knows he's had too much to drink and shouldn't be driving. Four glasses of wine—or was it five? As they stood there in the parking lot, stalling off the moment they'd have to go their separate ways, she took her cell from her purse. "I have to call a cab," she said. "I'd better not drive. If the mayor gets stopped for a DWI—"

She looked at him, with an expression... well, an expression that stirred thoughts he really shouldn't be thinking about the mayor.

"—she loses her influence," Angela went on. "Her political influence."

"Can I give you a lift?" he suggested.

She laid a hand on his arm. "Okay."

As if he knew exactly what was going to happen, he called Marjon, but she didn't pick up. He left a message: "I'll be late. I'm stopping off at Ariejan's." He'd better remember to warn Ariejan. He was home alone tonight, guaranteed. He was always home alone since Hanneke died. *Sad. Don't think about it now.* Angela had already mentioned that Hugo was spending a long weekend in the Ardennes, biking with a few friends, and that her son wouldn't be home until late. Interesting that she'd brought all that up....

He looks at her again, just as she turns toward him. Their eyes lock.

"The next right?" he says.

"Yes, and then the second left. So you know where I live?"

"Sure, the mayor's residence. We built it for Vermalen, fifteen years ago."

"You know, I don't really feel like going home," she says, before they reach the turn. "It's so warm."

It is indeed unseasonably warm for the time of year, humid, has been for more than a week. The heat gets into your head, into your body. In town, the men are all in shorts, the women in loose-fitting sundresses. *The silent killer.* He'd read a newspaper article about the danger the heat wave posed for seniors, and that's what they called it.

They pass a young lady on a bike wearing only short-shorts and a bikini top.

"Really *so* warm," says Angela again.

He nods. This is a direct invitation. A dare. She's had enough to drink that she won't drive, but this she'll do. Is she serious? Is she saying that she wants to have sex with him? The thought of it makes his blood race.

"Let's go to the beach. It'll be wonderful!"

"You want to swim?" he asks.

"Maybe."

The moon dimly illuminates the entrance to a small, dark parking area. All the beachgoers are long gone. A child's bicycle has been left behind, but there are no other cars. It's quiet, peaceful. He glances at his watch. Eleven fifteen.

"You need to get home?" Angela's voice is ironic. "Past your bedtime?"

He clears his throat. "No... I'm fine... absolutely."

She rests her hand on his thigh. He can feel the electricity course up and down his whole body and concentrate in his groinal region. She looks down there and must see that he's aroused. He tries to gather his scattered wits. Alone with Angela... an incredible specimen of womanhood. This can't be happening. He can't *let* it happen. But his body disagrees with his mind, and he can't resist. He unbuckles his seat belt and leans toward her. He seems to be on cruise control. He tastes the sweetness of her mouth. She pulls away for just a moment and eyes him greedily. A long soul kiss follows. Their tongues meet in wet heat. More, longer, he gasps, cups her breast in his hand, slips his fingers inside her bra, feels her nipple harden, caresses it gently. She moans.

And then she pulls away.

Dammit. Too much, too soon.

He's ruined it. He can see those city contracts dissolve into nothingness.

Then she gets out of the car. Stands there for a moment, walks around to his side and jerks open the door. A hot kiss, even hotter than before.

"Are you coming?"

Without waiting for an answer, she pulls him out of the car and runs ahead of him toward the sea. He follows her, almost stumbles but manages to keep himself on his feet. She vanishes down the narrow beach path. He gains on her, although he thinks she could run faster if she wanted to. She might break away and outpace him later, just to tease him. He tries to grab her arm. She falls—accidentally on purpose—and pulls him with her. He winds up on top of her. No thoughts of possible witnesses enter his mind.

No thoughts whatsoever, just lust, a wild animal greed that completely consumes him.

They walk hand in hand along the path. They could walk like this for hours. The party at the school was crap, with all those people, all their fellow students. Why should they hang out with that bunch, when all they want is to be alone? It's a little after midnight. Except for the song of a couple of noisy crickets, it's utterly quiet. No people, no sound. Well, sure, a rustling in the distance, as if some bunny or other little animal is hurrying away from their footsteps through the underbrush. The full moon lights their way, sometimes peeking out from behind a passing cloud, bathing the scene in a strange, almost unreal glow and casting sharp shadows, as if they're moving through the landscape of a video game.

Fedor comes to a stop, draws Bente toward him and kisses her. She runs her hands through his hair.

"I really like you," she whispers.

"How much is 'really'?"

"I'm not telling." Sometimes she can be a real tease—he loves that about her.

They kiss again. He touches the curve of her hip, slips a hand beneath her top and strokes her back. Tonight, he knows, this sultry night could be the night it happens. The first time. Him and Bente. Without saying a word, he knows that that's why they're walking here, hundreds and hundreds of meters from civilization.

Further on, they come out into an open area, a small parking lot. A solitary car stands there. Its lights are on, and the driver's door is open.

Fedor points to the BMW. "Check it out. It's just sitting there. Doesn't look like anyone's in it."

"I wonder why." Bente comes to a stop and looks around. "Where's the driver?"

"Maybe in the dunes," Fedor blurts, "with some hot babe."

Bente giggles.

On impulse, Fedor slides behind the wheel. Earlier in the summer, his father let him drive his Renault Mégane around a big empty lot. At first, he'd had trouble shifting gears, and sometimes he gave it too much gas before going into neutral and made the engine roar. But he picked it up quickly. Next year, if he passes all his classes, his parents have promised to pay for lessons and the driving exam.

"Shit, the keys are in it!" He turns the ignition key impulsively, and the car comes to life.

Bente slides in beside him. "Let's take a ride!" she says.

The idea shocks him back to reality. "No way!"

"Come on, Feddie, just for a minute. Just here in the parking lot."

"I don't even have a license," he argues.

"Like that matters? Come *on*, don't be chicken!" She covers his face with little kisses, each kiss promising something bigger if he gives her what she wants.

Reluctantly, he shifts into reverse and backs out of the parking space.

"You really know how to drive?" asks Bente.

"Well, sure. Just watch." He feels powerful behind the wheel of this fancy BMW. The car responds perfectly to his touch. He shifts into first and moves forward. As he approaches the tree line, he turns the wheel and lets up a bit on the gas, easing smoothly into a half circle. The suspension is amazing—they don't even notice the bumps and dips in the road surface.

"This is fun," says Bente. "Keep going!"

He drives on. A beautiful girl, an expensive car—this is a once-in-a-lifetime chance, and he's not about to let it pass him by. He glances over at Bente. Her eyes gleam with excitement in the moonlight.

After a couple of minutes, they come to the main road.

"We better go back," says Fedor. "I just need to find someplace to turn around." He taps the turn signal and makes a right out into the road. Just ahead on the left is the turnoff for the village, but he's not going to take that chance. Traffic, people, maybe cops. Best bet is to stay as far away from there as possible. There has to be a driveway up here where he can turn. He slows down and jumps nervously when a horn honks behind him. A convertible roars by, two guys in it. The driver flips him the bird.

"Jerk," mutters Fedor, and Bente pushes the button that lowers the passenger window and screams "Asshole!" into the night.

Fedor's knees begin to tremble, and his hands, suddenly sweaty, almost slip from the steering wheel.

"Let's go back," Bente says. There is anger in her voice.

Maybe he's spoiled everything, Fedor thinks, when all he wanted was to impress her.

"OK, fine," he says quickly. "Hang on." He turns carefully into a driveway, then backs out, spinning the wheel the other way. He can't get the shift lever back into first. There's a grinding noise, and the engine stalls.

"What's wrong?" asks Bente.

"Nothing. No problem." He turns the key. The car starts. Clutch in, shift into first, let up on the clutch and give it a little gas.

And then, out of nowhere, there's a bright light and a sudden jolt and a loud crash. Fedor and Bente are frozen in time and space.

· · ·

Fedor isn't sure how to get back to the parking lot. Bente is no help —she just sits there crying. They can't have been gone for more than fifteen minutes, tops. "He was driving way too fast," says Fedor for the umpteenth time, but it's as if Bente doesn't even hear him. "Crazy fast. I didn't see him. All of a sudden, he just *hit* us."

And then he sees the entrance to the lot, after all. He pulls the car right back into the space where they found it.

He rummages through Bente's purse for a tissue and carefully wipes the steering wheel, surprised that he's thinking clearly enough to do this. Then he gets out of the car. Bente sits there, paralyzed. She's shivering, though the evening is still warm. A dark cloud hides the moon, maybe indicating a change in the weather on the way.

"Come on, we gotta get out of here. They might come back any second." Fedor walks around the car, opens the passenger door and pulls Bente's arm.

"We should have done something," she sniffles.

"Are you nuts?" Fedor shakes his head. "Can you imagine the trouble we'd be in?"

"But maybe—" she begins.

"No, really. He was just shaken up a little. Good thing he had his helmet on. He'll be fine, trust me. But there's no way we could stick around and get involved."

As if they're glued together, not ready to break their embrace, Hans and Angela walk back up the path. It's more stumbling than walking. Their passion has intoxicated them. Hans suddenly remembers a beer ad with the slogan "Beer as beer *should* be." This was sex as sex *should* be....

They come in sight of the car. Stupid of him not to lock it. The lights are on, the driver's door wide open. He stops.

"What?" asks Angela.

He searches his trouser pockets. Nope, no keys. He hurries to the BMW and slides in. Whew, they're still in the ignition.

"Is something wrong?" Angela comes up beside him.

He gets out of the car and wraps his arms around her. He resists the urge to talk about the future. No promises, no obligations. He leans against the car, his right hand on the hood. Strange, it feels warm. Must take the engine longer to cool off in this heat.

"We'd better go," he says.

She nods.

When they've been driving for a while, they hear an ambulance's siren.

A hundred meters from her house, Angela says, "I'll get out here."

He tries to pull her to him, but her soft hands hold him off. "You gotta know when to hold 'em and know when to fold 'em," she murmurs.

He recognizes the lyric. An old American country song.

"You mean—?"

She presses her fingertips to her mouth and then touches his lips gently. Is she kissing him goodbye, or telling him not to speak? Before he can ask, she's gone.

Five minutes later, he's home. Marjon has apparently gone to bed. He pours himself a whiskey, drops in a couple of ice cubes, and goes out to the back terrace. When he closes his eyes, he can call it all back. Her voice, her perfume, her skin, her body. And they did it outside, in the open air, like a couple of exhibitionists. Maybe she gets a kick out of that, taking risks she really ought to avoid.

When his glass is empty, he goes back inside, locks up and takes a shower. As quietly as possible, he opens the bedroom door and crawls into bed. Marjon doesn't stir.

A few minutes later, her voice startles him: "Late."

"Yeah. I had a drink when I got home." The excuse seems superfluous.

"How is he?"

It takes a few seconds for him to realize she means Ariejan.

"Oh, okay. G'night."

She curls up against him and kisses him. "Sleep tight."

Betrayer, he thinks. *Cheat.*

Fedor hears the first notes of Coldplay's "Atlas," pulls out his cell phone, and sees Bente's name on the screen.

"Have you heard anything?" she asks.

"You mean about... the guy on the motorbike?"

"Well, *duh.*"

He clears his throat. "No, nothing. It'll be in the paper on Monday, I guess."

"I think we should go to the cops," Bente whispers, so low he can barely hear her.

"The cops?"

"We were involved in a hit-and-run, Feddie. That's a crime!"

"*He* hit *us*, we didn't hit him. And if we keep our mouths shut, no one'll ever know we were in the car."

The guy on the bike can't possibly have seen us. He doesn't say these words aloud.

Neither of them speaks for a while, and then she breaks the silence and asks if they're going to see each other today.

"I've got homework," he says, "and my mom wants me to visit my grandma with her this afternoon." He sighs.

There's a sudden rumble of thunder, and within moments the sky is full of dark-gray clouds.

"It's gonna rain." As soon as the words leave his mouth, Fedor knows it's a dumb thing to say. Gazing out his bedroom window, he sees the first drops begin to fall. And then it's pouring so hard he can barely make out the houses on the other side of the street.

"I'll see you in school on Monday, I guess."

"Sure, Monday." He presses his lips to the phone and listens for her answering kiss, but it doesn't come.

Half an hour later, she texts him: "We should go to the police."

He texts her back, tells her just to forget about it. "Please, Bente, trust me." And then five x's. Five more than she used to close *her* message.

More than once, Hans picks up the phone to call Angela, but each time he forces himself to cradle the receiver without dialing. It was a classic one-night stand, he knows, the sort of thing you always remember but never repeat. She'll remember it, too, he hopes. But it can't go on, that's impossible. Although it seems cruel, almost inhuman, to simply set aside such an hour of utter passion, to replace it with an eternal longing that can never be satisfied. Does he regret what they did? No, not at all.

While Marjon is busy in the kitchen, he calls Ariejan and quickly fills him in on what's happened. "I told Marjon I was with you," he says.

"So I'm your alibi," says Ariejan.

"Yeah, I suppose you could say that."

"Mr. Bergman? Mr. Bergman!"

He shakes his head to dislodge the memories.

Nienke holds up her phone. "I've got the police on the line. Can you speak to them now, or should they call back?"

"I'll take it now."

He lifts his own receiver and hears a few clicks, then a surprisingly high-pitched male voice. "This is Joris Bovenkamp. Is this Hans Bergman?"

Hans acknowledges his identity. Bovenkamp tells him that he's with the regional police. He'd like to come by and have a look at Mr. Bergman's car.

"My car? Why?" The only thing he can think of is possible traces of Angela's presence. A strand of her hair, a whiff of perfume?

"I can be there in half an hour. Is that okay?"

"Certainly."

After he cradles the phone, he tells Nienke that he has to duck out for a second. He goes downstairs and out to the parking lot and has a look at his car. Smells it, runs his hand across the passenger seat. No sign of Angela. As if it never happened.

Then he walks around the car—and, damn, there's a big dent and some deep scratches on the rear panel on the passenger side, and the right taillight is shattered. It looks like someone's rammed into the back of the car. Here in the parking lot? No, not possible. At home, he parks in the driveway, and the car was there all day yesterday. Earlier, then? But when? And is this why the police are coming? The questions echo inside his head.

Back in his office, he sits at his desk, flips open the folder for the shopping-center remodel and tries to make sense of the blueprints. The minutes tick by slowly. At last the phone rings. A Mr. Bovenkamp is asking for him at reception.

Bovenkamp offers Hans a hand and introduces himself. His voice is pitched deeper than it sounded over the phone.

"Hans Bergman. Pleased to meet you."

"Shall we go have a look at your car?"

Bovenkamp walks around the BMW and examines the damage thoughtfully. "What happened here?"

Hans shrugs. "Looks like somebody hit me when I was parked somewhere. I didn't see it until now."

Bovenkamp runs his fingers along the paint, following the line of the scratches. "Seems pretty recent."

It begins to drizzle.

"Should we go inside?" asks Hans.

It's as if Bovenkamp doesn't hear him. "You weren't on the Harkemaseweg around midnight on Saturday?"

"Saturday?" He has to force himself not to turn and run. He doesn't know what exactly is going on, but it must be something serious. The police don't show up at your doorstep just because of a couple of scratches.

"Correct, sir, Saturday night. A car was spotted driving slowly along the Harkemaseweg, as if the driver was looking for something. One witness said he thought it was a BMW. Right around that time, a man on a motorcycle ran into a car. He was pretty seriously injured. So we're checking out all the BMWs in the area."

Hans feels as if *he* has been run into.

They sit together at lunch.

"I saw it on the news," says Bente. "A guy on a motorbike, twenty-four years old. He's in the hospital, hurt bad. Our fault."

He sees that she's holding back tears, and he puts his arm around her. He tries to make it look like they're just having a little argument. Maybe nobody's paying attention to them, but the girls especially always seem to know when something's going on.

"Totally *not* our fault," he says. "We weren't even moving. We had our lights on, and he just smashed right into us. Honestly, it was one hundred percent *his* fault."

"If we hadn't been there, it wouldn't have happened."

"But that doesn't make it our fault." In his mind's eye, he's back on the road. He gets out of the car and checks out the poor dude lying draped over the curb. Ten meters off, the front wheel of the stalled-out motorbike is still spinning. If the guy's dead, there's nothing they can do about it. If he's alive, somebody must have heard the crash and will call an ambulance and the cops. Jesus, the cops! If his parents find out about this, they'll kill him. "The stupid bastard was driving like a maniac, way too fast."

"But—"

Bente loses her fight, and tears stream down her cheeks. "We have to go to the police," she gasps between sobs.

He looks up and sees Viviana, Bente's best friend, watching them.

Hans follows Bovenkamp to the police station "for further investigation of the vehicle," as Bovenkamp puts it. A young officer brings him back to his office in a patrol car. He tells Nienke that he has a meeting and can't be disturbed, so he's turning off his cell. He takes a company car and spends several hours just driving. It rains all afternoon. He pulls off the road at a café near the dunes, orders a cappuccino and a cheese sandwich, and tries to get his thoughts straightened out.

He's back at the office at four thirty.

"Mr. Bovenkamp wants you to call him," says Nienke.

Bovenkamp is all business. He wants Hans to come to the station.

"Why?"

"We'll discuss that when you get here."

Interesting that Bovenkamp doesn't offer to provide him with transportation. No way to know what that means. Hans calls a cab and has to wait half an hour before it pulls into the parking lot. The driver seems eager to chat about the weather, but Hans returns only the briefest of responses.

This time, Bovenkamp is accompanied by a second man, who introduces himself as Mulder. They get straight down to business. Multiple flakes of paint found on the damaged motorcycle have been matched to the BMW.

"But," says Hans, "there are lots of dark-gray BMWs." He suddenly remembers the siren he heard while driving Angela home.

"The paint came from *your* BMW, Mr. van der Berg, not *a* BMW. And don't forget the dent and the scratches on your car."

Hans shrugs. "I told you, someone must have run into it when it was parked somewhere. And then the jackass drove off without leaving a note."

"Must have happened pretty recently, seeing how you hadn't even noticed the damage until today."

"Maybe Thursday or Friday."

Mulder repeats Hans' words, but with an intonation that makes it obvious he doesn't believe it.

Then the question comes. Hans expects it. Where was he around midnight on Saturday?

"I was with an old friend. Ariejan Langhuis."

They write down Ariejan's name and ask for his address and phone number. As soon as he leaves the station, he'll have to call Ariejan. Then he realizes that, if he's a suspect, they may not let him go. He'll have to call home and have Marjon bring him a change of clothes, a toothbrush, toothpaste.

"So you visited him Saturday evening, after the reception at City Hall?"

They've done their homework. "Yes, he's an old friend. His wife died recently, and he's lonely."

"And Mr. Langhuis lives in the Oude Peppelstraat." Bovenkamp eyes Hans meaningfully.

It takes a few seconds for the penny to drop: the Oude Peppelstraat intersects with the Harkemaseweg.

"Is something wrong?" asks Marjon, when Hans has poured himself a stiff shot of whiskey, grabbed the paper, and settled in his favorite armchair.

He takes a sip. "No, nothing."

"You seem so... I don't know, preoccupied. Like something's on your mind."

He decides to tell her, since it'll be in the paper tomorrow or the next day. He gives her the same story he gave the police. His visit to Ariejan, the drive home. Nothing out of the ordinary happened, as far as he knew at the time, but it seems almost certain that some poor guy on a motorbike ran into the BMW at some point, damaging the car, totaling the motorcycle and winding up in intensive care.

"How can that have happened?"

"I don't know. But it did."

And then all at once he sees *how* it did. It's as if some invisible observer whispers an eyewitness account in his ear. While he was having sex with Angela, somebody took his car for a joyride. That's when the bike must have collided with the BMW. He remembers now that the engine was still warm when they got back from their tryst in the dunes. Whoever "borrowed" his car must have put it back where Hans had parked it, hoping the car's owner would wind up taking the blame for the collision.

"Goddammit," he whispers.

Marjon says again that it doesn't seem possible, must be some kind of a mistake.

"I'm tired of talking about it," he tells her.

After dinner, which they eat in silence, Hans goes into the home office he's turned into a man cave.

Marjon brings coffee. "Oh, you're in here?"

"I seem to be, don't I?"

She mumbles an apology and leaves him alone. He really should treat her more nicely, but he just can't manage it.

When he's finished his coffee, he calls Ariejan, who reports that he was just about to dial Hans' number, since the police have just left.

"And?" asks Hans.

"Well, I backed you up, except I didn't realize your story was meant for the cops."

"It wasn't. It was meant for Marjon. In case you ran into her, you know?"

"But now the police. Are you in some kind of trouble?"

Hans tells him the whole truth and nothing but the truth: the BMW, the accident, the injured biker. "And it happened in the Harkemaseweg, not far from your place, while I was in fact *not* visiting you."

"You're not going to tell them that, I hope."

"Well, I may have to. If I don't want to have to take the blame."

"And if they find out you weren't here last Saturday evening, then what happens to *me*? I've lied to the cops, given you a fake alibi." Hans hears the indignation in Ariejan's voice. "That makes me an accessory after the fact or something."

"Don't be ridiculous. You didn't know it had anything to do with the accident. You thought you were just helping me put one over on Marjon."

"But I still turn out to be a liar."

Hans sighs. He doesn't know what to say or think. The whole

business is so mixed up in his head, he can't even keep it straight himself.

He sits there for a long moment, the room quiet except for the ambient noise of the phone connection.

"Well, fine," he tells his old friend. "You do what you have to do."

And at that, Ariejan hangs up on him.

Hans closes his eyes. Then he opens them and looks up Angela's home phone number. They're going to have to come clean about what really happened Saturday night. There's no other option. If he can't duck responsibility for the accident, then who knows how long a prison term he might be facing. There's only one person who can help him now—not counting whoever it was who stole his damn car, but *that* bastard's not going to own up to the theft, Hans is sure of that much.

Marjon's bound to find out the truth sooner or later. She'll be hysterically angry at first. He'll let her scream it all out, won't say a word when she flings a few place settings at the walls, do whatever penance she imposes on him—and eventually she'll get over it.

He fetches the whiskey bottle, a glass, and some ice cubes from downstairs. Marjon doesn't seem to be around.

A stiff drink gives him the courage to call Angela.

"Hello," a teenaged male voice says.

"This is Hans van der Berg. I'd like to speak with your mother. It's urgent."

"I'll get her."

Hans can visualize the boy walking through the house with the cordless phone. He hears a quick rat-a-tat on a door. "Mom, phone. It's urgent."

Hans can't quite make out the response.

"I don't know," says the boy. "I'll ask. Can I tell her who's calling, please?"

"Hans Bergman. I've got to ask her something important."

Now that he's taken the step of calling, he absolutely needs to get Angela on the line.

"Hans Bergman," he hears the boy repeat. "He has to ask you something important."

A full minute passes before he hears Angela's voice. "I was taking a bath. What is it?"

She was taking a bath. Why would she tell him that? Maybe to get him thinking about her body. He tries to concentrate on the matter at hand. He tells her about the accident, but he has the impression she's already heard about it. "We have to go to the police—I think we should go in together—and tell them the truth."

"I don't know what you're talking about."

He forces a laugh. "You know exactly what I'm talking about. The empty parking lot by the dunes. You ran towards the sea, I followed you, and then—"

"You've certainly got a vivid imagination. And then *what*? We did it, is that what you're saying?"

"Well, yeah. We did a *lot* of it."

"And you thought this delightful little scenario up all by yourself?"

"Come on, Angela. Stop playing games. We have to—"

She hangs up on him. Hans stares at the receiver as if *it's* to blame for everything. He wants to fling it to the ground and kick it to bits. Instead, he yells out "Bitch!" at the top of his voice.

Fedor and Bente meet up after the last class period of the day.

"Did you see it in the paper?" she asks.

He nods.

"They've arrested that poor man, and he didn't do anything."

"We didn't do anything, either," says Fedor.

She lays a hand on his arm. "No, but we took his car. If we hadn't done that, then—"

"If, if, if," Fedor interrupts her.

"I can't stand it," says Bente. "We *have* to tell them. I can't sleep, I keep thinking about it. That poor man in prison, and he's totally innocent." She looks at him, her eyes wide. "Fedor, you can't want him to suffer?"

"You think *I* want to go to jail?"

"You won't, if we tell the truth how it happened."

"How do you know that?"

"I don't *know* it," she admits, and then a thought strikes her. "You can ask your mom. She knows all about legal stuff. Let's ask her."

Fedor hesitates, but Bente gazes at him with such concern, such love, that he almost loses himself in her eyes. "Okay," he says at last. "She should be home by six."

She puts her hands over his ears, pulls him to her and kisses him full on the mouth.

"No," Fedor's mother says, "I wouldn't say a word to anyone."

"You wouldn't tell the truth?" asks Bente, her head cocked in surprise.

"I don't think it would be a good idea, especially not for Fedor. He doesn't have his license yet, and you were on a public road. That's a pretty serious offense right there. And then he caused the accident—"

"He didn't *cause* it," Bente protests.

But his mother seems not to have heard her. "—and he drove away from the scene without reporting it to the police or calling an ambulance. I don't know what a judge would say about that, but

I'm guessing Fedor—and you—would wind up in some pretty serious trouble."

"But it's not fair to let that man take the blame!"

"Fair? Sweetheart, life *isn't* always fair. Is it fair for Fedor to lose his future because some idiot on a motorbike was too stupid to watch where he was going?"

Bente stares at the carpet, as if she hopes to find the answer to Fedor's mother's question written there.

"Well? Would *that* be fair?"

Slowly, Bente shakes her head.

The room is quiet for a while. And then the conversation turns to school, to the academic year just begun, the projects and assignments and examinations that lie ahead. At six thirty, Bente says she has to get home.

She stands up to go, relieved, almost happy. "Thanks for talking with us, Mrs. Boonstra," she says.

"Mrs. Boonstra?" says Fedor's mother. "You don't have to be that formal with me, Bente. Please, just call me Angela."

2

THE LAST RUN

BY MICHAEL BERG

Burger pulled around behind the hospital, backed the Packard into the space closest to the morgue's entrance and got out. The biting February wind made him shiver. He pushed open the door, and the stink of Lysol crimped his nostrils, calling up images of dead meat, images he'd be happier living without, this early in the morning.

He wheeled a gurney out to the back of the hearse, unloaded the coffin and headed back inside, asking himself for the umpteenth time what had made him think that starting a business transporting bodies across the border would be a good idea. A lot of Poles, Yugoslavians and Italians worked in the mines. Men who'd left their homelands and families behind in the years after the war and come to Limburg—a province in the deep south of Holland—for the promise of better jobs, better pay. Some of them died down there, below ground, and their families wanted to bury them back home. Burger had managed to swing a bank loan and buy a 1939 Packard Henney Super 8 hearse with less than five thousand kilometers on the clock. A beautiful vehicle. And it wasn't only good for ferrying the dead, just in case the business didn't work out—a possibility he hadn't considered when he'd applied for the loan. But fewer mineworkers were dying than he'd expected. Or he was spending the money he made too freely. He suspected it was probably the latter.

"You just piss the money away," Maria told him sourly. But she was right. It was like the guilders burned a hole in his pocket. If there was one thing Burger wanted, it was to enjoy his life. Drinking, laughing. Junkets to Paris with his friends to watch the Tour de France cyclists sprint across the finish line. And then stay on a few extra days to paint the town. Dammit, why not? The money wouldn't do him any good when he was dead.

He pushed the gurney through the swinging doors to the cold room.

"Cognac?"

Offermans was leaning against a mortuary table, his back to the body laid out on its metal surface. Burger got a glimpse of skinny white legs to one side of Offermans' own stocky torso, gray hair in a bun to the other. A brandy bottle and two glasses stood at the corpse's feet.

Burger nodded. "I could use one."

Offermans poured, and they emptied their glasses in silence. Meanwhile, Burger examined the body. The wrinkled flesh made him think of Maria. Her skin was beginning to show signs of age. He forced his mind back to the dead woman before him. She was probably around seventy. Her name didn't matter. Just so the age he wrote down on the form seemed right.

"When will you bring her back?" asked Offermans, putting away the bottle and glasses.

"Eleven?"

"Fine."

This was the way they'd handled things each of the three

previous times. Pick up first thing in the morning, return late the same night. That way, there was no risk anyone would see them.

Burger handed Offermans a twenty-five-guilder note. He'd pay the balance tonight. He saw Offermans glance furtively left and right. The man was afraid. If they were caught, he'd lose his job here in the morgue.

"So, see you tonight," said Burger.

"Tonight, yes."

He wheeled the coffin back out to the Packard. Before the garage opened for the day's business, he'd fill out the paperwork and seal the casket. And then he could set off for Vaals, a small town on the Dutch side of the Holland/Germany border. The first three times, everything had gone off smooth as silk. He started the engine. This one last run, and he'll have paid off the last of his loan.

Assuming Gesthuizen was a man of his word.

At the thought of Gesthuizen, the director of the Geldersche Bank, Burger stomped so angrily on the gas that his tires spat gravel as he peeled out of the parking lot.

"Coffee?"

Without waiting for a response, Maria poured a cup and slid it across the counter to the mechanic.

"Thanks, Mrs. B."

She turned a page of the morning paper. Out of the corner of her eye, she could see the young man appraise her appreciatively. Just because Burger never touched her anymore, that didn't mean other men found her unattractive. No, she still had it. A lot of the customers came in especially because of her. Men who—all right, she had to admit it, most of them were a little past their prime— flirted shamelessly with her, their comments ranging from the shy to the positively bawdy. As long as they ordered off the menu and paid for what they ate and drank, though, she didn't mind.

She glanced around the café. The furniture—oaken tables, heavy chairs, a raggedy pool table—hadn't changed since she'd bought the place. A reasonably solvent café, with a reasonably solvent auto-repair shop right next door. Not exactly what she'd envisioned when she and Burger had first gotten together. She'd fallen for his charm, his easy manner. A Dutchman, from The Hague. Straightforward, spontaneous. During the bad years, in the '30s, he'd moved south to Limburg. He understood cars. She'd been helping out around her father's shop long enough, she thought, and she wanted something of her own. There was a café for sale in Heerlen, on the corner of the Akerstraat and the Putgraaf, with an apartment upstairs and a big warehouse next door. With some help from her dad, she'd bought the parcel and converted the warehouse to a garage. She and Burger got married. Community property, although her father had tried to talk her out of agreeing to that. And now it was too late.

"Would you do me a favor?"

The mechanic perked up. "Sure, Mrs. B."

"Can you bring up a case of soda from the cellar?"

"Right away."

She watched him head for the stairs. His overalls were a size too small, and the fabric stretched tightly across his butt. A nice ass. Sighing, she looked back down at the paper. *Smuggler killed in Aachen*, a page-two headline ran. She read the story and thought of Burger, who'd gone out at the crack of dawn and come back an hour later, pulling the Packard into the garage and closing the wooden doors behind him. By the time she came down to see what he was up to, the doors were wide open again. Maybe he had another "delivery," which was what he called it when there was a dead body to transport. Or perhaps he was busy with something else. It had been a long time since Burger had bothered to keep her abreast of his activities. Now, she didn't much care about his crazy schemes, most of which led them nowhere. Except deeper into debt. A penny earned is a penny spent, that was her husband. The only people who ever got anything out of Burger's business dealings were Offermans and a few other so-called friends.

"Mrs. B?"

The mechanic set the case of bottles on the lunch counter and looked at her expectantly.

"Thanks," Maria said, and nodded at the clock on the wall behind the pool table. "Time to open the garage."

The young man trotted off obediently, and she gazed out the window at the bus stop. It was Friday. Fritz was usually on the nine o'clock bus. Visiting his sick aunt. And then, after that....

Scheiße. It wasn't just that Fritz had missed his bus, which meant an hour's wait before the next one came along. Worse than that was that Ilse, his wife, was beginning to suspect. At the very last moment, she'd handed him a shopping list. *Since it's so important you go to Heerlen anyway.* She didn't doubt his regular Friday visits to his bedridden aunt, but she wasn't buying the idea that, after sitting for a while with Tante Lena, he walked over to the Grand Hotel to take an afternoon course in Dutch. Where was his textbook, his notebook? It was conversational Dutch, he told her. No books. And why did a German need to learn Dutch in the first place? Because at his job they were working more closely with their counterparts in The Netherlands. A command of the language would increase his chances of promotion.

Ilse had eyed him skeptically.

Fritz flipped up his jacket collar and hurried on. His aunt lived in one of the old cottages by the church. When he pushed open her front door, which was never locked during the day, he came directly into her large living room, overfull of lovingly tended furniture and far too warm.

"Fritzi!"

From her sickbed, Lena smiled at him weakly, gratefully.

He kissed her cheek and excused his lateness. Then he did what he always did. He warmed up the last of the coffee on the metal stove in the living room, got two clean cups from the kitchen, and sat beside her on the edge of the bed. He usually stayed for about an hour. They talked about the old days, when she still lived in Aachen, about his work, about Ilse and the kids, about the horrors of the war that had ended so many lives and ruined so many others. Ordinary conversation. It quieted his conscience. If he was going to sin, it was better to do a good deed beforehand, like visiting his ailing aunt. Maybe then the good Lord would close an eye to what came after.

The old woman was considering him closely, the expression on her lined face midway between concern and surprise. Was everything okay between him and Ilse? Were they happy?

Sometimes she asked him questions he couldn't bring himself to answer. Now, when she wondered why it was that he'd suddenly begun to visit her every week, after years of little contact, he got to his feet.

"I have to go," he said gruffly.

"Already?"

Disappointment was written all over her. He stammered something about his language lessons and watched her nod understandingly. Of course. Fritz was preparing for the future. Fritz was going to make something of himself. He kissed her goodbye and left the house.

The Grand Hotel was around the corner. Passing the imposing structure, he thought that it wouldn't be much longer before Ilse checked and discovered that no language lessons were offered there. He crossed the square and turned into the Willemsstraat, a narrow street lined with dilapidated old buildings. The pension's dim foyer smelled of stagnant beer and cheap cigars. The old man at the desk nodded at him without expression and waited for his money. Fritz took the key he was offered and headed upstairs.

The moment Gesthuizen arrived, the other man—the German—swung the stable doors shut. The two of them shook hands. Gesthuizen never gave Burger more than a curt nod. Burger didn't care. He was just the courier. What bothered him was the idea that he'd taken out the loan from Gesthuizen in the first place. There was no way he could ever have paid it off if he hadn't agreed to get involved in this dirty business.

The two men huddled together in the corner, whispering. The German was probably also a banker. He looked like one: woolen suit, gold pocket watch, manicured nails, just as arrogant a bastard as Gesthuizen. His name was Kaiser. At least, that was the name on the mailbox set into the stone wall that surrounded the property. But Burger had never heard Gesthuizen address the man by name, so maybe the German wasn't called Kaiser, after all.

"Shall we begin?"

Gesthuizen had turned to Burger.

Yeah, sure.

Burger pulled a pair of work gloves from the pockets of his coat and saw the two of them turn their heads away. He took a deep breath and opened the coffin. This treas the worst part of the affair. The body's chill penetrated through the thick gloves to his hands. And then there was the nauseating stink of Lysol. He lifted the old woman out of the coffin and laid her out on the rough deal table dragged there for that purpose. Then he worked the false bottom loose and reached for the first of the platinum bars.

"I'll do that," said Gesthuizen dismissively.

He handed the bars to Kaiser, who placed them carefully in a leather suitcase. The two men counted aloud—Gesthuizen in Dutch, Kaiser in German—from one to twenty. They nodded, satisfied.

"Close it up," Gesthuizen said, not even looking at Burger.

Burger replaced the false bottom and moved the dead woman back where she belonged. He closed the lid, resealed the coffin and slid it into the back of the Packard. He could feel a weight lift from his shoulders. His debt was now paid off. He didn't expect a ceremony, didn't expect Gesthuizen to pull the loan documents from his overcoat pocket and tear them up, but the man could at least thank him for his help. Instead, all Burger heard was an uncomfortable silence.

"I, ah," he said. "I've done my part, and—"

"Wait outside, please," Gesthuizen interrupted him.

"But I—"

"Outside."

With an annoyed gesture, Gesthuizen waved Burger through the stable doors.

Maria and Fritz hugged tightly and began to undress each other. Impatient, greedy as always, they kissed and nibbled teasingly. The room was ice cold, the bed reeked, the harsh light from the ceiling fixture was anything but romantic, but they barely noticed. Maria wanted Fritz, and he wanted her. And that was all that mattered.

"When do you have to go?" she asked.

"An hour and a half," he said. "I—"

"Come on, then."

She was already under the blanket. Naked. Fritz slipped in beside her. He was still wearing his socks. But their time together was too precious to waste on trivialities. Their bodies melted together. It was all still new and exciting—and yet familiar, comfortable. They had grown up in the same neighborhood. As children, they'd been inseparable. They ran through the cobblestone streets together, biked together, played together. When Maria turned sixteen and the boys in Vaals began to notice her, she stayed faithful to her childhood sweetheart. As soon as Fritz finished his vocational training, they would be married. But then Burger had come along, and she'd made the biggest mistake of her life.

It had been many years before fate brought them back together. And now she lay on her side and stroked him tenderly, eagerly.

"Please," she moaned. "*Please!*"

He fumbled for the little cardboard box he'd set on the nightstand beside the bed.

"No," she said. "Not this time."

He stared at her, not understanding at first.

"I want to have your baby," she whispered.

"But—"

She rolled onto her back and spread her legs.

"Make me a baby," she begged him. "Now. We don't have time to argue."

It was cold and raining. Heavy drops, almost sleet. Burger huddled beneath a tree that offered little protection and worried about how long they were taking. Was there a problem with the delivery? If so, what did that have to do with him?

Burger had known from the beginning that this was bad business. During the war, Gesthuizen had played a questionable role. As the director of the Geldersche Bank, he was suspected of having collaborated with the Nazis. Afterwards, there'd been an investigation, and Gesthuizen's name had been cleared, but Burger couldn't imagine that the platinum bars had been obtained legally. And Kaiser also seemed shady. Maybe—

The stable doors swung open.

"Come inside, please," Gesthuizen summoned him.

When he re-entered the stable, Burger saw that Kaiser and the suitcase were gone.

"I—" Gesthuizen forced a smile. "There has been an unfortunate complication, and—"

"This was the last time," Burger burst out, surprising himself. "We had an agreement."

"We did." Gesthuizen raised his hands apologetically. "But I need you to make one more run in order to fulfill my own obligation."

"And if I refuse?"

"I'll find another driver, and you"—Gesthuizen pointed at the Packard—"you'll lose that beautiful car."

Burger was outraged. "I'll turn you in!"

"Good luck. I'll deny everything, and it'll be your word against mine. I'll have witnesses who will swear under oath that I'm leading a meeting at the bank at this very moment." Gesthuizen laughed. "One more run. Then I'll give you an official document releasing you from your debt."

"But I—"

"And I'll pay you a bonus."

Burger blinked. "How much?"

"Ten thousand guilders."

"Twenty."

"All right," said Gesthuizen, sighing.

"I want a written guarantee, right now," said Burger, cursing himself for agreeing too quickly.

Fritz lit a cigarette, trying not to think about what had just happened. A verse from the Bible murmured in the back of his mind: *The spirit is willing, but the flesh is weak.* My God. He'd allowed it to happen, and now he was consumed with regret. No, not regret. He'd always wanted this. Just himself and Maria, without protection, like a man and his wife. But God forbid she became pregnant. That would wreak havoc in both their lives.

"I'm leaving Burger," she told him.

Shocked, he turned toward her.

"I'm leaving him," she said again.

"And then?"

"And then you'll leave Ilse."

"But—"

"And we can be together at last." She snuggled into his arms. "With a little luck, we can have our own children."

"I—" Fritz could feel himself begin to sweat. "We're married. I mean—"

"We'll get divorced."

What therefore God hath joined together, let not man put asunder.

Fritz forced himself not to say the words aloud.

"Do you think the Lord approves of what we're doing now?" she asked, reading his thoughts, her face completely serious. "Instead of living together happily, we're deceiving our spouses. Is that what you want?"

"No, of course not." Fritz dragged on his cigarette. "A divorce costs money," he said. "I have to be sure Ilse and the kids are taken care of."

"That's why you need to get promoted as soon as possible."

Fritz sighed. As if a promotion would be his for the asking.

Burger counted four customers, three men clustered around a table and one at the bar. It was usually more crowded at six.

"Another?" He tipped a bottle above Offermans' glass, and his friend nodded.

As he poured, Burger thought ahead to tomorrow, to the very last run. Earlier in the week, Gesthuizen had called to say that his Citroën Traction was having transmission problems again. Could he drop the car off around eight Thursday evening, and would Burger check it out himself? This was a coded message. The words, the tone, were the same as the previous four times. Burger knew exactly what was expected of him.

He leaned across the bar and lowered his voice. "We have to talk."

"Talk?"

Offermans said the word so loudly that the men around the table looked over at them.

"Ssssh," Burger hissed. He glanced back over his shoulder at the door to the kitchen. Maria might be lurking in the hall. Or else the mechanic. *No*, he thought, *he's already gone home*. "I'm waiting for your answer," he said in a friendly whisper.

"Answer?" Offermans' eyes were glassy. He emptied his glass in one quick gulp. "What do I owe you?"

Burger gestured that the drinks were on the house.

"Thanks."

Offermans slid off his stool and stumbled toward the door. Burger hurried out from behind the bar to help him. Outside, the east wind howled in their faces, and they turned the corner of the Putgraaf together.

"I need to know," said Burger, steering Offermans into the garage's doorway, out of the wind. "I need a—a load, tomorrow."

"A load?"

"For the coffin."

"Oh, that," Offermans snorted.

"This is the last time, I swear it."

"I'm not helping you again."

"I'll pay double."

"No, it's too dangerous."

"Triple."

"No!" cried Offermans. "I'm finished. This time you'll have to go without a 'load.' You tell me they never even check the coffin. So—"

Burger knew it was pointless to argue. He let go of Offermans' sleeve, and his friend staggered off down the street.

Maria watched the low-slung black Citroën pull up to the closed garage doors, Gesthuizen behind the wheel. The banker usually had a chauffeur and sat in the back seat, puffing on a fat cigar, acting as if he was busy shuffling through a stack of important documents. Showoff. Maria had always detested Gesthuizen.

A horn honked.

He was always impatient, Gesthuizen. She heard footsteps in the hall. Burger, scurrying off to let him in like a good little lapdog. It was eight o'clock. Customers often turned up at the garage well after closing time. Regulars, who worked during the day and came by late for an after-hours oil change. Or people to whom Burger owed money, like Gesthuizen. The bank director had shown up unusually often, these last months. Suspiciously often.

She glanced around the bar, saw that everyone's glass was at least half full, and eased open the door. At the far end of the hall, the connecting door to the garage was closed. She tiptoed along the corridor and put her ear to the door, but she couldn't hear a sound. She crept back the way she'd come, returned to the bar, and picked up the phone.

She dialed a familiar number.

Gesthuizen lifted the bars out of the Citroën's trunk, one by one, and handed them to Burger, who laid them carefully in the coffin.

"Forty," said Gesthuizen, as Burger fitted the last bar into place. "You counted them?"

Burger nodded.

This was twice as many as usual. Forty platinum bars, worth a fortune. He thought again that he ought to have demanded an even larger bonus. Too late now. In his safe was a handwritten note from Gesthuizen, absolving him of his debt. This would assure Burger a comfortable future. For now, at least. If the corpse delivery service failed to pan out, he could always come up with something else. In any case, there'd be plenty of money. After this last run, he'd take a trip to Paris with his friends, pile the usual crowd into the Packard, and head straight for the Folies Bergère. Well, not all of them. That prick Offermans could stay home.

Burger wondered for a moment if he should let Gesthuizen know of the minor change in their usual arrangement. No, of course not. Just drive. He'd never had a problem before. Why worry about it now?

"The usual time and place tomorrow," said Gesthuizen tightly. "Agreed?"

Burger nodded again. Gesthuizen got behind the wheel of his car, and Burger opened the garage doors, waited for the Citroën to back out and disappear around the corner, then closed the doors. He slid the coffin into the back of the Packard. The paperwork could wait until morning. There was plenty of time. He locked up the car and dropped the keys into his pocket. He needed a drink.

Burger was snoring like an ox. No surprise, Maria thought, given the amount of booze he'd taken on last night. She eased out of bed and into her robe and slippers. Before he'd passed out, he'd dropped his trousers on a chair. She crept around to his side of the bed, found his keys in the front right pocket of his pants, and left the bedroom. Down the stairs, along the corridor, into the garage. Holding her breath, she snapped on a light. The Packard was parked directly beneath one of the overhead fixtures. She'd always wondered how her husband had been able to afford such an expensive vehicle, and now she had a hunch she might be about to discover the answer. She could see the wooden coffin through the back window. With trembling fingers, she found the right key, opened the hearse's rear door, slid the coffin partway out, and raised the lid. Inside, the box was lined with zinc. Empty. She was disappointed at first, but then a gap around the bottom of the coffin caught her eye. She pried up the false bottom and saw the metal bars. They were packed in tightly, like sardines in a can, and it took her a moment to work one free.

In the light from above, she saw the words *CREDIT SUISSE* etched into its top surface. *10 OUNCES PLATINUM* 999.0.

Platinum, she thought. *Much more valuable than gold.* She counted forty bars. What would happen if she hid half of them someplace Burger would never find them?

"Goddammit!"

She hadn't heard him coming.

"What are you doing?" he demanded.

"Half of these are mine," she said, shivering.

"Bullshit."

"I'll turn you in."

"You wouldn't dare." He grinned at her crazily.

"I'm entitled to half," she insisted. "Community property. Otherwise—"

"Some changes to the schedule," Customs Inspector Merkelbach announced, when he showed up that Friday morning at the border station. Merkelbach didn't usually work on Fridays, but today was going to be special. He knew it.

A ray of sunlight broke through the cloud cover and lit up the trees that lined both sides of the road. The wind had died down, and there was a hint of spring in the air.

The striped barricade on the Dutch side opened, and a long American car slowly approached. Merkelbach recognized the driver, but doubted that Burger would know *him*, after all these years.

"*Ausweis, bitte,*" Merkelbach's colleague from the *Bundesgrenzschutz*—the German border patrol—demanded, and waited for Burger to produce his passport.

Now it was Merkelbach's turn. "*Haben Sie etwas zu verzollen?*" Do you have anything to declare?

Burger handed over a thin sheaf of documents. His confident expression had given way to a frown.

Merkelbach studied the papers. The dead woman being transported was thirty-eight years old. The death certificate seemed authentic. The embossed seal, the doctor's signature. Any of his colleagues would have fallen for it. But not him, not today.

"*Aufmachen!*" he snapped, gesturing for Burger to step out of the hearse.

Beads of sweat trickled down Burger's back. He suddenly realized where he'd seen the man in the green uniform with the stylized eagle on the cap before. It had been a long time ago. Carnival. The man had been wearing lederhosen then, and the pretty girl at his side had sparkled in a blue dirndl. Burger hadn't thought of the man in years, couldn't remember his name. Frans Something.

Frans, or Friedrich.

"Aufmachen!" the man said again, louder this time.

The customs agent didn't seem like a person you could keep waiting. And now other men in uniform were gathering around. Burger got out of the Packard and opened the door in the back.

Merkelbach pushed his colleagues out of the way. This was *his* moment, his triumph. He broke the coffin's seal and lifted the lid himself. But when he looked down into the zinc-lined wooden box, the world stood still and his heart broke.

She lay there, motionless, her skin an unnatural gray.

Maria, beautiful Maria, his darling girl.

There was a gash on the side of her head, the dark blood crusted around the edges of the wound—evidence she hadn't died a natural death. Merkelbach's eyes burned. A voice deep inside him screamed. He wanted to grab Burger by the throat, beat him without mercy until he, too, was dead.

But with a tremendous effort of will, he forced himself to remain calm. He turned to his colleagues and said, *"Festnehmen."* Arrest him.

This is the man who killed her, he wanted to add, but grief had eaten the words.

As Burger was led away in handcuffs, Merkelbach took one last look at his Maria. Her eyes were wide open. He could see the fear in them, the shock, the horror. In his mind, he heard her call for help. But where had *he* been when it happened? He remembered the last time they'd spoken, her phone call. *Tomorrow morning,* she'd warned him. *This is our chance!*

Why hadn't he called her back and told her to leave? Why hadn't he been there to save her? Coward. Their chance for a future together, and now there was nothing before him but emptiness.

I don't know what he's up to, she had whispered, afraid Burger might hear her, *but he's up to* something.

The coffin, Merkelbach thought. *Of course.*

He'd have to search it. No, let someone else deal with that. With the last of his strength, he gently laid the wooden lid back atop the box and waved over two of his colleagues to take it away for further examination.

Seven hours later. End of the workday. Fritz Merkelbach stood at the bar and drank. It didn't help. With every swallow, the pain only became harder to bear. All around him, his colleagues were in high spirits, celebrating, laughing. Merkelbach wore a smile on his face, artificial as a carnival mask. Inside, he wept. His drunken colleagues had no idea he had known Maria, let alone loved her.

A murderer captured, forty bars of platinum confiscated, that was all they knew or cared about. The arrest of the decade. And it was all thanks to Fritz. A promotion was practically assured. Ilse would be pleased.

"Hey, *Zolloberinspektor!*"

A friendly hand clapped him on the shoulder.

"Next round's on you, *ja?*"

He caught the bartender's eye and signaled him to fill their glasses.

3

—————————————————

WHAT'S BECOME OF THE BABY
BY DOMINIQUE BIEBAU

In every river, there are beings that envy our ability to breathe. Some people claim that the Molenvliet—the river that cuts through the middle of our village—provides a home to creatures that only emerge at night. Their voices drive travelers mad and attempt to seduce them beneath the surface of the water.

Pieter always laughed when he heard these old wives' tales. That was my brother for you: there was only room in his head for facts and figures. Credits, debits, and—perhaps most important—the difference between them, which was what kept increasing his wealth.

The river was his most important employee. Its current turned the mill's waterwheel, and that's where his money came from, all summer long. The farmers brought their grain from kilometers away, and grinding it into flour turned Pieter's jet-black hair gray and spread a downy white blanket across the interior of the mill. During the warm summer months, the mill was a lively place, with the rasping of the wheel and the voices of our customers, their throats and wallets loosened by smooth Dutch gin.

In the summer, when the fields grew fat in the rhythm of the sun, you might think of the river as a friend, a troubadour whose gentle song accompanied the life of the village. Only in the autumn, when thunderstorms caused the water to spill over the river's banks and relentlessly pounded the wheel in violet waves, did the Molenvliet reveal its true colors. It shrugged off its chains and bucked like an angry bull against the banks that held it captive. At night, my fellow villagers lit candles at the feet of the statue of St. Anthony, the patron saint of, well, just about everything, praying for the storms to abate and the water to return to its usual calm. Little did they know....

For me, the true horror began in the winter, when panes of crystal ice hid the Molenvliet beneath their sparkling surface. That's when I heard the voices.

I always used to wear white dresses, and my laughter was loud and frequent. Dressed in white and laughing, I strolled our village streets. I sang, too: old songs no one had taught me. And I told stories the villagers had long since forgotten. Of course there were eyes that watched me pass, most of them misty with emotion, because they saw in me—just for a moment—another, more beautiful world.

Other eyes were less kind. There are always some people who see beauty and think only of possessing it, see flowers and think only of plucking them.

And so, one day, I too was plucked.

Some people say that ice has no smell, but they're mistaken. It smells of fear and grief—and blood.

. . .

I no longer wore white dresses. And that's not the only thing I stopped doing. I no longer sang. I sat in my room and listened to my brother and Ellen, his bride, fight—mostly about me. I sat on my bed and stared straight before me, my eyes narrowed, as if focused on something that wasn't even there. If I looked closely enough, though, perhaps I would finally be able to see the past.

But my efforts produced no results. A stubborn quilt with the weight of a thousand tears covered my memories, the elusive remnants of forgotten dreams.

Ellen was always kind to me. Sometimes she brought me a little something extra to nibble on—a piece of sugarloaf, a slice of cake. In exchange for her kindness, I would tell her one of my stories, one of the ones I still remembered. She liked ghost stories best, full of blood and looming creatures. Sometimes I looked anxiously at the baby sleeping peacefully in his crib. When Ellen noticed, she smiled. "Are you afraid your stories will harm my baby?" she asked.

I nodded.

"But everything's fine so far, isn't it?" she said.

So far. She attached those two words to all the shadows in the room. I thought back to when we were both pregnant, both filled with hope for the future.

I thought of Lukas.

They found me late one night a kilometer outside the village, lying on the ice, in a spot where the Molenvliet had risen several meters above its banks, like a clenched fist. No one could say how long I'd been there or how I'd come to be there. It was a miracle I hadn't fallen through the ice and drowned.

It was Pieter who found me. His warm hands lifted me to my feet. "What happened, sister?" he whispered in my ear. "In the name of God, what happened?"

I felt frozen, as if an icicle had grown within me.

"The baby," I said. "What's become of the baby?" I rested my palms on my belly and felt nothing.

Only then did I see the red stains on the ice. Pieter put his hands over my eyes.

"What happened?" he repeated, more emphatically this time.

I shook my head. "I don't know," I stammered.

Pieter's strong arms—miller's arms—carried me back to the village. All the way, I fixed my gaze behind us. A chorus of dead souls droned from beneath the ice, a skein of voices that included that of my stillborn child.

I'd known Lukas since we were children. His mother never breastfed him, so he was always a sickly boy, fragile, pale as milky glass. But his mind sparkled like water in the sun. Because his hands were too delicate for a farmer's life, his father apprenticed him to a weaver, so he would learn a trade. When his apprenticeship ended, we married.

There are two types of people: those who look into the water and, like Narcissus, see only a reflection of themselves, and those who in its depths discover new realities.

Lukas lived with his eyes wide open. He belonged to the kingdom of ghosts and mythical creatures, the land where writers and poets abide. He told me wonderful stories, and I gave him my music and my body. We were happy, an emotion that only grew stronger when we learned that I was pregnant.

Not long after that, it turned out that Ellen was also with child. Everything was perfect for all of us.

Until that one bloody night.

The gentleness that had attracted me to Lukas turned out to be his downfall. What happened to me that night drove him mad. Two days after I lost my baby, a new singer joined the underwater choir.

Ever since the birth of his son, Pieter wanted me gone. "She's been touched by Death," I once overheard him say to Ellen. "That can't be good for our boy."

I was standing at the head of the stairs, about to come down, but when I heard those words I froze. I wasn't ready to leave the Molenvliet behind.

Ellen's voice, clear but faint, drifted up from below. "Leave her be, Pieter. She helps keep me from being bored. She tells lovely stories. Please, Pieter... for a while longer."

I could imagine the way she looked, a fragile statue of resistance.

"But we could turn her room into a nursery. And she can go to the Magdalene sisters. They accept fallen women."

Ellen's resolve remained firm. "She's not a fallen woman. She was married, and her husband and baby died. Perhaps when our son is a little older. Right now, her grief is much too fresh."

I coughed, so they would know I could hear them. Pieter had the decency to close his eyes and change the subject.

Later, I heard him throw a tantrum in the millroom. He slammed doors and flung sacks of flour against the wall. I wasn't the only dangerous occupant of that house.

When Lukas died, I stopped singing. I tried, once, but my voice was so scratchy I wept in frustration. I traded my white dresses for black ones. "The Crow," the villagers began to call me. "The Mill Crow."

It didn't bother me.

A few days after my miscarriage, Ellen gave birth to her little boy. It went as such things always go in Molenvliet: quickly and without much of a fuss.

Pieter later told anyone who would listen how he'd heard a sudden scream from the stables and ran cursing, his hands dusted with flour, to find Ellen lying in a pool of blood with a squalling infant in her arms. The new mother had cut the umbilical cord herself. He always ended the story the same way: "Our Molenvliet women are as hard as ice."

I missed out on the birth. I was a ghost, locked in my room, swaying between life and death.

Pieter called his son Gideon, a Leysen family name that went back several generations. He invited all the region's farmers to toast the child's health. Even I was handed a glass of table beer. I was an island of silence amongst the exuberant company.

In the middle of the crowd sat the new mother, a pale Madonna, her baby boy on her lap. She looked exhausted, with black circles under her eyes. Pieter stood beside her, strong and healthy as ever, a proud papa—yet clearly aware of the potential financial benefit of the occasion.

What wouldn't I have given to see Lukas there in Pieter's place? That thought filled me with horror. How could I be so inconsiderate of my own brother, the man who had rescued me from an icy death?

Suddenly there was a commotion. Ellen had taken ill. Two of the farmers' wives supported her on either side and led her to her bedroom. I took charge of Gideon. The baby purred with pleasure, but Pieter saw us and pulled the lad away from me.

"Don't you *touch* my son," he snarled.

He glared at me, his eyes aflame. I didn't understand his anger, but from that day forward I was never permitted to come anywhere near little Gideon.

Gideon was a sickly child. Ellen wasn't producing milk, and she tried to feed the boy cow's milk, but that didn't satisfy him. He cried a lot. Once I suggested that I could nurse him; my own breasts still strained with milk. But Ellen refused with a stubbornness I wasn't accustomed to seeing in her. "My child," she insisted. "My milk."

Ever since she became a mother, the distance between us had widened.

At least I still had my stories. Like a clever Scheherazade, I tempted her with tales I always broke off before the end. In that way, I bound our lives together with words. But I had no illusions. My skill as a storyteller was the only thing that kept me out of the convent.

Life went on. Despite the traumatic events, I seemed to achieve a sort of balance.

But when Gideon turned two, something unanticipated happened. Ellen proposed that we go for a walk. "Some fresh air will do us both good," she said.

We left Gideon in the care of a neighbor and strolled beside the Molenvliet. It was November, and in some places the river had already begun to overflow its banks. We carefully navigated around occasional pools of stagnant water. And eventually we came to the place where I had been found unconscious on the ice. I wanted to move on as quickly as possible, but Ellen held me back.

"What do you remember about that night?" she asked. We stood in the shadow of a willow whose branches brushed the ground. Ellen's pale face shone like a death mask in the darkness that surrounded us. I didn't know how to answer her question.

And then she grabbed my wrists with surprising strength. "What—do—you—remember?" she repeated, emphasizing each word.

"Nothing," I gasped. "Absolutely nothing. I fell, and then—I woke up on the ice. Pieter found me. Please let me go."

My response seemed to calm Ellen. Her expression softened. "I'm sorry," she said, and I believed that she meant it. "This place —there's blood here. Terrible things happened here. Let's go home."

On the way, I told her the story of Medea, a mother who murdered her own children rather than allow her ex-husband to raise them.

"What a horrible woman!" She shivered, but her eyes glistened with excitement.

That night, I lay with my ear to the floor of my room and listened to the voices that drifted up from below—not so very different in tone from the voices in the water.

"She has to go," hissed Pieter, and this time there was no answering protest.

I pressed the side of my head harder against the floorboards.

"I'm going to Vereeckens tomorrow to fetch pork lard to grease the millstones," I heard my brother say. "That takes me right past the convent. Mother Superior still owes me some money. With a little luck, I'll convince her to take Lore in."

The convent. The thought of it stabbed into me like needles. The Magdalene sisters were known for their rough treatment of their sinful "guests." Long days slaving in the laundry. Both physical and mental abuse. And I would be leaving forever the place where I once was happy, the place where I heard the echoing voices of those I had lost. It would be the death of me.

I awoke very early. It had snowed during the night, and the Molenvliet lurked beneath a coat of frozen armor. It was still very cold. I went outside and hid in the stable, waiting for Pieter to come and saddle his horse. I prepared myself to deliver a plea that would melt the polished ice caverns of my brother's heart.

When I stepped out of the shadows, he clutched a hand to his heart. "Lore," he said. "You startled me." He looked as if he'd seen a ghost.

"Don't do it," I whispered.

He didn't take my meaning at first, but then his expression hardened. He turned his back on me and hoisted his saddle.

"Don't send me away, brother!" That last word made him hesitate for a moment, but then he led his horse outside. I followed him and laid a hand on his shoulder. He wrenched away, and I lost my balance and tumbled headlong into the snow. Dazed, I felt him lift me from the ground—just as he'd done that fatal night on the river —and carry me to my room. He laid me on my bed and closed the door behind him when he left. The sound of a key turning in the lock confirmed my suspicions. I was a prisoner.

From my window, I watched Pieter spur his horse and disappear in the direction of the village.

I wept and brushed the snow from my hair. The smell of fresh-fallen snow awakened memories within me. For the first time, the blanket that had long hidden those memories from my sight was ripped aside. I opened the window and listened to the voices arise from the water.

.   .   .

We stroll beside the river, Ellen and me, our bulging bellies hidden beneath loose maternity dresses. We waddle like old ducks through the snow. It's cold, the frozen Molenvliet not yet cracking. The wind takes hold of our skirts and shakes them.

"Pieter is so eager to have a child," Ellen says.

I smile. I know my brother well enough to know that what Ellen says isn't entirely true. Pieter is eager to have a son, someone he can entrust the mill to when his hair is gray year-round.

"Would you like to see something?" asks Ellen, and she raises the hem of her dress.

"I don't know if," I begin, but she waves away my objection.

"Look," she says. The word is no longer an invitation but a command. The thick woolen fabric rises up past her waist.

A pillow falls to the snow, and I look a question at her.

"I lost it," she says. "Yesterday, there was blood on my sheets. I burned them. And the rest, I—I threw into the water." She stares at me with huge feverish eyes. "I'm afraid there's something wrong with me, and I can never have children. Pieter will leave me." She gestures shyly at my belly. "Can I have—your baby? You're still young."

Her suggestion is so ridiculous, I have to laugh. Ellen's face changes, and a second Ellen appears, one who's lived in her body for years but I've never before seen. Her pupils contract, and she spits like a lizard. "I need your baby, Lore."

She produces a knife.

I fall from the path onto the ice.

I pulled hopelessly at the door of my room, pounded on the walls, stamped on the floor. Ellen didn't react. And why should she? I leaned out of the window and considered jumping. Then I saw them, two black shadows in a white world. Ellen had taken Gideon outside, far from the racket his real mother was making. They were playing in the snow on the other side of the Molenvliet. Ellen threw snowballs at Gideon, who ran in laughing circles in an attempt to avoid them.

It should have been *me* playing with him.

After an hour, they both collapsed at the foot of a crooked alder and stretched out in the evening sun like lazy cats. The ice on the river cracked. The thaw had begun.

I leaned out my window and sang, and my voice had returned to its former power. Gideon looked up, surprised, but Ellen slept on, a satisfied smile on her face.

This was my chance.

I sang the songs I had never forgotten, songs of longing and loss, of birth and death, of a never-ending always, of the paradise that lay just beyond the next hill. I imagined that the ghosts in the river were listening. Did they brush tears from their eyes? Did they still have hearts?

Gideon stood, transfixed by the strange songs that echoed from the house. With a face as perfect as the dawn, he turned homeward and began his final walk. Every step brought him closer to the river. I sang.

"You delightful child, come with me," I sang. The words were Goethe's, from his ballad *The Erl-King,* but I sang them as if I had written them myself. "I'll play wonderful games with you. Colorful flowers grow on the shore."

The ice cracked. I jumped. I flew, then fell like a songbird frozen in its flight.

And two new voices joined the river choir.

4

ANCHORED

BY WOUTER BOONSTRA

"*Getverdemme!*" growled Tjalling Siebers, fire streaking through his body. He had been welding for decades without incident, but this once he had somehow managed—while stripping off his thick work gloves—to brush an arm against the glowing steel. The heat and hurt dizzied him for a long moment, and he staggered across to his armchair and dropped into it. Sweat poured down his face. He closed his eyes and felt for the minifridge behind him, fished out an icy bottle and pressed it to the burn. When the chill had finally soothed the pain, he twisted off the cap and drank the beer in one long swallow.

Tjalling opened his eyes and saw that dusk had begun to settle. Mist floated above the surface of the Amsterdam canals. "Enough for one day," he said aloud, and reached back into the refrigerator. This time, he took a box of fish sticks from the freezer compartment.

Soon he was sitting at his kitchen table, chewing happily. His thoughts drifted back to the West-Terschelling harbor, where in days gone by he had fished for crabs with Auke and Boele. That was a long time ago. He remembered his father, remembered giving the old man the burial at sea he'd always said he wanted.

The pounding woke Tjalling up, but it wasn't only his head that pounded. The arrogant asshole who'd moved in upstairs had the obnoxious habit of playing loud music in the early morning hours. "Anything goes in Amsterdam," the bastard had grinned, when Tjalling—struggling to keep his anger under control—had politely asked him to turn it down. The guy was a student, Jan-Joris de la Bretonière, if you could believe it.

Tjalling got the name from the name plate he'd watched the klutz waste half an hour attempting to screw to the street-door jamb. He'd finally taken over the simple task himself, only to get the spoiled baby out of his sight. "Oh, so *that's* how you do it," said Jan-Joris, and he climbed the stairs without so much as a thank you. It wouldn't be long before the building's owner would be in the market for a new tenant.

"Another ear infection, I'm afraid." Pediatrician A. Jonker lay down his otoscope and took a seat behind his desk. "Your son's got delicate ears, Mr. Siebers. I'm sorry, but there's not much I can do for him. He'll have to learn to live with it."

Tjalling began to sniffle.

"Quiet, you!" his father ordered. "Thanks, Doctor. We'll be going home. Come on, boy!"

Outside, Tjalling's father rolled a cigarette. He lit it and gazed out at the sea. There was only the slightest breeze. A boat was moored in the harbor, crewed by men with long hair and beards, dressed in colorful clothing. The girls on board were practically naked.

Tjalling watched his father observe them. "I give those hippies two hours," he muttered, "and they'll be on their way back to Amsterdam."

Tjalling stared at one of the girls. She winked at him and smiled. He could feel his heart race.

His father bent down and shouted in his ear: "You like that one, son?"

Tjalling almost collapsed in pain, and his father laughed.

"I like to move it, move it!"

Without turning around, Tjalling knew it was his favorite homeless man behind him. The creaking and squeaking of the guy's shopping cart full of trash hurt his ears, but Tjalling had a weak spot for the old man, whose schtick was announcing the neighborhood news like an old-time town crier.

"Tomorrow in the Rembrandt Park, a performance by El Mariachi, the Spanish guitarist!"

With his long beard and hair, his shabby clothes and scuffed shoes, Tjalling could have passed for homeless himself, but around here no one seemed to notice. No one around here noticed much of anything. Sure, sometimes someone in the neighborhood died. There were assaults. A jeweler was killed. That got a lot of attention for a while, but eventually people lost interest. The street had gentrified, was populated with hipsters, some of whom wore beards as long as Tjalling's. And then there were the damn students, like Jan-Joris.

"Nice work, Tjalling!" Gerard van Diepen, who managed the Osiris yacht basin, knew a well-made anchor when he saw one, and he generally bought most of what Tjalling offered him.

Tjalling knew he would turn around and resell them at a big mark-up, but that was fine with him, as long as he himself got what he felt he deserved for his labor. And this way he didn't have to spend his time going from one potential buyer to the next.

Back on Skylge—as the locals called Terschelling—they'd been more critical. Except on a couple of the older boats, people wanted modern gear. If things hadn't gotten uncomfortable for him there, his business had pretty much dried up, anyway, and he would still have had to move. No way he could ever retire there.

He certainly missed the island: the smells, the sea, the open air, even the sounds. But it was his trade that kept him afloat. Without his anchors, there would be no Tjalling—and without Tjalling, there would be no anchors.

Waves lapped gently against the bow of Tjalling's little motorboat. In the early mornings, he enjoyed slowly traversing the city's canals. As the last of the previous evening's revelers staggered home, Tjalling drifted over the water alone, in silence, past the De Schinkel sports fields and onto the Nieuwe Meer, the New Lake. He soaked up the serenity of the misty dawn. Sometimes he went all the way out to the IJ and puttered past the rusted cranes of the Western Harbor. The best time was between four and five AM. On rare occasions, the sight of an endless line of illuminated sailboats approaching up the Kostverloren Canal would jolt him out of his dream world. The Tall Mast Route was much loved by sailors, who used it to go through the city at night, past the airport and southwest toward Rotterdam. He had nothing in common with those people, except that it was during one such night crossing he'd first run across Van Diepen.

The wealthy sailors were a sociable lot. And they were always in the market for authentic handmade anchors. *Authentic.* They were crazy for authenticity. But Tjalling liked the canals best when he had them to himself, when he could float through the darkness undisturbed.

The smithy had been a School of Hard Knocks for Tjalling, but he'd learned his lessons well. He was forty years old when his father—against Tjalling's wishes—had turned the business over to him. "You go ahead and sink the whole enterprise, boy," he'd said, in a normal tone of voice for once, not roaring into Tjalling's bad ear. He still played that terrible game. When he was working or hanging out with his friends at the harbor, Tjalling usually wore ear protection.

The smithy stayed afloat, though times were hard. Tjalling was an artisan, not a businessman. There were times when his father still stepped in and managed the workflow. "You've got to be tough," the old man screamed in his bad ear, and collapsed in masochistic laughter.

Tjalling opened his second bottle of brandy and lit a hand-rolled cigarette. Dizzy, he rested his head on the table. The numbers didn't lie. That gray February afternoon in his father's claustrophobic office, he had decided for the first time to dig into the smithy's books. The situation was even worse than he'd thought. The winter months were always slow, and he'd already had to let quite a few of the employees go. Men he'd known for decades. But there'd been no alternative. He'd been protecting them for too long as it was. Now the business was well and truly heading down the tubes.

"Doesn't look good, does it, son?" He started awake. His father. "I knew I could count on you. If Kremer hadn't pulled back his offer at the last minute, I could have stuck him with the corpse. But he was right. There's no money in anchors anymore.

At least, not the way you've been running things. You're no businessman, Tjalling; you've never been any good at it. Too sensitive. Jelmer went to the university, and Koos went to sea. They found their own way, your brothers. But you? You don't belong here."

Tjalling was furious. His father turned away, heading for the door, but Tjalling grabbed the silver anchor the men had made to celebrate the smithy's fortieth anniversary and flung it at the old man's head. For an instant, it seemed to hang in the air, but then the crack of his father's skull broke the silence. Anchor and father dropped together to the floor.

The cleaning fluid and the icy air made his hands tingle, but Tjalling resolutely trundled his wheelbarrow along the path. Local kids sometimes used the wheelbarrow to take old iron and other trash to the junkyard. There would have been easier ways to transport his father's body, but Tjalling figured the wheelbarrow was likely to leave the fewest suspicious traces. He'd dumped the corpse into the barrow, which was always left out in the smithy courtyard, then covered it with the canvas sail from his father's boat.

There was no one out on the streets at this hour. The harbor was nearby, but how was he supposed to move the body onto the boat without being observed?

After killing the old man, he'd sat in the office for a while to calm himself. The pool of blood beneath his father's head slowly widened. Tjalling studied his father's lifeless face. He felt nothing. He downed several stiff shots of brandy, then got to his feet. He cleaned the office floor and got the body stashed in the wheelbarrow. As he pushed it toward the harbor, he had time to think. Glancing furtively from side to side, he thought he spotted Hiemstra, a neighbor, standing at his living-room window, peering out through the lace curtains, frowning.

The harbor was completely deserted. Afternoon had melted into night. It was dark and misty and cold. If he took the boat out now, someone might see him. Tjalling hesitated but finally decided to risk it. A few hundred yards from shore, he unwrapped the canvas from his father's body and heaved the old man overboard. He let out the rope he'd tied to his father's ankles, until all that was left aboard was the lead anchor at the far end of the rope. He dropped the anchor into the frigid water of the North Sea.

It bothered Tjalling that he didn't know for sure just what Hiemstra, the neighbor, had seen. When Hiemstra "dropped by" the morning after the murder, "just for a cup of coffee," Tjalling's darkest fears seemed at first to be confirmed, but the man acted just the same as always, which reassured him. As they sat in the office and talked, though, Hiemstra began acting suspiciously, and Tjalling realized he'd forgotten something important. His head buzzed with a terrible pain. The silver anchor was leaning against a filing cabinet, still stained with the old man's blood.

"Nobody 'disappears' from an island," Detective Henk Sietsma said.

In the days after Tjalling reported his father missing, the cop was a regular visitor. The disappearance of both Tjalling's father *and* neighbor Hiemstra in the same week set the island's tongues to wagging. People who would ordinarily never visit the smithy just happened to be passing by and stopped in to say hello. The old women whispered about his mother's death at an early age. His father's friends proposed far-fetched theories. Former employees, despite having been let go, showed up to offer their condolences. Their feigned grief over his missing father, the approaching bankruptcy of the business, and the blind panic that had assailed him ever since the murder of Hiemstra led Tjalling one evening to Café Bruijnis. He preferred a café without music, where it was quiet enough to talk, though conversation was the last thing he wanted.

After several shots of Dutch *jenever*, though, his own tongue loosened.

"You don't think your dad and Hiemstra went off together?" asked Barend, a regular customer. "It's too cold for a pleasure trip. By the way, what were you doing with that wheelbarrow out at the harbor the other night?"

Tjalling felt as if he'd been stabbed in the heart with a rusty blade. He looked up, instantly sober. Gulfs of pain assaulted his eardrums.

"Just dumping some rubbish," he said, his voice as casual as he could make it.

"You must have had a lot of rubbish," Barend said. "I saw you out there two nights in a row."

The doorbell rang. Tjalling's head was practically exploding. He knew he had to hang in there, turn off his emotions.

Sietsma looked like he'd had a long night of it. "You understand we're at the end of our rope, Tjalling. I'm sorry to bother you again, but you seem to be the last person who saw him. Do you remember what you talked about?"

So they'd found Barend already. Foggy as he was, Tjalling hadn't tied the anchor tightly enough to Barend's legs. And he couldn't risk using the boat again, so he'd simply rolled the body off the end of the pier. Thank God they hadn't found the anchor, since the body had floated some distance by the time it was spotted the next morning by the crew of the day's first seal-watching excursion.

Tjalling pretended to think it over for a moment, said they hadn't discussed anything in particular, but he'd noticed that the man had definitely been drinking. "When he left, he was heading for the harbor, and he was staggering drunk. Did he fall into the water?"

Sietsma nodded. "We think so. It's a plausible explanation, but you know how people talk. They're saying it's strange that you were the last one to see him. First your father goes missing—which I know how awful that has to be for you—and then Hiemstra, and now this. I've convinced the mainland police to send out a team."

Tjalling froze. The pain in his ears was almost unbearable.

Sietsma saw Tjalling's face tighten and changed the subject. "Did you talk about your father?"

Tjalling shook his head. "Not really. More about the business. It's finished. *I'm* finished, too. I'm going to close up shop and leave the island."

Sietsma frowned. "You're not going to like this, Tjalling, but you can't leave until we finish the investigation. You're not in any trouble, it's totally routine, but you're a witness, so you have to stay available for questioning. At least until the guys from the mainland get here."

Tjalling had expected something like this. Sietsma was a capable cop, he'd known him all his life. The pain was so intense, now, it was as if an electronic howl was penetrating his brain.

"Say, Henk, you were asking about my wheelbarrow. You want to see it?"

Sietsma eyed him suspiciously. "Your wheelbarrow? I don't remember—"

Tjalling cut him off. "Come out back to the courtyard."

Sietsma stayed put. He wasn't sure what Tjalling was up to, but in a criminal investigation any detail might turn out to be important. He'd known Tjalling all his life. As a kid, he'd worked for Tjalling's father on odd occasions. They were hard people, the Siebers, but honest.

"Come on back. You look like you could use a cup of coffee. I was just about to make some."

Sietsma's day had indeed gotten off to an early and chaotic start. "Sure, I'd like a cup."

Tjalling held the door for him. The wheelbarrow stood in the middle of the courtyard, a piece of canvas draped carelessly across it.

"Oh, that old thing. Why did you want me to see it?" Sietsma tugged at a corner of the canvas. "I never thought I'd—hey, are those bloodstains?"

Tjalling knew Amsterdam mostly from when he was a boy. If his father had anchors to deliver, he'd sometimes get to go along. They'd stroll through the Red Light District, and his heart would throb when he got a glimpse of the whores behind their plate-glass windows.

"Ladies of pleasure, Tjalling," his father crowed, making obscene gestures at the women. "You can look, but don't touch!"

Returning to the city as a grown man awakened a feeling of freedom within him. No one paid him any attention here. And he liked it that there was water everywhere he turned. The bustle and noise were a problem, but still Amsterdam was the first place he thought to go when he left the island.

With what he'd inherited from his father and the proceeds from the sale of the smithy, he had enough money to rent an apartment along the Admiral's Canal in De Baarsjes, a densely populated neighborhood in Amsterdam-West. He blended right in.

He convinced his brothers to hold onto the family home on Terschelling, at least for now. If they sold that, too, his leaving would raise one red flag too many. The islanders already thought his departure strange, but when all was said and done, they understood his desire to start afresh, now that his father was gone and the business had failed. On the other hand, though, they wondered if he'd had something to do with Barend's death.

They hadn't found Sietsma. They never would, since Tjalling had broken up the wheelbarrow into firewood and incinerated the body.

Life in the big city agreed with Tjalling—at least at first. He was now a freelance blacksmith, a craftsman, which earned him due respect in the digitalized hip capital. Nowhere else in The Netherlands were there as many boats as here. The Admiral's Canal was lined with them. And where there were boats, people needed anchors.

Tjalling didn't go out much. When he climbed onto his cargo bike to deliver an anchor, the pressure on his eardrums soon overpowered him. It was only after dark that he felt comfortable exploring the canals in his little boat, blanketed in the beauty and the splendor and the silence.

During the daylight hours, he worked. And when he returned from his nightly boat rides, he went straight to bed—though the blare of his upstairs neighbor's stereo often jarred him awake.

A strange sensation overcame him as he steered his boat through the Admiral's Canal, heading for the Nieuwe Meer. He had done it again. In Amsterdam, this time. He hadn't wanted to. He'd left the island to get away from this sort of thing. But the pain had become impossible. And it seemed easier here. No one paid him the least attention. His boat was right outside the front door of his building, close enough to carry an anchor in his arms, without a wheelbarrow. In a few minutes, he'd reach the deepest part of the lake. Against his ankles, he could feel that Jan-Joris de la Bretonière's body was still warm.

"You've got a nice collection." Detective Dijkstra glanced admiringly around Tjalling's workshop at the more than fifty anchors in various stages of completion. "And I see you don't mind a little drink, now and then." He waved a hand at a group of empty brandy bottles standing in a corner of the shop. "Don't get me wrong, I understand. It's a lonely profession."

Tjalling had already told him what he knew about Jan-Joris. He was a student, they hadn't had much to do with each other, he threw a loud party once in a while.

The last few days, Tjalling had slept like the dead.

"I've got an old barge in the harbor," Dijkstra said. "Maybe you could make *me* an anchor."

This took Tjalling by surprise. "Why not?" he said.

The disappearance of Jan-Joris was reported on the television news, and the whole neighborhood gossiped about it. But after a while their attention moved on to other things. No one made the connection between Tjalling and the similarly unexplained disappearances on Terschelling.

Before putting the student's apartment back on the market, the landlord decided to renovate it. That meant drills and electric sanders, hammers and saws—there was no end to the clamor. Tjalling considered anchoring the construction workers, but there were too many of them. The noise was so disruptive he couldn't work. Alcohol dulled him, softened the constant pain. He rarely took his boat out anymore. He woke up in the middle of the night, drenched in sweat, from terrifying dreams crowded with walking corpses and flying anchors. He could hear his father screaming in his ear: "You don't belong here, Tjalling!"

"They're all gone. They're dead." The words came out slurred, hard to understand. Late that Thursday afternoon, Detective Dijkstra had stopped by to pick up the anchor he'd ordered. It wasn't ready, was barely begun.

"Who's dead, Mr. Siebers?" Dijkstra asked. "Your father?"

The detective was well aware of the disappearances of Tjalling's father and neighbor Hiemstra, and of the mysterious drowning of Barend. The mainland police were still investigating the disappearance of Detective Sietsma. At first, he'd been unable to link these events to Jan-Joris' case. But now he saw the connection: Tjalling. The bearded islander was fading away into an alcoholic stupor. Dijkstra debated bringing him in for questioning but wasn't sure this was the right time for that.

"Mr. Siebers," he said, "I need to make a phone call."

Dijkstra turned away. Without the slightest hesitation, Tjalling grabbed for the closest anchor. That crack about his father had made the pain in his poor head intensify horrifically.

They knew.

At last.

But he couldn't quite reach the anchor, couldn't find it through the haze.

His brains thudded against the inside of his skull, and he saw flashes of light and stars before his eyes.

Dijkstra watched him, shaking his head sadly. He looked down at his phone. The reception in the workshop was poor, and his call hadn't gone through. Maybe he could send a text.

He looked up again and saw the sharp point of an anchor whistling toward his face.

That was the last thing he ever saw.

Fifteen minutes later, Tjalling was in his boat, heading for the IJ. It was broad daylight, and the Western Harbor would be quieter than the Nieuwe Meer.

He tied up at a deserted pier beside an abandoned warehouse.

The last swallow of brandy from the bottle he'd brought along tasted bitter.

For the first time in weeks, he felt at peace.

It would be better this way.

He made sure the rope was tightly fastened around his ankles and tossed the silver anchor overboard.

5

THE RED MERCEDES

BY THEO CAPEL

From where I stood, I had a clear view of the red Mercedes E240. It was bathed in afternoon sun, which made it seem even redder. If you gashed your hand and watched it bleed, you'd see the exact same shade.

So the car *did* exist, after all, which meant we had a chance to get it back. Klop's uneasiness had been misplaced.

Klop runs the Personal Loans department of the Geldkrediet Bank. His job is, on the one hand, to lend out as much money as possible, then, on the other hand, to get it all back with interest. It doesn't always work out the way it's supposed to, and that's where I come in. My one-man firm is called Stammer's Collections, but Klop and I know each other from way back and are on a friendly basis.

That morning, he'd sounded more nervous than usual, and the fact that he was waiting for me when I presented myself at the reception desk was a clear sign that something out of the ordinary was up.

"Seen the paper, Hank?" he said, as we walked down the

bank's cool corridors toward his office. "The accident in the Keizersgracht?"

I shook my head. Klop and I read different newspapers.

"Guy's lived his whole life in Amsterdam, run over on his doorstep by a French tourist. Must have had too much wine at dinner, the Frenchman. And then, while the guy's lying there in the gutter waiting for the ambulance, he's robbed by a German drug addict. What a world, Hank. What's it all coming to?"

In my newspaper, they're called "junkies," not "drug addicts." Maybe that sounds more interesting. I didn't answer Klop's question—his paper'd already done that for him. The world was going to hell, you could read about it every day.

We walked on in silence, me still wondering what was up. The answer came at Klop's office door.

"You hear about Schepers, Hank?"

"Schepers? No, what's the old man done now?"

"He's dead. Heart attack."

This *was* news. I'd known Schepers during my own time at the bank. He was an old-school manager, totally authoritarian. His fight against women in pants had made him notorious.

"But, Mr. Schepers, pants cover up more of my figure than a skirt," one courageous secretary had dared to argue.

"Pants accentuate, madam," was his honeyed response. "A skirt conceals."

Since that day, those words had been used around the bank to put an end to uncomfortable conversations.

"It was a disaster," Klop said. "You see, it happened in a—in a club."

"A club?"

He gave me a pained look. "You know what I mean."

The penny dropped. "A sex club? Schepers? Really?"

He winced. "You don't have to say it out loud, Hank. The walls have ears. Let's just call it a club, okay?"

That was fine with me, but I knew there had to be more to the story. Klop might be a latter-day Puritan, but he didn't really care what other people did with their private lives, as long as they didn't scare the horses. Work, that's all he was interested in.

He ushered me into his office and sent his secretary for coffee.

I sat there quietly, waiting for the rest of it. It took Klop several moments to work his tight mouth around the words.

"He left a hell of a mess, Hank. He broke more rules than I can count, and it looks like he knew exactly what he was doing. I'm afraid the bank stands to lose a bundle."

His face reddened. Klop was convinced that his customers were always trying to rip the bank off. But he couldn't bring himself to believe that his colleagues were capable of the same bad behavior.

"So far, we've been able to keep it quiet. Only Internal Affairs knows anything about it. We're talking about a hundred thousand. Euros, Hank. A hundred thousand euros."

Klop hadn't really adjusted to the euro yet. He still thought in guilders. Personal loans were generally in the five-to-ten-thousand-euro range. It would be the end of Klop's world if twenty such loans suddenly went up in smoke.

"Is the money gone? What did he do with it?"

Given the scene of Schepers' death, there was an obvious answer to my question.

"You know Schepers was in charge of Auto Loans?"

I hadn't known.

"Well, for starters, he seems to have approved two car loans which ought to have been denied. He took care of all the paperwork himself, didn't go through the ordinary channels. Then he made it look like the payments were coming in on time—but actually it turns out that the man who got the vehicles never paid a cent on the loans."

"How did he manage that? If no payments were being made, it'd've shown up in Accounting, wouldn't it?"

Klop shook his head sadly. "He made the payments himself. Well, not really. He made it *look* like the payments were coming in, juggled the books, sort of a robbing-Peter-to-pay-Paul situation. And because he's been here so long and knows our systems, he was able to cover it up."

"Until he died."

"Well, yes. When he stopped faking the payments, the loans were red-flagged and investigated, and that's when the truth came to light. Now we need to repossess the cars. You think you can handle that?"

"We'll see," I said. "But why did he do it? What did he get out of it? And why *two* cars?"

Klop scowled. "That's where the story turns really nasty. Schepers was speculating on the dollar market—apparently with embezzled funds. He bought an option for three months, the dollar fell against the euro, and he lost it all. Naturally, he was hoping to make a big enough profit to pay everything back."

For a man in Schepers' position, it would have been easy to place a large dollar order with a small upfront investment.

"If he could have held on for another two weeks," Klop said, "everything would have worked out the way he intended. The dollar turned around, and it's still going up. Schepers saw it coming—but he got the timing wrong and lost it all."

Klop looked like he'd made the doomed investment himself. He was far too cautious for such speculation, though.

"Upstairs has put me temporarily in charge of Auto Loans. They're positive there's more bad news to come."

Upstairs meant the bank's directors.

"Will you take a look at this for me, Hank, see if you can at least find out what happened to those two cars?"

Before I'd finished my coffee, Klop's telephone provided another shock. Auto Loans also handled insurance, and it turned out that one of the two Mercedes had been reported stolen several months earlier. Quite quickly—suspiciously quickly—Auto Loans had paid off on the claim.

"It could be worse, Klop. At least it was the cheaper of the pair, just a C320," I said, only half joking. "The buyer must still be driving the other one, and that one's a lot pricier. Second time around, he had a better idea of what he really wanted."

Klop was not amused.

"Do you realize how much even the C series costs, Hank? You can't find one for under forty thousand."

Disgust, despair—Klop's tone spoke volumes.

From my vantage point, I watched the blood-red Mercedes E240 sit there glittering in the sun. You could almost smell the wealth and privilege, especially in that neighborhood. The cars parked around it were mostly midrange, none of them new. They were all on at least their second owners.

The little square in Amsterdam-South was intersected by a wide cross street. The Mercedes was registered to Marco de Bruin, salesman. That didn't really fit the neighborhood, either. You'd expect to find a salesman on the other side of the irrigation canal, where the houses were bigger and there was even the occasional villa to be seen. Of course, salesmen come in all shapes and sizes. Maybe de Bruin was just a minor hustler, but then what was he doing with a Mercedes? Maybe trying to look like a major hustler....

In this part of Amsterdam, many of the blocks were housing

projects, originally thrown up for laborers and office personnel. The buildings, most of them, were due for their first major renovation. Trucks full of construction materials offered excellent cover for the itinerant investigator.

There was a playground on the other side of the square, with a jungle gym and a sliding board, a knot of kids clambering up the one and *woosh*ing down the other. The word *Fuckaduck* had been spraypainted on the side of the slide. The children looked Turkish to me. It surprised me to think that they knew English on top of Dutch and their own language.

I stepped out from behind the truck and crossed the street, heading for the Mercedes. Klop had warned me that the E240 might also have been stolen by now, same as the C320—"stolen" in quotation marks, he'd said. I took a good look at the license plate, though, and it was the right car. All four doors were locked.

"Hey, you! Get away from the car!" someone shouted.

I turned and thought I saw a figure behind the curtains in one of the downstairs apartments. I couldn't make him out clearly, but that didn't bother me. What bothered me was the pistol pointing straight at me.

The downstairs apartments had tiny front gardens, with access from the apartments via sliding glass living-room doors. On each side of these doors was a small curtained window. There was a broken pane in one window, and the pistol's barrel was sticking through the hole in the glass. A man held the curtain a little to one side, so he could aim in my direction.

"That's right, you see it. You want to *feel* it, too? Get the hell away from my car!"

"Mr. de Bruin? Marco de Bruin?" I called in an official voice.

It was quiet for a moment.

"What if I am?"

"My name is Stammer. I'm representing the Geldkrediet Bank."

The pistol disappeared, and a few moments later the dark-green front door opened. I saw a thin young man. As I walked toward him, I saw that he'd been threatening me with an air pistol. It had seemed far more dangerous when I hadn't known what it was.

"They're always messing with my car," he said.

He made a sweeping gesture with his arm, encompassing the children crowding the playground but also, apparently, everyone else in the neighborhood. Even the grownups. Even me.

"Every once in a while, you have to scare them a little. And don't get me wrong, this thing can *sting*." He raised the pistol. "I shot a pigeon right out of a tree last week. Thought I was out there washing the car just to give it a clean place to take a dump."

"I'd be careful, if I was you," I said. "Especially around the kids. All you need is a bunch of pissed-off parents banging on your door."

He shook his head stubbornly. "Not a problem. They find out one of their brats touched my car, they'll beat the crap out of him themselves. Those foreigners know exactly how much a Mercedes costs. One of them came by the other day, wanted to know what I'd take for it."

"As long as the bank still holds the paper, though, you wouldn't try to sell it, would you?"

He stared at me in silence. I noticed that he'd cut himself shaving. He didn't look like he could afford a new razor, let alone a car. He definitely fit the minor-hustler mold. His trousers were wrinkled, and his striped shirt was a Goodwill special. On his feet were cheap, off-brand sneakers.

"I'm here for the keys," I said. "No payments, no car."

For a second, I thought he was about to spit on my outstretched palm.

Then, "What's your problem?" he said. "That's not the deal I made with your dude. I'm waiting for the cash. You guys know that. It won't be much longer—you'll get your money."

"We want it now, Marco. A deal's a deal. You haven't kept up the payments, so we take the car back. That's the way it works. You signed the papers yourself."

"Papers? What papers?" he said, stroking his chin. He glanced down at the air gun and stuck it clumsily in his pants pocket. "Mr. Schepers was supposed to take care of all that for me."

"Mr. Schepers isn't with us anymore."

"Naturally," he muttered. "I knew this would turn to shit. Look, I can explain everything."

"Including the stolen C320?"

He was dumbstruck.

"What are you talking about?" he demanded. "Somebody stole it. Stuff happens. But the insurance covered it, it was all taken care of."

"I see," I said. "So then why did you need to finance *this* car, too? Why didn't you just pay for it with the insurance from the first one?"

He stared at me. "What do you care about the insurance? The insurance company doesn't care. They've got zillions."

"The insurance company is owned by the bank."

There was a momentary pause, and then he grinned. He was missing a tooth, I noticed.

"So you took quite a hit, then," he said.

He was starting to annoy me.

"The keys," I said.

I took a step toward him, which put me practically inside his apartment. He was getting nervous: he took a step back and looked shiftily from side to side.

"You don't mean that," he said. "It's all gonna be fine, the money. I need the car for work. I can explain everything." He thought a moment. "You know what? We'll go see the dealer. They know the whole story."

"I'd be happy to believe you," I said, "if you let me see some cash. I'm not leaving without three thousand euros or the car. You pick."

"Three grand!" His voice was suddenly shrill. "You know I haven't got that kind of money. You have to give me a little time!"

He started in again about business, without explaining exactly *what* business he was in. I kept quiet. I knew the routine.

Finally, I agreed to ride along with him to the Mercedes dealer —who was sure to advance him a few thousand, he insisted. After all, he was a good customer.

What changed my mind was the realization that he was inviting me to sit inside the car, with the keys within hand's reach. And I was going to have to check out the dealer, anyway.

De Bruin went inside to get a jacket. I watched him poke around for a piece of cardboard to prop inside the broken window-pane. He came out in an old leather bomber jacket with a wide collar and epaulets. The keys were in his hand.

Crossing the street, we had to jump out of the way when a heavy black Honda motorcycle carrying a rider and passenger roared past.

"Hey!" de Bruin called after it. "Watch it, you jerk!"

The biker slowed down, and his passenger turned back to face us. Both of them wore full leathers with the Honda logo on the back. You couldn't see their faces through the tinted visors of their helmets.

"Bikers are such jackoffs," said de Bruin, opening the

Mercedes' passenger door for me as the motorcycle picked up speed and disappeared around a corner. "They think they own the road."

During the drive, de Bruin bragged nonstop about the beauty of the E240, and I had to admit he was right. You barely heard a whisper from under the hood. It accelerated smoothly and ran like a dream. When I didn't argue with him, his self-confidence accelerated as smoothly as the car. He assured me four separate times that the Mercedes dealer would lend him the three thousand euros I was demanding. He even chewed me out when I made a minor readjustment to my sideview mirror.

The dealership was in Buitenveldert, in a big showroom on the ground floor of a huge apartment block. There was a parking area in front, no kids around to smudge the car's brilliant paint job with their greasy fingers.

We were the only customers at that hour. A fellow about my age came out to meet us. He wore a spiffy blue-gray suit, a white shirt, a striped silk tie. He was perfectly cleanshaven. His gaze seemed slightly clouded, and he forced a smile when he saw de Bruin.

"Ah, Mr. de Bruin. What can we do for you? No problems, I hope. I saw you pull in, and everything looks just right—I told you, it's a heck of a car." He turned to me. "Is your friend interested in a Mercedes?" He said it dubiously, unsure whether I *was* de Bruin's friend or something else.

"I'm with the Geldkrediet Bank," I said, as we strolled towards the showroom. "Mr. de Bruin has been having some trouble making his payments, and the bank has decided to repossess the car."

"It's not gonna come to that," de Bruin snapped. "I told you, they'll take care of it. Just give me five minutes to work it out!"

The salesman had edged away from him, and I also stepped back, leaving him standing by himself, like a shipwrecked sailor on a desert island.

"Well," the salesman said hesitantly. "This can't be very pleasant for you, Mr. de Bruin."

"Pleasant?" de Bruin snarled. "You want to talk about pleasant? I'll tell you what won't be pleasant. If you don't hand me three thousand euros, I'm going straight to your wife, and I'm gonna let her know what you've been smoking back there in your office between customers. You knew damn well I didn't have the money when I bought the car, but you were happy to sell it to me, and you haven't said no to those bags of herb I tip you with. Now you're going to help me out of a jam—three thousand euros doesn't mean a thing to you."

He grabbed the salesman by the lapels. He didn't really seem dangerous to me; his bluster looked more like begging than a threat. But the salesman took him seriously. He kneed de Bruin hard in the groin, and de Bruin staggered back, his face drained of color. For a moment it looked like he might throw up on the showroom floor. He collapsed and covered his crotch with shaking hands. If I hadn't been there, the salesman would have kicked him in the head with a perfectly polished wingtip.

"I should have done that when you first came in here, you dirty loser," the salesman hissed. "You think I let a nobody like you threaten me in my own place? You watch yourself, little man. You ever set foot in here again—you go anywhere *near* my wife—I'll have a couple of my mechanics teach you some manners."

His face was red with anger.

"Okay, now," I said, just to be doing something.

"It's *not* okay," the salesman cried. "You've got your own problems with him—otherwise, you wouldn't be here."

"Well, you're the one who sold him the car," I said. "Wait a minute, what am I saying? You're the one who sold him *two* cars. You figured you could make some money off him. Or am I missing something?"

De Bruin had risen to his knees and was sucking in deep breaths. His hands were still clutching his privates.

"Sure, I sold him two cars," the salesman argued, "but only because Mr. Schepers vouched for him. You don't think *I* sent *him* to Auto Loans? They came in together, and Mr. Schepers guaranteed me the financing wouldn't be a problem. What was I supposed to do? I mean, I sell cars, that's what I *do*. And you can't always judge by appearance. I had a rock singer in here, he looked to me like he was stoned to the gills, but he had a pocket full of five-hundred-euro notes. Fifty-thousand euros, cash, and he wasn't leaving without a Mercedes, he said. I had to go to the bank with him to make sure the bills were real. Not that I was worried. I've seen him on TV, his records sell like crazy. My own kids buy them, so do all their friends. The guy's rich, but you wouldn't know it to look at him."

"This one says he's a salesman," I said, pointing down at de Bruin, who reached out a hand to me.

I helped him up.

"Jesus," he groaned. "Jesus, that hurts." His face spasmed. "I gotta ralph."

Before I could make a move, the salesman took him by the arm and had him halfway back to the big glass showroom door. I tagged along, and a minute later de Bruin was tossing his cookies on the asphalt of the parking area. He didn't have all that many cookies to toss, but it took him quite a while to toss them. When he was finished, he stood there bent forward at the waist, gasping.

"Sit in the car," I said. "Try to pull yourself together."

He nodded and handed over the keys. I opened the door on the passenger side and helped him in. He leaned back against the leather, but he didn't seem to appreciate the comfort he'd been bragging about twenty minutes earlier. I got in behind the wheel.

After a while, de Bruin seemed to be tracking again.

"Bastard," he said, looking over at the showroom.

The salesman was nowhere to be seen. He'd apparently gone back to his office.

"He's a freaking liar. He's the one who put me and Schepers together. I'll tell your boss the whole story, if you want, he'll be very interested. I could write a book about all the dirty games he and Schepers were playing." He was getting his nerve back. "You saw it yourself, he attacked me. I'll get even."

I thought about it. I had the keys. I had to deliver the car to the bank, anyway. Why not take de Bruin along and let him talk to Klop?

De Bruin insisted we stop off at his office to pick up what he called his "evidence."

"Where *is* your office?" I asked.

He glared at me as if I'd insulted him but told me to head for the Central Station.

"And be careful with my car," he added, when a light turned red and I didn't come to a stop quickly enough to suit him.

By the time we hit downtown, I was feeling more comfortable behind the wheel. All I had to do was stop thinking about my own car, an old VW. Every once in a while, de Bruin did some backseat driving, but for the most part his attention was still focused between his legs.

"Stop here," he said at last. "I'll be right back."

I watched him go into an old warehouse in the Spui Street, not far from a line of pricey tourist hotels. An illuminated yellow sign over the warehouse door said *Club Kitty* in English. *Open all day and all night.*

"That's some car, mister," a voice said.

A slim young woman, maybe twenty-three or twenty-four, had appeared beside the Mercedes, running the tips of her long white acrylic fingernails slowly along the edge of the half-open driver's window. Her hair was dyed the same dead white as her fake nails, and she wore a faded black microskirt over fishnet stockings and a V-necked T-shirt with the sleeves slit off. It too had been white, once upon a time, but too many wash cycles—or too few—had left it a dingy gray. Her face was probably the same color beneath too much clumsily applied makeup.

"Can you spare a cigarette? Or maybe we could take a ride?"

The way she said it suggested she wasn't really interested in smoking or riding. Her Dutch was clumsy, her accent Slavic.

"Buzz off, Vera," said de Bruin, swinging open the passenger door. He eased himself carefully into the seat.

"This is your office?" I said. "So you run the sex club where Schepers died, is that it?"

"Like you didn't already know," he said. "Yeah, this is my place. At least, I'm one of the partners. Why do you think I needed that insurance money? And I use the car to pick up customers and bring them home after. It makes a nice impression. I was supposed to take Schepers home that night, and then all of a sudden he was dead in one of the rooms. We had to straighten him up a little—didn't want it to look like the girls had killed him." He gazed over at his sex club. "I thought the publicity would be bad for business, but go figure: soon as the story leaked out, the thrill seekers started showing up, wanting to see where it happened. A couple more days like this, I'll be able to pay off all my debts. You'll get your share, don't worry." He groaned, but that was still because of the pain. "And that bastard at the dealership, he'll get what's coming to *him*, too."

I started the car and pulled carefully out into traffic. I gave a little gas, then stomped on the brake when the car in front of us unexpectedly came to a halt.

"Hey, watch out!" cried de Bruin. He hadn't fastened his seat belt. "What are you doing?"

Two men jumped out of the car.

"Police!" they shouted. "Step out of the Mercedes. Step out!"

"Dammit," de Bruin muttered, reaching inside his leather jacket.

I jumped when he pulled out the pistol. My seatbelt unclasped easily, but de Bruin still beat me out of the car. He aimed his weapon at the detectives, who dodged behind their vehicle. I heard a motorcycle behind me, and then a man in black leathers and a helmet with a tinted visor grabbed me by the neck. A second man, similarly outfitted, was dismounting from the bike and setting it on its kickstand. I recognized them by the Honda logos on their leathers.

"Police!" the second biker screamed from under his helmet. "Don't move! Drop the gun!"

"Don't shoot," I cried. "Don't shoot! It's just an air pistol!"

"Right, I'm an idiot," said de Bruin. "You think I'd go up against that ripoff artist at the dealership with a stupid airgun? This one's the real thing. You bastards want my car? Come and get it!"

To my astonishment, he shot a giant star in the rear window of the car the officers had been driving. I saw one of them waving a badge folder from behind the front bumper. I don't know why he bothered. Nobody was doubting they were cops.

Out of the corner of my eye, I saw that the biker had unzipped his leathers and pulled out a gun. His colleague pushed me onto the asphalt and pressed his knee against my spine. On the other side of the Mercedes, de Bruin fired again. Two more shots sounded from much closer to my ear.

I lay with my cheek pressed against the road and could see de Bruin's legs and feet on the other side of the Mercedes. I watched him slump to the ground.

"He's hit," the man holding me down called out. "His buddy's unarmed."

He let me go. I slowly got to my feet and assumed the position. De Bruin wasn't moving. One of the cops pulled his jacket open. The brown leather was drenched with blood, which had also spattered onto the hood of the Mercedes.

"There's nothing on him," the man yelled. "Where's the damn weed? I don't see anything in the car."

My policeman slapped the side of my head.

"Where is it?" he demanded.

He patted me down, but I had nothing for him to find.

"This one hasn't got it, either," he called to his colleagues. "You check the club, maybe it's still in there. I'll check the trunk." He pulled me away from the car. "Open it."

I wasn't really paying attention. I was looking at de Bruin's blood on the hood of the Mercedes. They weren't quite the same shade of red, after all.

6

GARAGE 27

BY DE PAEPE & DEPUYDT

Thanks to me, the folks who live in the big apartment block on Ganzendries Street in Ghent are well taken care of. Thanks to me, Remi De Sutter. I know them all. I know who lives in each apartment. I know that the old man at #113 always takes out his trash on the wrong day of the week. First thing in the morning, I see one girlfriend or another slip out the young stud who lives at #107's door. All summer, I check the widow Colle's balcony at #121 to make sure the nurse who looks after her positions her wheelchair in the shade and not the bright morning sun. When the kids at #143 dump their bikes and block the building's entrance, I wheel them to the side of the path. I look after my residents. I'm the concierge.

There's a row of garages across the alley that runs behind the building. It's a squat brick structure with a corrugated tin roof. When it rains, the drops pelt the tin, and the *rat-a-tat-tat* ricochets through the alley like a machine gun. The metal garage doors are old, with rusty handles and squealing hinges. Most of them are used by the building's tenants. But some are rented out to commuters who live in the suburbs, park their cars here, and walk to the nearby Sint-Pieters station to take the train to their office jobs in Brussels. I know every car: make, model, color, driver, passengers. And I have a master key that fits all the garage doors.

Garage 27 is the odd one. It's always open, day and night. I was thirty when I came to work on Ganzendries Street, so I've been here for eleven years now, and I've never seen a soul use it. Except me: when I make my rounds at night, I sometimes duck in there to get out of the rain, or for a few minutes' respite from the nasty wind that whistles down the alley on a brisk autumn day, chasing dry leaves along the asphalt. I shine my flashlight carefully around the interior. There's a limp tire leaning against the far wall, stitched with cobwebs. Beside it stands a cheap particleboard cabinet. Once, curious, I looked inside the cabinet. It was empty, but there were circular stains on the shelves, which suggested it was long ago used to store bottles or jars.

I'm a guy who's never had much luck with the ladies. I weigh about two hundred and fifty pounds, and my thinning hair is giving way to male pattern baldness. My walrus mustache is going gray. My mother says I should lose the 'stache—it scares women off, according to her. But I've got a birthmark shaped like a cockroach on my upper lip, and that would be worse.

Every night, I grab a coffee from the rundown snack bar behind Sint-Peters. They're always running out of coffee, tea, sugar, plastic cups, and spoons, so I picked up a big supply of all that stuff and stashed it in the empty cabinet in Garage 27 and put a lock on it. After I finish my evening rounds and before I head over to the snack bar, I call the woman who runs the place—a fat Thai who answers to Sun—and see what she needs. I bring it over and sell it to her under the counter. I mark it up fifty percent, cash on the barrelhead, no sales tax—and she doesn't charge me for my coffee. A good deal all around.

My tenants are an ungrateful lot. Doesn't matter how well I look after them—day and night, weekdays and weekends—most of them act like I don't even exist. They draw their curtains when I'm checking on the garages. They glare down at me from their balconies, snatch their wash from their clotheslines and hurry back indoors. The kids sometimes chuck stones at me, or insults.

Fatso!

Freak!

Your mama's a hooker!

I puff myself up and put on an angry face and shake my fist at them, and they peel off on their bikes and disappear around the corner of the building. Little devils.

Things go on like this for years. The widow Colle dies, and a group of noisy students move into her apartment. The kids at #143 grow older, and their bikes are replaced by sputtering mopeds. The guy in #107 finds himself a steady girlfriend, a tattooed skank he constantly fights with as they sit in his open window passing a joint back and forth. One thing never changes: though trash pickup is on Fridays, every Tuesday the old man in #113 drags a single garbage bag out to the curb.

The summer heat shimmers the air above the garage roofs, and cawing swifts swoop and dive through the tempting aroma of balcony barbecues. Winters bring snow and ice, and I sow the asphalt between the building and the garages with salt, my boots crunching pleasantly on the snowpack, strands of Christmas lights twinkling merrily from the balcony railings. My side business, headquartered in the locked cabinet in Garage 27, flourishes. I am one contented concierge.

But this fatal fall, something happens. It's the first week of October, and we're enjoying an Indian summer. Then we get a couple of back-to-back chilly nights. For the first time this year, my breath puffs visibly from my mouth as I sweep up the broken branches which have dropped from the chestnut tree in the back garden next door. Chattering magpies on the tin garage roofs warn each other of winter's approach, their feathers rustling in the descending dusk. Sun has called me from the snack bar to tell me she needs a delivery. I wait for full darkness, then lean my broom against the fence and head for Garage 27.

The door is shut. First time in eleven years.

I blink my eyes in surprise, cautiously touch my ear to the rusted metal door. There's someone stumbling around in there, a man, breathing heavily, clearing his throat. An intruder? A homeless person? Or has the garage's owner come back, after all this time?

My heart pounding, I slip through the apartment building's rear door and hide myself in the bike room. I wait for the motion-activated hall light to click off, then peer through the grimy window that looks out across the alley. One eye squeezed tightly shut, I watch Garage 27 with the other. Light dances in the cracks around the door. What's he up to in there? Though it's chilly in the unheated bike room, I break out in a sweat. What if he breaks open the cabinet I've locked and finds my stuff? If he reports me to the building management, I could lose my job. This is definitely not good.

And then the door swings open, its rusty hinges screaming. A backlit figure emerges from within. The man is unkempt, his clothing tattered, his age impossible to determine. He looks around wildly, his eyes sunk deep in their sockets. Cardboard boxes and bulging shopping bags are piled up on the concrete garage floor, but as far as I can see from my hiding place, he doesn't seem to have opened my cabinet. There's a toolbox at his feet, so he wouldn't have any trouble breaking into the cabinet, if he wanted to. And why *wouldn't* he want to? I know I'd be curious if some unknown person hung a lock on *my* cabinet.

The stranger buttons his greasy jacket and scurries off into the night. He leaves the garage door open and the light on. I count slowly to a hundred and leave the bike room. I sweep my flashlight slowly left and right across the alley. No one there. The commuters are long gone, and the residents are parked at their TVs behind drawn curtains.

I check my watch. It's nine thirty. My cellphone buzzes in my pocket. Probably Sun, wondering what's keeping me. I ignore it and go into Garage 27. I hadn't seen it from the bike room, but there's a filthy mattress lying in the back. So maybe *not* the owner, but some drifter who's stumbled across a comfy place to get some shuteye? If so, it's my job as the concierge to get rid of him.

All righty, then.

I take a deep breath and slowly let it out.

If I make too much of a racket, the tenants may be alarmed. They'll come out to see what's going on, and one of them might call the management, which could put an end to my little side business. No, I'll have to deal with the situation as discreetly as possible.

I unhook the ring of keys from my belt and open my cabinet. Everything's right where I left it. I'd better get it out of here, and best is to move it all in a single load. But how? A garbage bag? I can probably find one in the maintenance closet off the bike room, but that'll take a bit of time. Faster would be to empty out one of the newcomer's cardboard boxes and use that. I fish my pocketknife out of my pocket and cut the tape that seals the box at the top of the pile.

When I open the flaps, the flesh at the back of my neck crawls.

The box is lined with dusty glass jars of various sizes. Their labels are gone, but from the lids I can see that they once held some handy homemaker's canned fruits and vegetables. Now, though, each jar is filled with a brown liquid in which a fleshy white object floats. I frown, take a jar from the box at random and examine it more closely. The white object is an ear. A human ear. I shudder and reach for another jar. Another ear. I begin to hyperventilate and pull jar after jar from the cardboard box. A human ear floats lazily in each of them. And the jars are exactly the same size and shape as the round stains on the shelves of "my" storage cabinet.

Gasping, I kick the empty box over to the cabinet. One shelf at a time, I sweep my stuff into the box. Suddenly I realize that the garage light is blazing. Anyone who happens to be spying on the alley from behind his living-room curtains can see exactly what I'm doing. Dammit, what crazy dangerous hornet's nest have I gotten myself into? I drag the box out of the garage and across the asphalt to the apartment building's back door and into the bike room. I feverishly fold the box flaps shut so no one can see what it now contains. I catch my breath. A cardboard box holding coffee supplies, tucked away behind the bike rack. No problem there. Happens all the time. If a tenant leaves personal items other than bicycles in the bike room for too long, the management tapes a nastygram to the door, but that's all. So no worries. I'm safe for now.

My cell vibrates again, but I'm pressed up against the little window, watching too intently to answer it. A quarter of an hour later, the guy is back. He's carrying two big shopping bags, and they seem pretty heavy. He staggers into the garage and sets them down, puts his hands on his hips and stands there for a solid minute, eyeballing the glass jars I removed from the box I "borrowed" and the unlocked cabinet door. He scratches his head and leaves the garage and looks around. Then he goes back in and swings the cabinet door open and feels around inside it, like he can't believe his eyes and needs to make sure the cabinet's really empty. And then he bends over and starts loading the jars onto the shelves, two at a time, carefully setting them in the spots where the stains tell him they used to be.

So this *is* the owner. Probably thrown out of his house by his wife and now planning on bunking in the garage. You hear stories like this. And it explains why he's got so much stuff with him. But what's up with those jars, those *ears*? I'll have to look into this and figure out what to do.

After a while, the guy swings the garage door shut. From the inside. Light leaks through the cracks for another couple minutes, and then Garage 27 goes dark.

That same evening, I come to a new arrangement with Sun. I've lost my warehouse, and she agrees to store my stock of goods at the snack bar in exchange for a better deal on the prices. Plus from now on I have to pay for my coffee. I sign off on that. Sun is a good sport about it, and our negotiation is amiable and enjoyable. I'm glad to have her as a friend. Her broken English cheers me up, and she encourages me to tell her about my old mom and the antics of the tenants I look after. She's impressed by the level of responsibility I bring to my work. She admires my calm attitude. For now, of course, I don't say a word about those eerie jars.

The next few weeks, the door to Garage 27 stays closed during the daylight hours. I begin my rounds at dusk, but I don't dare press my ear to the door. When it's completely dark, I have my coffee at Sun's snack bar, then squirrel myself away in the bike room for the night. A couple times, the students reel in drunk at a godless hour. I tell them I'll rack their bikes for them, and they can go right on upstairs to sleep it off. They slap me on the back and disappear, giggling and shushing each other.

And every night I witness the same sequence of events: the unkempt guy shows up dragging boxes and shopping bags, empties them out, moves his treasures from one box to another, folds his bags neatly and later unfolds them and refills them. From my vantage point, his treasures seem to be nothing but junk—garbage, really. Doesn't look like his wife's letting him move anything of actual value out of their house. No more jars, thank goodness. The ones he brought in that first night are stowed away in the cabinet.

He no longer checks to see if he's being observed. Around four or five AM, he emerges, switches off the light, pulls down the door, and locks it and drifts away. And while the magpies scratch around on the tin roof above and the commuters park their cars and go off to their day jobs, it's quiet in Garage 27. Until the following night.

I keep watch for weeks. It's exhausting work, but I endure. I sleep during the day, just like him. I owe this to my tenants because, after all, I'm the concierge and it's my job. Sun comments on my dedication and smiles shyly at me. Finally someone who sees me for who I really am. Unlike the tenants, those ingrates. But there's something rotten in the state of Ganzendries, and it's my responsibility to get to the bottom of it. To protect them. To make sure they can go right on sitting behind their drawn curtains watching TV, without a care in the world, secure in the knowledge that everything is fine in their little community because Remi De Sutter has the situation under control.

Three weeks after the owner moves into Garage 27, there's another new development. As abruptly as he appeared, the mysterious man disappears. Maybe he's gotten back together with his wife, or found himself a decent place to live? I hope so, so I can move my stuff back into that cabinet. But there's something fishy going on. The garage door stays closed around the clock. I continue my nightly sentry duty, but it's pretty boring in the bike room with nothing whatsoever to see. Cold, too, because by now it's November, and Old Man Winter decorates the tin garage roofs with a glittering layer of frost each night. Far above the Ganzendries, the constellations dance slowly across the sky. The sounds of braking freight trains and barking dogs in distant gardens provide a soundtrack for my vigil. My tenants spend their evenings indoors. They've already brought in the carved pumpkins from their balconies. Ghent shivers in the cold gray weeks that lead up to the holidays.

On the fifth quiet night after the stranger vanishes, I can't contain my curiosity any longer. I find the right key on my ring and stick it in the lock on Garage 27's door. I have to jiggle it a little until it fits. When I pull the door open, the hinges protest more loudly than I expect.

It's pitch dark in the garage. There's a bad smell inside, like the stench of rotting meat. Before I turn on the light, I ease the door shut behind me. I don't want my tenants to see their concierge poking around in a garage they by now may have begun to identify with someone else. The stink in the air is more pungent with the door closed. I hold my breath and feel for the lights. When I flip the switch, there's an electrical hum as the fluorescent bulb hanging from the ceiling stutters into life. I blink my eyes against the glare and practically faint from the shock that awaits me.

In the far corner of the garage, Sun lies stretched out on the concrete floor. She is naked and filthy, and her wrists and ankles are tied with dirty lengths of rope. Her skin is blue from the cold, and there are ugly scabs around her mouth. A bandage clotted with dried blood has been wrapped clumsily around her head. She's lost a lot of weight. Where two weeks ago there were love handles bulging the hips of her patterned house dresses, now there are flaps of useless white skin. A milky film clouds her eyes. Her toenails are broken—she's apparently been kicking the concrete in a vain attempt to loosen her bonds—and her shoulders are slumped forward, hiding her bare breasts from my sight.

I kneel beside her and ease a hand beneath the back of her head. "Sun, can you hear me? Who did this to you?"

"Water," she pleads, her voice hoarse, barely audible. "Please."

I look frantically left and right, but there's nothing for her to drink. I know there's a faucet on the apartment building's back wall across the alley, but I don't dare open the garage door and let in the frigid outside air.

"I'll find you some water, Sun," I promise her. "But first tell me what happened."

"Water," she says again, "and something to eat. I'll cook for you. Give me a knife, a cutting board, an eggplant, some red peppers and ginger, and a little ground beef."

I ignore her ravings. The poor woman is out of her mind with hunger and thirst and pain and fear. "Was it the man who brought all these boxes and bags in here? Is that who tied you up?"

She nods.

"I'll get you out of here, Sun," I whisper. "I'll save you. Where do you want me to take you?"

"Untie me," she murmurs.

I carefully slide my hand out from beneath her head and undo the rope from around her ankles. And before I can do a thing to stop her, she kicks me in the chin with everything she has.

The world around me whirls, as if an earthquake is shaking the neighborhood. Choking, I hear the magpies on the tin roof overhead scream in panic. Sun scrambles to her feet, flings the metal door open and flees. I try to follow her but lose my balance. By the time I emerge from the garage, she is nowhere to be seen. Muted television colors illuminate the curtains of the apartments across the asphalt. The students in #121 are clustered on their balcony, laughing and flicking glowing cigarette butts into space. I feel dizzy, and the icy air clutches my lungs in its fingers. There's a sudden rush of warmth in my groin, and I realize I've peed my pants. I rush drunkenly down the alley, turn away from the direction of the snack bar, and lose myself in the city's back streets. At dawn, I wake up in the rail yard on a bed of hogweed, my extremities numb, my teeth chattering.

I don't dare return to the Ganzendries. All day I wander aimlessly through town. I throw my cellphone in the river Leie. I scoop up abandoned bottles of beer left behind by tourists and drain them of their final drops. I eat breakfast, lunch, and dinner from dumpsters. I sing a foolish song on the corner of a pedestrian shopping street and collect more than four euros from passersby.

In the evening, I finally wind my way back. Garage 27's door is closed. I find my key and try to slide it into the lock, but it doesn't fit. I push and pull on the door, but it defies me. I slip into the apartment building and go down to the basement, to the furnace. I keep a crowbar hidden there, in case I need it to chase away a burglar. I carry it across the asphalt to Garage 27 and slip one end beneath the bottom of the door and force it downward with all my strength. The lock gives with a loud *sproing* and the door pops open. I straighten up and feel cold steel touch the back of my head.

"Police! On the ground! Now! Clasp your fingers behind your neck!"

Iron hands press me down. A bolt of pain lances through my knees as I fall forward. All I can think is what a shame I never had the chance to take Sun's other ear.

"Finally!" I hear from behind me, from one of the balconies. I recognize the voice: it's the old man in #113. "That bum's been sneaking around here for years. I always said there'd be trouble, sooner or later."

"Eleven years!" another voice adds indignantly. "I must've called you guys fifty times. 'Oh, no,' you always tell me, 'there's nothing we can do about it. The man inherited the garage from his brother. He can do whatever he likes with it.' Thanks for nothing, fellas. Now you see what he's been up to!"

I begin to laugh. Eleven years. For eleven years, I've been their concierge. And I never got one red cent for my services. They didn't even know about it. What a bunch of ingrates. How dare they call the cops on me? Well, fine, the hell with them.

The last thing I see as the officers drag me off is seventeen-year-old Emma from #138. She's leaning against the building, her hands in the pockets of her jeans. "I'm not sticking around this madhouse," she tells her girlfriend, who's standing next to her, blowing big pink bubbles with her gum. "No way. Next summer, I'm getting a job as an au pair in America."

I've never gone back to the Ganzendries. I live in a nice quiet place in Zelzate now. My therapist is a tall, strange man who tells me to write it all down, my whole story. So here it is. I've done my best, and I'm really sorry if it makes for boring reading.

With all best wishes,
  Remi De Sutter

7

AFTER THE FALL

BY BRAM DEHOUCK

Standing on the doorstep of her house, clutching the front of her housecoat tightly over her pajamas, Alice Mortier makes what will turn out to be the most important decision of her life.

A little girl pedals by on a bicycle. Only her blond hair is visible above the hedge that encloses Alice's front yard. Her training wheels could use a little oil—there's nothing wrong with Alice's hearing. She nods a good morning to the child's mother, who follows along close behind her daughter.

A car rolls past. Two scurrying teenagers are apparently late for school. But Little Mister is nowhere to be seen. Normally, when he's been out on the town all night, he's waiting for her at the front door early the next morning, his eyes revealing nothing but the desire for a good breakfast.

What do the neighbors think of this daily ritual, Alice at the door in her nightgown, waiting for her cat's return? No one ever says a word. He angrily refuses all her attempts to get him to come and go by the back door. The back door is obviously beneath his dignity. Either you *are* a Little Mister, after all, or you're not.

Alice shrugs her shoulders. His problem. She leaves the door open a crack. He can push his way in when he's ready. But he can forget about breakfast.

She climbs the stairs easily—okay, she can't take them at a run anymore, and she has to hold on to the railing, but she's not ready for one of those stair lifts they advertise. She doesn't need adult diapers, either, or a grab bar for the shower, an elevated toilet seat, or a hearing aid. No, thanks, she's not lonely, and she's not interested in a course in preventing falls at the local senior center. Although it *is* depressing when she thinks too much about the sad reality that, from the age of sixty-five on, the only things they bother trying to sell you are assistive devices. And she's already *seventy*-five, believe it or not.

It's nice and warm in the bathroom. She smiles at herself in the mirror. Her hair is a mess, but—

And then her legs fly out from beneath her.

In a fraction of a second, she's flat on the bathroom floor with a terrible pain in her hip. In shock, she stares up at the underside of the sink, a strange sight she vaguely remembers from the days when she cleaned the house herself. The bathmat is bunched up at her feet. When she tries to stand, the pain forces her back to the floor. She manages to turn to the door.

"Help!" she cries.

What time is it? Beneath the shattered glass of her wristwatch, the hands are frozen at eight twenty. The worst of the pain has faded and only returns if Alice tries to move. So she lies still, and her muscles cramp. She's stopped yelling for help. There's no one to help her.

Has the mailman already come and gone? Could he see from the street that the door is slightly ajar? It's worth another try.

"Help!"

It comes out not a cry but a hoarse cough. For the first time, she finds herself unable to hold back the tears.

She has imagined this moment completely differently. Although she's become almost resigned in recent years to the inevitability of death—at her age, it would be pitiful to fear it—she has wanted it to come with a bit of style, or at least as painlessly as possible. She has hoped that it will take her in her sleep, or in a hospital bed with a morphine drip in her arm. If need be, let it be unexpected and quick: a fall down the stairs and a broken neck, or a slab of tile blown from the roof to smash her skull. But not like this. Not on a cold bathroom floor, having slipped on a stupid bathmat.

How long can she lie here before her body gives up the ghost? When will someone find her? The mailman, when her mailbox overflows? She hardly *gets* any letters. The cleaning woman, five days from now? She'll have begun to decompose, a cloud of flies buzzing around her....

She gazes at the door, wants to scream again, but lays down her head and sighs.

The light changes. Or, rather, it fades. She can't tell if clouds have covered the sun, or if it's already evening. In the quiet of the bathroom, she has waited for some sound to tell her that help has arrived. But there has only been the occasional drip of a faucet, the crack of the house settling on its foundations, the far-off burr of motor scooters.

Now, though, now at last she hears something.

On the stairs. In the hall. Outside the bathroom door.

The door swings open a few centimeters. It's Little Mister. Her savior. He looks at her for a while, as if he's trying to make sense of the situation. Then he pads up to her and licks her face.

"Hi, Little Mister," she says. The black patches on his chest look like a necktie—whence his name. She wants to pet his back. There's a big black patch there which—if you really use your imagination—could be seen as a tuxedo jacket. And the patch on his head suggests a stylish hat. Little Mister lies down beside Alice and begins to snore as, with great difficulty, she lifts her arm—she has no control over the dead weight of it at first—and scratches gently behind his ear. Her fingers tingle as the blood resumes its flow.

As she strokes him and inhales his damp catty smell, she thinks: *Dying like this wouldn't be so bad.*

It must be night by now. Only the orange glow of a streetlight illuminates the bathroom, revealing its contours to Alice. She is cold, her mouth is dry. Little Mister is gone, off searching for his dinner. He came back upstairs one more time, meowing, his bowl probably empty. *The way to a man's heart is through his stomach.* When he understands that she can't help him, he stalks grumpily off.

Has she slept a little, or did she faint?

And what has awakened her?

The orange of the streetlight is dappled with quick white flashes, abruptly coming and going. Headlights? No, the motion is too irregular.

Are the neighbors having a party?
There it is again. She watches the white light dance.
It's a flashlight.
And it's here in the house.

Holding her breath, she listens to the voices. Men. Two of them. She can't make out their words, but she can hear where they are. In the living room. They open the top drawer of the buffet. Now the bottom drawer—she recognizes its squeak. The voices sound angry. Alice understands. Behind the nineteenth-century gable and the lovely wooden front door, they expected to find cascades of jewels, envelopes stuffed full of banknotes. Unfortunately for them, they've chosen the wrong house.

The kitchen. Silverware clatters. An angry voice.

You want the neighbors to hear you? He must have said something like that, Alice imagines. Or *Watch out, you fool!*

She listens intently. Waiting for them to come up the stairs, she works her mouth full of saliva. When the time comes, she doesn't want her throat to be dry.

They move from the kitchen back to the living room.

Alice prepares herself.

Footsteps in the stairwell.

"Help! Please help me, whoever you are!"

Feet pound up the stairs. Alice's heart is in her throat, her eyes glued to the door.

The men storm into one of the bedrooms. They talk.

"Help! I've fallen! Here, in the bathroom!"

Something breaks. A bedside lamp?

The men burst into the second bedroom.

"Help me."

Her voice is weak.

Unidentifiable noises. Footsteps in the hall, a short conversation.

Are they arguing?

It's quiet for a moment, and then she hears someone head down the stairs.

One someone.

Blinded by sudden light, she curls into a fetal position. She feels a pain, as if the light has reawakened her nerve endings. She squeezes her eyes shut tight.

"Take whatever you want," she says hoarsely.

The man laughs. "Not much to take." He speaks Dutch with a slight accent.

Alice opens her eyes, blinks until she can see him. It shocks her that his face is uncovered. A burly man. Short black hair, bushy eyebrows.

"Your front door was open," he says. As if that had been an invitation.

"Take anything you want." She has to cough several times before she can go on talking. "There's a coin collection behind the TV. But help me—don't leave me lying here."

She stares at her feet, at the little bathmat. That stupid mat.

The man goes downstairs. With her eyes closed, her head resting on the bathroom floor, Alice prays he will come back to help her.

He comes back. Her cordless phone is in one hand, a glass of water in the other.

He sets the phone on the floor and offers her the glass. There is dried mud on his work boots, she sees, gulping the water greedily.

"Can you use the phone?" he asks.

She nods.

"This is all I can do. I'm sorry."

And then he's gone.

Two weeks later, Alice is still recovering from her fall. She can't seem to shake the stiffness that crept into her muscles that day, and the neck brace is a constant irritation. It's a given that, from now on, she's going to need some help around the house. But it could have been worse. Much worse.

It takes forever for her to get to the phone.

"Ms. Mortier, this is Tess Jonkman from the police."

Alice smiles. She has fond memories of the young detective who questioned her about her burglars. An "impulse crime," she called it, not planned in advance. They saw the open door and couldn't resist the opportunity.

"Hi, Tess."

"We've picked up a couple of guys trying to fence some stolen property. We think the same pair may have broken into other houses in the area, including yours."

"Oh," says Alice. Suddenly she sees his face before her. And those muddy work boots.

"But we haven't got any proof. Since you say you got a good look at one of them, we'd like you to come in for a lineup."

"And?" Tess bites her lower lip.

Alice shakes her head.

"No," she says.

"Damn. Are you sure?"

Alice takes another look at the men. Her eyes linger on number six. The short hair, the thick eyebrows. No mud on his shoes today. New shoes. He must have gotten a good price for those coins.

"No," she says, "none of them."

"Dammit!"

"I'm sorry."

"We'll have to let them go." Tess sighs.

The next time Alice sees him is at the newsstand. She plucks a paper from the pile and, holding her breath, hurries home as quickly as her old bones can carry her and settles in at her kitchen table.

In the photo, he looks straight out at her from the front page. It gives her goose bumps. The picture is at least five years old, might have been taken for his identity card. His name is there: Franciszek Radzka. There's a short bio in a sidebar: ten years in the country, a long police record.

She sighs as she reads the headline: *Jeweler shoots burglar dead.*

Little Mister jumps onto her lap. She pets him, strokes his tuxedo jacket and the funny little spot on his head. He curls up and purrs happily as she turns the page.

8

THE STRANGER INSIDE ME
BY LOES DEN HOLLANDER

Monday

Ted Bundy came again last night.

Ted always comes around midnight on Sundays, every other week for a year now. He says I'm his friend, his *best* friend. I'm proud of that. It's great to finally have a friend.

Mother says I have to take a shower. She says she can smell me, and other people will say I stink and blame her. Mother's been nagging me more and more lately. She says I eat too many eggs. Eggs are bad for my cholesterol, according to her. The blood vessels in my brain will get all sludgy. She also wants me to go back to getting my meds by injection, because the pill I'm supposed to take every week is bad for my stomach. I don't like needles, and the pills never actually *get* to my stomach. I don't need them, anyway, but try explaining that to someone who believes God knows best and medication can make the negative thoughts in your head disappear.

Mothers. There ought to be a law.

Against mothers *and* caseworkers.

I can't stand anybody who has anything to do with the psychiatric profession. They think they know everything about your mental ability. They label you without any idea who you really are. They ask questions, arrange your answers in their spreadsheets, and—presto!—they slap you with a diagnosis you carry around for the rest of your life. And of course you're stuck with *them* for the rest of your life, too.

Caseworkers should all be exterminated.

My mission is scheduled for this Thursday. The woman will be wearing a short brown leather jacket, a tight black skirt, black stockings, and high-heeled black boots. She'll have long blond hair, and here's the important thing: it'll be parted in the middle. Ted really made a point about that parted-in-the-middle part.

The place: Amsterdam's Central Station, Track 13B. The time: Thursday, between 11:30 AM and 2:37 PM. Not one minute sooner, not one minute later.

Ted knows he can count on me.

The first time he came was the night before my eighteenth birthday. I woke up and saw him standing in a corner of my bedroom.

I wasn't surprised, and I was aware that I wasn't. It would have been normal if I'd screamed and run out of the room, because I can really overreact when I'm startled. Instead, though, I just lay there in my bed and folded my hands behind my head and asked him who he was.

"They call me Ted Bundy," he said.

"Is that your name?" I asked.

"I was born Theodore Robert Cowell, but it was changed to Bundy when my mother married a loser and he adopted me. You can call me Ted." There was laughter in his voice.

"What's so funny?" I wanted to know.

"Me, being here. You, letting me in." He looked at me with an intense expression in his eyes. "Letting me *inside* you, do you understand?"

I didn't.

It got very quiet in my room, and I didn't know what he expected of me.

He came closer. "They stopped me," he said. "I want you to pick up where I left off."

At that moment, I heard Mother in the bathroom. I turned my head toward the sound. Water ran out of the tap, then stopped. The toilet flushed.

When I turned back, Ted was gone.

Anja, the psychiatric caseworker I have to see every month, always asks me if I hear voices or have visitors. She wouldn't ask, if I'd just ignored Mother always grilling me about who I talk to late at night. But I had to go and tell her someone was coming to see me, someone *she* couldn't see. She should have known that was private information, not something she was allowed to pass on to anyone else, but Mother doesn't understand things like that. It doesn't surprise me, since every man she's ever gone out with in her life has wound up dropping her. What *does* surprise me is that, with all those guys, she's only had the one child.

Mother lives in a world of her own.

I don't tell the caseworker anything about my visitor. I'm polite, I answer her questions, I tell her I take my penfluridol every week. It's important I stay calm when she asks me trick questions. I know for a fact she's trying to trap me.

Tuesday

Ted told me about Track 13B months ago, and today I went to take a look at it.

Mother had a migraine this morning and stayed in bed. She can't stand the least bit of light or sound when she gets a migraine, so I shut the living-room drapes, made sure the windows were latched, and disconnected the doorbell. Then I snuck out of the house.

She didn't come right out and say so, but she made it clear that the migraine was my fault. In her indirect way, she let me know that I'd disturbed her sleep by making a racket until all hours, not even quieting down when she banged her cane against the wall that separates our rooms.

See, Ted showed up again last night, which was a surprise. When I realized he was there, I tried to make a joke: *Don't you have days of the week up there in Eternity*, I asked him, but I don't think he got it. I backed away from his angry reaction and apologized profusely. He raised his voice, and that made me start screaming. When Mother wouldn't quit banging on the wall, I begged him to calm down. I lowered my voice and started asking him questions. Open-ended questions, full of empathy. That helped.

He was clearly in the mood to talk, and to brag. Full of pride, he told me that, right before his execution, he confessed to more than twenty murders, but in fact his count was much higher. He explained what it had meant to him, the killing, the raping, the kidnaping, and he especially wanted me to understand how much he missed it, and how happy he was to be able to enter into me, and we were going to be a team, an amazing team that would always be there for each other.

I was so touched.

I feel this powerful connection to Ted, because we're both children of unwed mothers and we never knew who our fathers were. That's why I don't think it's weird that he picked me to be his special friend. And that's why I'll do whatever he tells me to. I won't be surprised if he shows up every night this week, though he didn't promise that he would.

He's always welcome.

I go into the Central Station by the main entrance. The gates from the main hall to the tracks never close, so I can walk right through.

There are two women in front of me, and they keep looking around. I go past them as quickly as I can and hug the right side of the broad shopping area. First I check to make sure all the stores are in the right order. De Broodzaak: check. Swirls Ice Cream: check. Smullers: check. The Amstel Passage is closed. The Doner Company: check. No changes, so that's good.

There are two sets of fifteen steps up to Track 13B. I have to be sure to remember to count them again when I come down.

My mission is so exciting! I can feel that it's all going to go just right for once. The woman I'm supposed to look for will be there. Everything will work out perfectly. I know it, and that sense of certainty makes me happy.

I've never been so happy in my life.

. . .

The man is only a few feet away from me, and I can smell his cigarette. "There are special smoking areas," I say, and I point to the standing ashtray not far off. He inhales deeply and blows a white cloud at my face.

I lower my head and count to ten. Every time Ted gives me a mission, he tells me not to raise my voice and not to argue with anyone. If I say something to this man....

I count to twenty.

I feel like Ted is watching me, but I can also feel Anja's eyes aimed in my direction. Let that frustrated caseworker find herself another victim! A piece of advice: make it somebody who'll give her a good roll in the hay. Somebody her big boobs will make all horny.

"Watch where you're going," a voice beside me snarls.

I'm standing beside a woman whose buttons are practically popping off her blouse. I mumble an apology and walk away.

As I approach the stairs, I see a woman in a short brown leather jacket coming toward me. Black skirt, black stockings, black high-heeled boots. Her long blond hair is parted in the middle. But it's only Tuesday.

I hurry down the thirty steps.

Mother has left me a note. She's gone to the beauty parlor and wants me to do the shopping. There's a list in the linen bag on the inside of the kitchen door. The money is in an envelope.

The thought hits me the second I touch the bag.

Mother is going to poison me. She's letting me do the shopping, so I won't be suspicious, but she's already bought the poison, see? She tells me to get the ingredients she needs to make her endive stew with bacon, and that way she figures I'll never stop to think how easy it'll be for her to stir the poison into the stew. She'll serve me a poisoned dinner, a meal I know *she* doesn't like and won't eat.

She wants to get rid of me.

I don't fit in here.

I wish Ted would come, wish just once he'd come during the day instead of at night. I could talk with him, explain my suspicions. He would give me good advice. Maybe if I sit very quietly on the sofa and stare straight down at the floor. I listen for his footsteps, not moving a muscle.

The clock in the hall strikes four. He's not coming. I'd better go do the shopping. But I won't eat the stew, not one bite. I won't let myself be poisoned. Not by *anyone*.

Wednesday

The new day is only ten minutes old. I slipped into the kitchen half an hour ago to make two cheese sandwiches. Mother loves cheese, so that's something she won't poison. And bread is safe. And butter. And milk. Anything Mother eats, I can eat.

She was insulted I wouldn't have any of the endive stew. She asked me what was going on with me, was I taking my penfluridol. She's always bitching about those pills. I have to stop myself from kicking a kitchen chair to bits.

I told her I had a stomachache and couldn't keep anything down. Then I went to my room and watched TV. With the door locked.

I'm positive Ted will come tonight. Maybe he'll tell me about the city where he was born. He's done that before, and that's why I

Googled Burlington tonight. I found out it's a city of interesting contradictions: it's the biggest city in Vermont, but the smallest biggest city in any of the fifty United States. When you think that Ted's not only a serial killer but also somebody's best friend, you can understand why he was born in Burlington.

I have to tell him I saw her in the station yesterday afternoon, a woman who fit the description for tomorrow's mission. Should I have talked to her? That question weighs on my mind.

He's told me many times how he approached his victims. If you go up to a woman and you're friendly but you don't bug her, most of the time she'll talk with you. But the best way to get her attention is if there's obviously something wrong with you: your arm's in a sling, you're using a cane and limping, you've got a big bandage on your head and you act like you're dizzy. Then they'll be all concerned, they'll ask if they can help you.

When Ted found out I don't have a car, not even a driver's license, so I can't drive women to some remote place and attack them there, he was mad at first. But later he said I was a new kind of challenge for him, and he gave me instructions I had to memorize but not write down. He decided the starting point would be Amsterdam's Central Station, and he told me which track and what the victim would look like. It wasn't until he'd come to see me a dozen times that he told me he wanted to concentrate on women who looked like the victims who'd escaped from him his first time around.

I have an old school bag that's just the right size to hold my bat. It has a long shoulder strap, so I can clutch it tight to my stomach when I carry it.

Up to now, my first seven tries were no good, because the women I was supposed to find didn't show up at the right track when they were supposed to. Ted says I have to pay closer attention, be sharper. Tomorrow is my eighth chance, and this time it's going to be just fine. I've already seen the woman, and I know she'll turn up right when she's supposed to. I'll bandage my left hand in the morning, and I'll walk with a cane. When the woman gets off her train, I'll catch her attention by the stairs, and I'll ask her to help me down. Halfway, I'll say I'm dizzy and I need some fresh air. Track 13B is closest to the station's back entrance, and that's where I'll have the best chance to use my bat.

And to get away without anyone seeing me.

I know it's risky. But I'll take my chances. I'm not worried. Ted will protect me.

And if the woman I'm waiting for isn't *arriving* on the train but *leaving* on it, I'll just climb aboard with her, with my cane and my school bag. I'll sit near her and make sure she notices me.

Then I'll grab her right before the train pulls into a station. Or maybe it'll be better to wait until the train comes to a stop, so I can get off right away.

Thinking about the woman on the track and about finally carrying out my mission is exciting. It's giving me a boner. I like the way that feels.

I hope Ted's coming tonight, and he tells me more about what he did with the bodies. He is *so* cool!

Thursday

Ted didn't come last night. I'm really disappointed. It would have been helpful to discuss the plans for today one more time. Maybe he didn't show because he thought it would be too much of a distraction. Maybe he's afraid I'll back out at the last minute.

You never know.

My mission begins at eleven thirty, and I'll be sure to take a tram that'll get me to the station on time. Better to arrive half an hour early than one minute late. Because what if the woman turns up exactly at eleven thirty and I'm not there?

I have to get this right.

Mother thinks I look exhausted, and she wants to know why that is. I don't have a job, and I don't really *do* much, so why am I so tired? She thinks I don't get enough physical exercise but work myself up too much mentally. That needs to change, she says.

I'll have to find a way to fake her out.

She's made homemade jam, but I say thanks but no thanks. She wants to know why I'm barely eating anything, do I still have a stomachache, and then of course she gets on my case again about changing my meds from the pill to an injection.

I try to tune her out and concentrate on my cheese sandwich and the glass of milk I made sure to pour for myself.

Track 13B, I think. Woman with long blond hair parted in the middle. Brown leather jacket, tight black skirt, black stockings, black boots with high heels.

The bandage and the bat are in my bag. I hid the cane in the bushes by the garden gate, I'll fish it out as I pass.

"She'll be here in half an hour," I hear Mother say.

I sit up straight. "Who'll be here in half an hour?"

"Your caseworker, Anja. I called her. You're not well, you need an extra visit. And a shot."

I get up. "Tell her I said hi. I have to go."

A second later, she's all up in my face. "You're not going anywhere until you've talked with Anja. I'm doing this for your own good, boy. You'll thank me later."

I look at her. She means it, she's not going to let me go.

But I *have* to go.

Why isn't Ted here when I need him?

The front door is locked. Where is the key?

Mother smiles.

I feel myself becoming calmer. Okay, fine, she has the key. It's obviously in her apron pocket. She always cleans the house after breakfast, and she's already wearing her apron.

It's almost ten o'clock, it's a five-minute walk to the tram stop, I might have to wait another five minutes for a tram, and then the ride takes twenty minutes. That gives me just enough time to get the key, and, if she won't give it to me willingly....

I go into the living room and sit in my chair. Mother is puttering around in the hall. She's probably getting the vacuum cleaner from the closet at the top of the basement stairs.

The basement!

The bag with the bat is still in my bedroom, but the base of the lamp that stands on the armoire in the living room will do just as well.

I've put on a clean shirt and also a clean sweater. The key was indeed in the pocket of Mother's apron. The vacuum cleaner is back where it belongs, and so is the lamp. The basement door is locked. I can go.

The doorbell rings.

"I rode my bike," says Anja. "It's actually quicker than coming by car, so I'm a little early. Is it okay if I leave it outside?"

"You'd better bring it in," I recommend.

· · ·

There's a detour, because they're working on the tramline. Signs show you which way to go.

I haven't ridden a bike in a long time, but I don't have any trouble. It's nice, the wind in my hair. I'm careful not to let the wheels drop into the tram rails.

I've got my bag on my right side. I bandaged my hand before I left the house. I have to hurry, because it's already five minutes to eleven. I pedal past the Bijenkorf, and I can see the station up ahead. I know for sure the woman will be there, and the thought gives me wings.

The big clock in the station's main hall says eleven fifteen. I'll leave the cane in my bag until I get to the stairs to Track 13B. There's a strange noise behind me, and as I'm about to turn around to see what it is, a man in an electric wheelchair zooms by.

I'm panting a little.

Calm down, calm down, calm down.

Quickly check the stores.

There's the stairway. Count carefully, two sets of fifteen steps.

It's eleven twenty-five.

I'm positive I looked everywhere. I didn't miss her, she just isn't here. Didn't get off the train, didn't get on. This can't be happening!

The train that leaves Amsterdam at 2:38 PM is slowly pulling into the station. It comes to a stop. The doors open, and people come out. I have a good view from where I'm standing.

It's two thirty-seven. The time is up. I feel all the energy drain out of my body.

And then I see her.

She walks past me, close enough to touch, and hurries to the train. I follow her without thinking, and the second I get on board I hear the conductor's whistle and the doors *whoosh* closed behind me. She heads for the first-class compartment and holds the connecting door for me.

I lean on my cane.

"You should sit down," she says.

I obey and see that she takes a seat in the middle of the car.

It was one minute later than the end time I was given, but I don't think Ted will have a problem with that. I found her, and inside my head I'm cheering. She's sitting there talking on her phone, laughing.

But not for long.

Pretty soon, I'll be the one who's laughing.

We're the only passengers in the compartment. Ted must have arranged it that way.

I'm not happy about that minute.

But I've got her!

What day is it?

I've lost track of time, and there's a gap in my memory. The last thing I remember is the woman on the train, the way she looked. After that, there was a lot of commotion, somebody dragged me away, I was in a cell, people kept asking me questions, someone told me I had to be examined.

I've got a room and a bed, but all the doors and windows are locked. The food is good. Everybody here is crazy, but the man who comes to talk with me three times a week is far and away the craziest. He tells me I tried to molest an old lady on the train, though I keep explaining that she was young. When I describe her, he contradicts me. The lady he talks about isn't blond with a middle part, doesn't wear a short brown leather jacket, no tight black skirt, no black stockings and high-heeled boots. When I say we must be talking about two different people, he says no, we're absolutely talking about the same person. So he's a total nutbag.

Each time he comes, he's got new idiotic comments. He thinks Mother has been dead for a year, and I haven't seen my psychiatric caseworker, Anja, since she died. He says I've been skipping my appointments, and he keeps insisting that, given my condition, isolation is my worst enemy, because if I'm alone I don't have anyone to correct my behavior and my thoughts.

According to him, when Mother was still alive I used to take medication that kept the weird thoughts at bay. It's apparently pretty much a miracle I didn't go off the rails until now. If I go back on my meds, I can learn to think straight again. I'll have to go to trial, but a good lawyer should be able to convince the judge I wasn't accountable for my actions when I attacked the lady on the train. The shrink will recommend confinement to a psych ward. The doctor emphasizes that everyone wants what's best for me.

I'm allergic to people who want what's best for me.

When I very carefully describe what I did to Mother and Anja, the doctor doesn't react.

He ought to go take a look in the basement.

They force me to take the pills. When I refuse, I get a shot. The meds make me dull, I sleep away half the day.

Ted doesn't come to see me. Now that I can't do anything for him, he's abandoned me. With friends like him, who needs enemies?

What month is it?

They're fed up with my continued insistence that Mother and Anja are in the basement. The doctor thinks it would be good for me to see Anja. She's coming this afternoon.

I bet she won't look too good.

They've decided that the meds they've put me on are too strong, so now they're reducing the dosage. But they make darned sure I swallow the pills. I have to put each one on my tongue, and after I swallow it the supervisor looks down my throat, probably all the way down my esophagus. I don't feel as foggy now, and I don't drag my feet when I walk.

And Anja's coming to see me.

Party time!

I sit beside the shrink and across from the caseworker nobody seems to realize is lying in my cellar. I have to admit she looks pretty healthy, and she doesn't seem to have had any work done. I probably ought to keep my mouth shut, otherwise before you know it they'll up my meds again. But I can't stop myself from telling her that, even though she thinks she's sitting here, she's actually dead.

She leans a little closer.

I pull back. She stinks like a corpse.

She tells me everything will be okay, and she'll always be here for me.

Those words rock me, and I have to hold onto the table to keep from falling over.

How could I ever have thought Ted would leave me in the lurch? How could I have doubted his intentions? When I see him again, I'll beg his forgiveness on bended knee, if that's what it takes. The more I think about it, though, the more I realize he won't be mad. If he was truly angry, he wouldn't have sent Anja to me. The only explanation for her presence is that she's joined up with Ted. And I'm the only one who knows.

See, this is what friendship is all *about*.

Now I know for sure Ted's coming back.

With Anja.

I wonder what my next mission will be?

9

STINKING PLASTER

BY BAVO DHOOGE

I tasted blood, sweet blood, but that was just an appetizer. A second later, a pair of hands gripped my head and gave my hair a quick rinse in a tub of plaster. The stink permeated my nose and mouth and lungs and weighed on my tongue like a charred steak. I struggled free of the tub and felt wet plaster bite at my eyes. There wasn't a mirror handy, but five'll get you ten I looked as sexy in gray as Richard Gere. The trick would be to get the stuff off me before it hardened and turned my perfect profile into a Greek bust with a busted nose.

But there wasn't time for a self-beautification project. My attacker was still on the loose, somewhere in the atelier. Every lightbulb in the place had been shattered, one by one, and the studio was dark as a tomb.

I scooped up a plaster limb from a pile of debris. It could have been an arm or a leg—hell, for all I knew, it might just as well have been a giant toe. Contemporary art goes right over my head. Whatever it was, it'd do as a club in a pinch, and it might just help me avoid ending up stiff and cold as a statue myself.

It was almost pitch black, but just enough light leaked in around the edges of the drawn drapes to allow me to pick my way. The plaster figures that surrounded me were like angels guarding a crypt. I hoped they'd look out for me, too, while they were at it.

Then my attacker stumbled into a statue and cursed loudly, and I ducked behind a gargoyle the size of a basketball.

"Hey, watch your language!" I yelled.

No response. I reached the worktable where I remembered having noticed a flashlight the day before. A lot had happened in the last twenty-four hours....

The previous morning, I was admitted to a stately home in Millionaire's Row, the wealthiest neighborhood in Ghent. My old nemesis Inspector Bonte, who'd invited me, hadn't been happy about it. He and his minions were there to investigate the disappearance of a girl.

"Somers," he said, as I entered the atelier, "this is Jaak Froger."

He nodded toward a lanky figure with long gray hair and a beard. Froger didn't seem to recognize me in my detective outfit, but that's the story of my life: nobody pays any attention to private dicks—or butlers, either.

"My pleasure," I said, sticking out a hand. "I'm Pat Somers. 'I stay awake, so you can sleep.'"

"That's his advertising slogan," Bonte explained. "He makes more sense in person."

Froger ignored my hand, and I put it back where it belonged. "I take it you didn't ask me here to critique my business card, Bonte?"

"Hardly. Mr. Froger is an artist. A sculptor."

"You'll have to find me a toga. I don't pose in the nude."

"You're always posing," Bonte growled.

"Jealous of my Greek profile?"

"Somers, I wouldn't be jealous of you if you owned your own island in the Caribbean."

"We haven't seen each other in a while," I told the sculptor confidentially. "We need to catch up."

He looked like some ancient sage or philosopher, lost in a world of Higher Ideals. He stood there with one hand resting lightly on a wooden worktable, its surface littered with knives and spatulas and other tools of his trade—and, oddly, the black barrel of a flashlight.

"You ever want to carve up the inspector here, I'd be happy to help. I'll bring sandwiches, we can make a day of it."

"All right, Somers, enough chitchat. The girl we're looking for modeled for Mr. Froger. Her mother hasn't heard from her in three days, and she didn't show up here yesterday for her session."

Froger awakened from his pensive moment and rejoined us in the land of the living. He uncrossed his arms and dug his hands into the pockets of his white smock. He looked like a tramp who'd dressed up as a surgeon but had forgotten to wash his hands.

"Maybe she didn't like the finished product," I suggested.

"It isn't finished," said Froger, like a politician discussing a bill that was still in committee. He had a Dutch accent.

"Maybe all that posing gave her cramps."

"For five hundred euro, she can damn well deal with cramps," said Froger. "I've already paid her, and I'm not finished with her yet."

"So your interest is in finding your muse, is that it? You don't really much care about the girl herself?"

"She'll be worth far more as a statue than she's worth as a girl," he said, his words as cryptic as Sanskrit.

I glanced at Bonte. "I'd love to go right on chatting with Lord Froger, here," I said, striking a match against the rough surface of a plaster grotesque, "but it's like trying to get straight answers out of a block of marble."

Bonte took my arm and led me outside. Through a dusty window, I watched the Dutch Rodin's face go blank, as if he was a table lamp and someone had just pulled the plug. His shoulders slumped, his eyes fell closed.

It was misty out, and the garden smelled like a graveyard.

"Jaak Froger's about to break through, Somers."

"Ask me, he's about to break apart."

"The city's going to commission him to do a monument for Millionaire's Park."

"Yeah? I hope he comes up with something better than those." I waved at a pair of incomplete figures that glared out from the atelier at us like a couple of juvenile delinquents behind bars.

"They're supposed to be abstract, Somers. You don't know about Froger?"

I knew. Jaak Froger's first success had come with an exhibition in the S.M.A.K., Jan Hoet's Museum of Contemporary Art. After that, he'd pulled off an impressive stunt, erecting twelve plaster monstrosities along the Graslei in a single night—the city awoke the next morning to their miraculous appearance, as if they'd been delivered from outer space by aliens.

In my opinion, Froger himself was the alien.

I also knew there were collectors who'd paid as much as half a million euros for one of Froger's plaster tchotchkes. Come to think of it, the plaster cast I'd worn on my broken leg after crashing my Taunus was still lying around my apartment somewhere. It wasn't all that big, but give it the right title and maybe Hoet would buy it for his mantlepiece, pay me enough that I wouldn't have to waste any more of my time dealing with the Old Philosopher.

Anyway, I knew about Froger. In fact, I'd *seen* him, the day before. Him *and* his muse....

. . .

A day earlier, I crossed the atrium and shimmered into the atelier. In amongst the ugly headless statues, I spotted a true work of art. She sat like a Roman goddess with a white sheet draped over her shoulders, facing the artist. Jaak Froger stood at an easel, sketching her with broad pencil strokes. I doubted that he generally needed sketches for his misshapen, hulking projects—but with a still life like that in front of me, I would have found some excuse to stand and stare at it, too.

She was simply irresistible. She held her proud chin high, and her red hair seemed to be in constant motion. Froger wasn't satisfied with his sketch, and he strode up to her and readjusted the sheet to bare one of her shoulders and reveal another ten centimeters of creamy thigh.

I took a seat on a huge plaster head that lay on the floor near the easel.

"What is this, a city map?" I said, examining the sketch.

"If you don't mind your tongue," snarled Froger, "you'll *need* a city map to find your way home."

"I thought artists only got moody when the *work* wasn't going well."

"I have no idea what you're talking about."

"You apparently get moody when your *seduction* isn't going well."

"Get out of here, James. You're throwing me off balance."

"I was born off balance." I winked at the red-headed model.

"You're in the wrong room, James. My wife wants a foot massage."

I tried to read the look on the model's face. Her head was as motionless as a corpse's, but the twinkle in her eyes was intended to reassure me. I nodded at her. Then Froger faced her and tipped his head at an angle. He smiled affably, but the girl didn't react. Froger laid a hand on her thigh and patted it gently, to indicate that it was time to take a break. She stood up and strolled off to smoke a cigarette.

"Even a butler ought to know that an artist and his model share an intimate relationship," Froger told me.

"Would you have an intimate relationship with Margaret Thatcher if she was posing for you?"

"I make statues out of plaster, James, but I'm a man of flesh and blood." He strode over to his easel, examined his sketch intently and added a line here and there. If he needed that drawing to make his next sculpture, then I needed to fly to the Bahamas to eat a banana. His real motive was as obvious as Gene Simmons' makeup.

Froger went on looking at the sketch and muttered, as if he were reciting a poem, "If you disturb me again while I'm working, James, you'll need some plaster yourself—for the arm I will break. It's up to you, you little bastard."

"You've got strong hands, but that doesn't mean you scare me, Jaak. You can play with your plaster titties as much as you like, but if I see you lay a finger on that girl again, the next project you work on will be your own tombstone."

He barely looked up. I brushed past him as if he were one of his own white monsters. A row of them glared at me as I left the room, and I expected a cold plastery hand to grip my shoulder at any moment. They were truly awful creatures, disgusting, reflections of a twisted soul. Their faces had dripped and run in long white streaks that trailed down their cheeks like the frozen tears of the damned.

On my way out, I told the lady to holler any time she needed me.

She'd needed me a day earlier....

. . .

Before the cops had called me in to assist in the search for her, she'd hired me herself. Her name was Helga, she studied art history with a concentration in classicism. Jaak Froger had found her phone number posted on a "Models Available" bulletin board at the art school, and now he was concentrating on her curves.

The first time she'd posed for *me* with those piercing green eyes was when I'd run into her in a hallway at the house. It was like an eighteenth-century rendezvous in a country manor, where the ticking of a grandfather clock was louder than the whispered conversation of a pair of secret lovers. But Helga wasn't exactly walking around in a hoop skirt and petticoats. She was stark naked when she turned a corner and bumped into me, and she was visibly upset. I gently pushed her off me. Dried, gritty plaster was smeared all over her, like salve on an arson victim's burns.

"You better hustle to the bathroom and wash that stuff off you," I said, "before one of us gets hard."

She giggled. "Who are you?"

"I'm the butler who's going to have to clean up this mess."

"Forget the mess. I need you to protect me."

"From what? A plaster avalanche?"

"They're all crazy here."

"You're one to talk," I said. "You need to get some clothes on before somebody nails you... to a pedestal."

I shrugged off my black morning coat and draped it over her shoulders. Her red hair was white with plaster, and flakes of it drifted down onto the collar like a hobo's dandruff. She stood there looking around her like a madwoman out of a Virginia Woolf novel. I touched a match to a joint and handed it to her as a peacefulness offering.

"That's pot," she exclaimed. "You're a strange sort of butler."

"I get paid just like a normal butler," I said. "I throw in strange for free."

"I'll pay you extra if you'll protect me," she whispered. "This place is a madhouse."

"Why don't we pretend you're not naked, and you tell me what the trouble is?"

At that moment, I heard footsteps approaching on the thick carpet. Jaak Froger ran towards us in his dirty smock, as if he'd been called to the OR for an emergency appendectomy. But from Helga's expression, it was obvious he'd already been operating. Or at least trying to. She backed away from him nervously. Froger had a look in his eyes as if God had sent him a text message telling him he was on the right path to salvation. But I suspected that his wild expression had a more earthy cause. He held a nasty looking metal file in his hand.

"So, here you are, Helga. I've been looking all over for you. You said you were just going for a cigarette."

"She was in the mood for something a little more potent," I said, exhaling pot smoke in his face.

"Who the hell are you? This is a private home."

"I'm a private kind of guy. So that's all fine, then."

Helga wrapped her arms around my waist and held me close. Froger was salivating like a cop who's spotted an expired parking meter. He stormed up to me and raised the file.

"I don't know how you got in here, buster, but I know exactly how you're going to leave."

I buttoned my coat across Helga's ample chest. Outside, it had begun to rain, but the heat was on in the house, and I really didn't need the coat, anyway. We were all so cozy together, I was ready to ring the bell for tea. Then I remembered that, since I was supposed to be the butler, fetching the kettle would actually be *my* job.

"What happened?" I asked Helga again.

"He wanted to cover me with plaster. My whole body."

"I hired you as a model," Froger snapped. "This project is bigger than you are, girl. You're not going to go all prudish on me now, are you?"

"I thought you were supposed to be a sculptor," I said, "not a standup comic."

"And who are you again, my man?"

"I'm James, the new butler," I said. "And what are *you*? A sculptor or a fetishist?"

"I'm in a difficult stage at the moment. A transitional stage."

"What stage *is* that, exactly? Puberty?"

"My earliest works were cast aluminum," he explained, as if either of us really gave a damn, "and then I tried working in carved marble. But now I'm searching for something more naturalistic. Plaster allows me to replicate the human form almost exactly. So—"

"—so you figured you could dunk her in a vat of it?"

"I'm making a life cast, James. I—ach, why am I explaining myself to a fool like you? My wife will call the police to have you removed, and then you and I can get back to work, little one."

He gazed intently at Helga. Not in a decadent or dirty way, but strangely, insistently, as if she belonged to him and he could do whatever he liked with her. And then, abruptly distracted, he wandered over to the living-room door and stood there scratching his head with the business end of his file.

Helga, meanwhile, was stuck to my side like superglue.

"Your wife's already made a phone call this morning, Jaak," I said.

He glanced up, surprised.

"She called *me*. I'm your new butler, and I'm supposed to make sure you don't sweep too much dirt under the carpets. You artists think *you're* perfectionists, but I'll see your perfection and raise you."

He blinked absently. "Excuse me?" he said.

"You heard me. I don't care what 'stage' you're in, Oedipal or narcissistic or whatever. You better play well with others, because the butler's here, watching every move you make."

He waved the file dismissively and stalked into the living room. The door swung shut behind him, and, behind it, an argument erupted. Helga gazed up at me playfully, as if inviting me to make a sandcastle from the plaster that still clung to her breasts.

"I want to hire you to protect me from his crazy moods," she said.

"Make me an offer. You're the third person who's wanted to hire me this week."

"I need the money he's paying me, James. If you help me, though, I'll split it with you."

So in addition to private detective and butler, I was now also a model's bodyguard.

But before the cops and Helga, yet another prospective employer had promised to treat me like a servant but pay me a king's ransom. One day earlier, I'd waltzed through this same living-room door to meet a distinguished gentlewoman who sat in a wooden rocking chair by the window....

She was a study in contrasts: white hair, black sunglasses, pale skin, jet-black high heels. We all have our signature accessories. Mine is my battered Ford Taunus, hers was the expensive pair of sunglasses perched on her fine nose, despite the drizzly weather and the room's subdued lighting. She'd introduced herself over the telephone as Francine Marie-Christine d'Oplinter Cruz, and I felt like it was the first day of school and I was about to be tested to see if I could remember all that.

"You are Mr. Somers?"

"Patrick 'Pat' Isaac M.J. Somers, Jr.," I said, trying to keep up with the d'Oplinter Cruzes.

"Will you sit, please? I can't see, but I prefer to *be* seen straight on, not in profile."

I pulled up a chair and sat and winked broadly at her. Then I slowly drew my upper lip up to reveal my top teeth, à la Bogey. I decided to think of the woman with half a telephone book for a last name as Franny and undressed her with my eyes. I'd never had any problem with that stunt before, but it was more enjoyable when the woman could see me do it.

"I've been blind for three years, Mr. Somers."

"I can beat that," I said. "I haven't been able to see or smell a thing in *five* years."

"The agency told me you were amusing." She forced a tight little laugh. "But let's get down to business. Jaak Froger is my second husband. He's an artist and spends most of his time in his studio in the back of the house. I need someone to keep me company during the day."

She coughed away a catch in her voice. I raised my eyebrows.

She seemed to feel a change in my attitude.

"I hope I haven't offended you," she said.

"You've seen right through me. In my business, I have busy periods and slow spells. Right now, things are slow as molasses."

"I might as well be dead for all the attention I get when my husband's busy with his stinking plaster."

She seemed a pleasant woman, well into her middle age, who didn't mind looking the other way when it came to questions of etiquette.

"Well, I'm afraid I'm not very good company. I'm really more of a loner."

"That doesn't matter. I just want someone in the house for a few hours a day. Perhaps you can read to me a bit."

I got to my feet and crossed to the baby grand on the far side of the room. I hadn't played in a long time, but I ran my fingers across the keys and brought Erroll Garner back to life for a few moments —a zombified version of him, maybe, but still. A copy of Fitzgerald's *The Other Side of Paradise* lay on top of the instrument. Yeah, Franny seemed to be the sort of dame who belonged back in the Roaring Twenties. I carried the book back to the chair and sat, flipped it open and cleared my throat, but before I could get out a syllable, she stood up and groped her way to the window, almost knocking over a vase as she went.

"Mr. Somers, I told you that my husband no longer pays me any attention. Why don't you go have a look at what he *does* pay attention to these days?"

She leaned forward, her forehead touching the window. Her pale calves were well worth looking at.

I nodded as I realized what she was really hiring me to do.

As I stood in the dark atelier, trying to brush the plaster out of my hair, I thought back to the phone call that had set this whole chain of events in motion. Four days earlier, before the cops, before the model, before the lady of the house, I'd been hired by an insurance company. It seemed that a certain Francine Marie-Christine d'Oplinter Cruz had suffered from poor vision her entire life, but the company wanted to find out if the lady had truly been stricken blind four years earlier.

"We suspect," my caller had told me, "that her claim is fraudulent."

"Tell me about it," I'd said.

"The woman receives a hefty payment every month because of her 'blindness,' and we think she's concluded that *we* must be blind ourselves. You'll be taking a position as a household servant, but in fact you'll be working for us."

"I don't do windows," I'd said—but I'd taken the job.

And now, four days later, I located the flashlight on the worktable by the atelier's window. I flicked it on and followed its beam of light like a bloodhound on a scent.

Something glittered behind one of the plaster grotesques. I headed that way and stumbled over a work in progress, which shattered like a china plate in a Greek restaurant. My attacker whirled toward me, but I swung my right arm in a wide arc and felt my elbow connect with its target.

In the flashlight's beam, I saw a black pair of sunglasses lying amongst the plaster shards that littered the floor. I picked them up and set them on the bridge of a statue's nose.

Then I told Franny the game was up, and she crawled out from behind the gargoyle where she'd fallen. Even with one eye swollen shut and ass over teakettle, she held herself with perfect dignity.

"Enough already," I said.

"This time I really *couldn't* see where I was going."

I forced a tight little laugh.

"I can see where you're going," I told her, "and you're not gonna like it there."

"How long have you known?"

"I suspected it when you almost knocked over that vase the other day. A blind woman would know exactly where every object in her house was located."

I put out a hand and helped her to her feet. She leaned against a giant plaster sculpture. It seemed to be the only finished piece in the studio. Froger had apparently found his inspiration after all, although it really didn't do much for me.

"I know it's none of my business," I said, "but there are easier ways to make a living."

"I wouldn't know," she responded coldly. "I've never worked a day in my life."

"You've been busy," I said, "filing your nails."

"You have no idea what it's like, living with an egomaniac like Jaak."

"I can imagine there were times when you couldn't stand the sight of him, but there *are* limits."

"I'm not a maid, Mr. Somers. You don't think I'd spend my life cooking and cleaning for him?"

"No, not that, but you'd help him get away with a murder. Or did Helga realize you were faking, so you did what you had to do to protect your secret?"

She lowered her hand from her eye. It was already turning purple, but oddly enough, on her the color looked good. I wondered why a woman would hide herself away like this. She lived in another age, with other values and other norms. She called it elegance, but to me it read like pure indolence. After four years of putting on an act, she'd become literally blind to the world outside her home.

I shuffled my feet, wiping plaster from the soles of my Pumas.

"I don't know what you're talking about," she said.

"You're not the only one who's suddenly seen the light, darlin'."

"Jaak and I went through hard times, Mr. Somers. My 'blindness' was the only way we could think of to generate an income—and it was barely enough to keep us going. Perhaps I'm old-fashioned, but I've never known a woman who'd go out and get a job while her husband stayed home and stared at other women's nakedness. I believed in Jaak's talent, but I wasn't *that* blind."

"But Helga didn't like Jaak staring at her—so Jaak lost control of that file he was holding?"

"Jaak's not just an artist. He's like some kind of omnipotent god. If he can't have what he wants, then *no one* can have it."

"These bastards who think their 'art' entitles them to gallop off in any direction their dicks are pointing make me sick."

Her head swiveled to gaze at the giant grotesque figure against which she was leaning. I shoved her into it, and they both fell to the ground with a crash. The statue cracked open like Humpty Dumpty.

She swallowed a scream and looked away.

I didn't need the flashlight to see what Franny's god had wrought. Froger's poor beautiful model had been immortalized in stinking plaster, and all the king's horses and all the king's men would never put Helga together again.

10

THE FINAL STAGE
BY INGRID OONINCX

Huong was wearing her favorite nightgown, white, embroidered with little red roses. Mr. Li set her empty glass on the night table, took his wife's timeworn hand and stroked it. He spoke softly, his voice droning.

"Close your eyes, my dear, and think of the olden days. Feel the warmth, smell the orchids, gaze out across the rice paddies and let the river's gentle current carry you. Time flowed slowly then, do you remember? Our life together was about to begin. The day you first held my hand, Huong, you rescued me. I felt as if I had been chosen. It was your love that gave me strength to face the terrible times. I knew from that first moment that I would do anything to protect you."

Mr. Li watched her suspicious eyes flutter closed. She was trapped within her calcified brain, where there had been no room for him for years. He sat there for several minutes, but she was sound asleep. He wiped tears from his cheeks with his shirtsleeve. There was no time to lose: he had work to do.

He rose and left the second-floor bedroom of their well-kept row house. His joints cracked as he descended the stairs and rolled the vacuum from the hall closet. He rested for a moment, caught his breath. He was getting old. At work, the younger employees joked about his old-fashioned manner of speaking. Sometimes they called him the Poet, sometimes Buddha, on difficult days the Eggroll King. He laughed along with them, but even after all these years he found the Dutch humor and directness impossible to get used to.

Mr. Li carefully vacuumed the Persian carpet he and Huong had purchased with their first vacation bonus. Despite a few worn spots, it remained in fine condition. They had never even considered spending their hard-earned money on a pleasure trip. Huong was pregnant with their first child, and furnishing their home was their top priority.

Li smiled. During that first pregnancy, Huong had been a caterpillar, preparing itself to become a butterfly. He had observed her metamorphosis happily. Today's transition would unfold in exactly the same manner.

In the kitchen, he cleared the table and started the dishwasher. Then he checked to make sure the bills had been paid. The children would find a clean house and all the paperwork in order. *Don't cause trouble*: that was his first rule.

The letters he had composed so carefully were in their place on the coffee table in the living room. From the moment the solution had presented itself, he had debated how to explain it to the children. They were grown and flown and had no idea how much worse their mother's situation had become. In the end, he had written a separate letter to each of them, filled with wise advice for the future, concluding with a straightforward description of what he was now about to do. The youngest would be furious, the middle one would weep, and the oldest would accept his responsibility and be strong. Eventually they would understand, he was sure of that.

Facing the altar, Mr. Li lit two sticks of incense. He knelt and with due deference asked his ancestors to take care of Huong's spirit. He remembered that she had once packed away the altar, after a Dutch neighbor had made an offensive remark about it. Li prayed that the ancestors had forgiven Huong's foolish mistake.

He looked at his watch. It was time. *Don't delay, stay focused.* Just like at his job: deal with the tiresome tasks first, and then nothing would prevent you from having a pleasant workday.

He felt a sharp pain in his belly when he slid the brand-new carving knife from its wooden block. He had asked many questions in the cookery shop, and this particular model seemed perfect for his purpose. Li traced his fingertip along the razor-sharp blade. A thick drop of blood splashed on the kitchen counter and took the shape of a lotus blossom. He examined it in pleased surprise. The red lotus was the symbol of their homeland. The ancestors were apparently granting him permission.

As he went back upstairs, a hammer began to pound inside his head. Had he thought of everything? Was there nothing he'd forgotten? Had he used enough of the sleeping pills? He had carefully researched the proper dosage and had added a little extra—under no circumstances would he want Huong to regain consciousness.

His hand trembled as he opened the door of the darkened bedroom. He remembered the suspicion in her eyes and hid the knife behind his back. He slowly approached her. A band of bright light from the hallway fell across her face. She was sound asleep. In the absence of the accusing glare he had grown accustomed to in recent years, she appeared once again as the innocent girl he had fallen in love with. His heart ached. Dear, beautiful, happy Huong. Giggling at his foolish jokes, deeply touched by the stream of poems he sent her, blushing when he whispered in her ear that her chastity was driving him crazy, completely devoted to him when at last they became man and wife.

A shiver ran through her wasted body. The sight of it pushed Mr. Li back a step. The doubts he thought he had left behind loomed up again in his thoughts. He took a deep breath and shook his head. *Don't give in to them!* That thing in the bed was not Huong. It was nothing more than a withered relic of the lovely flower she once had been.

It had begun at the party celebrating his twenty-five years on the job. His employer had made a gracious speech, and Huong's face shone with pride, but she was silent in the car on the way home. For a week, she stubbornly spoke not a word more than was absolutely necessary. When he finally begged her to explain the reason she was ignoring him, she pronounced the name of his colleague Wies, a cheerful, flamboyant woman whose desk was three over from his.

"She wants to steal you away from me," Huong hissed, her voice that of a poisonous snake.

Li was dumbfounded, but she refused to let her anger be soothed.

"Wies is married," he protested.

"So was my father. To *three* women!"

Mr. Li smiled. "What has that to do with us? Polygamy is illegal in The Netherlands. In Vietnam, too, these days."

She frowned. "But if you could, you would take another wife. I know that for certain."

"Nonsense, my darling. You know I could never love anyone but you."

He approached her, intending to wrap his arms around her

and, as always, to comfort her and convince her of the purity of his love. But she pushed him away as if he were a filthy dog.

Upset, he reproached her. "Why do you treat me in this manner?"

"You're attracted to other women."

"Since the day of our wedding, Huong, I have never looked at anyone but you. You are everything to me. You *know* that."

"You lie! I have eyes, don't I? That Wies was hanging all over you at your party."

"What was there for me to do about that? Dutch women are different, Huong. Freer. She meant nothing by it. It's just the way she is. She treats every man like that."

But Huong would not be convinced. She had always been jealous and insecure. Long ago, he had seen that as evidence of her love for him, but over the years it had gotten worse. Much worse, and finally unbearable. Unbearable for him, but also for her. The doctors called what was happening in Huong's brain "early-onset basal ganglia calcification," and it had turned his wife into a devil and their marriage into a battlefield. It had reached a point where she would call him at work many times a day to check up on him, and he would have to hurry home to prove that she was the only one he cared about. The situation had become hopeless. He could no longer stand to watch her suffer.

The weight of the carving knife seemed to burn his hand. But he had to keep to his plan, the only possible way to resolve their problems. Step by step, he drew closer to the bed. She lay there exactly as he had left her. He turned back her blanket and ignored the red roses on her nightgown. This shell of a woman had to die, so the Huong who was trapped inside her could be free.

Mr. Li had seen it happen time and again during the Vietnam Conflict, had seen it with his own eyes. Those images still haunted him, half a century later. One steady cut across the carotid artery would do it. Even were she not sedated, she would barely notice the killing blow.

He took several slow, deep breaths. There could be no mistake. He pressed the point of the knife against her arm, then again, the second time harder. No reaction. Reassured, Mr. Li rolled her body onto its side and spread a clear plastic tarp across the mattress. Images from their hellish boat ride, many years ago, flashed across his mind: a similar plastic sheet had been their only protection from the constant rain and howling wind. The cold, the hunger, the uncertainty, and especially the fear that the other refugees might turn against them had been nearly fatal.

A squeaking sound escaped him and brought him back to the present. *Don't think of the past! Concentrate on this moment!*

Mr. Li rolled his wife's body back onto the plastic, pulled her to a sitting position, and crawled into the bed behind her. He stiffened when she muttered a few words he could not decipher. If she were to awaken, there would be no way to explain what he was doing in her bed with a knife in his hand.

The time had come. He drew the blade quickly across her throat. Warmth flowed over his hand, and he knew that it was her blood. She sank deeper into his arms. He repeated the slicing motion he had studied, and Huong's head tilted to one side.

Li carefully laid her down and got out of the bed. A dark pool spread from her wounds and welled at the edges of the plastic. His body shook uncontrollably when he realized that his shirt was drenched with blood. He fisted his hands and beat himself on the legs and backside in an attempt to stop the spasms, but the pummeling had no effect. There was no time for this. *Don't think. Just act, just follow the plan.*

Her body was warm when he wrapped it in her blankets, then lowered it to the floor, where he'd spread another plastic tarp. Li stripped the sheets from the bed and put them in the washing machine with his shirt. The mattress was also bloody. He flipped it over and hoped the children would never think to look beneath it.

He wrapped the plastic on the floor around the blanketed figure of his wife and lifted the bundle with some difficulty. The tiny woman's weight surprised him. Staggering beneath this burden, he managed to get her down the stairs. He was horrified to see a blood-smeared man in the foyer, then realized he was looking at his own reflection in the hall mirror. He turned away quickly and hurried through the kitchen to the attached garage.

The Daewoo's door was already open. He eased Huong into the passenger seat and buckled the safety belt around her. Her head drooped to one side. He gingerly peeled the plastic and the blanket away from her face and rewrapped it around her neck to support her head. That worked. She looked unnatural, but that was not a cause for concern. No one ever paid attention to a pair of elderly Vietnamese in an ordinary Korean car.

In the shower, Li stared at the drain until the pink water ran clear. He rubbed himself dry with a rough towel and went to the guest room, where his best suit and a clean shirt hung ready for him. He put them on and smoothed away a wrinkle with his hand. Earlier, he had neatly packed the rest of their clothing in cardboard boxes. The children could take them to Goodwill and give them a second life. He and Huong had always objected to waste.

His next chore awaited him at the kitchen table. The sleeping pills were already crushed into powder. He had calculated that he would have at least fifteen minutes before the dosage took effect. That would give him all the time he needed. He dumped the powder into a glass of water and added a tablespoon of strawberry syrup to camouflage the bitter taste.

This was it, then. There was no need to be mournful. A better existence awaited him. He emptied the glass in one long swallow. *Done.*

Mr. Li was on his way back to the garage when a familiar ring-tone sounded from the hall. Hesitant, he looked at the phone. His daughter's name was on the screen. A yearning to hear her voice one last time welled up inside him. He ignored his common sense and lifted the receiver.

"Dad, where were you?"

"What do you mean? Were we supposed to be somewhere?"

"Iris had her swim test tonight."

Mr. Li slapped his forehead. "That was today? We completely forgot, sweetheart. I'm so sorry. Did she pass?"

"With flying colors. She's standing right here. Do you want to say hi?"

A dagger pricked his heart at the thought of a conversation with his favorite grandchild. In the background, he could hear Iris whining for a present.

"Congratulate her for us. We're on our way out the door."

"Where to?"

"Just going for a drive."

"So late? Can I talk to Mom for a minute?"

"She's already in the car. I really have to go."

"I'll call her tomorrow."

He could hear the disappointment in his daughter's voice. "I love you, Lily. Don't forget that."

"It's okay, Dad. I'll talk to you tomorrow."

Mr. Li bit his lip. There was no way back, this was the only solution. He had to finish what he had begun, as he had finished everything he had begun, from the moment that—after that hellish sea journey—they been given their second chance in The Netherlands. Soon, they would be together again. Their twin spirits would find each other in the next life. Healthy and unencumbered by care, unburdened by dark thoughts and false accusations.

His wristwatch informed him that too many valuable minutes had already elapsed. He would have to hurry. He opened the garage door, started the engine, and backed into the driveway. When he stepped out of the car to close the door, he became aware of the icy raindrops pelting the road.

Driving faster than was permitted, he wound his way through the dark, empty streets of the village, where once he and Huong had been able to consider themselves happy.

He glanced at his wife. Her blood had soaked through the blanket and adhered to the plastic in elongated bubbles, like the beads in a kaleidoscope. No one would see them. No one would pay them the least bit of attention. Her face was paler than he had ever seen it. Her thin lips were turning blue.

His sense of time became distorted. Mr. Li had the feeling that time was slowing down, was stopping entirely, then suddenly jerking forward in a rush. He understood that he would have to press harder on the accelerator to reach his destination.

The streetlamps on both sides of the road formed long lanes of light, reflecting up from the wet asphalt. Mr. Li saw an infinite wind tunnel stretching out before him, saw himself passing through it like a knight in shining armor. Struggling against the odds, heroic....

Stop all this! Pay attention! Stay awake! You're not finished yet!

Li opened his window. A frigid wind blew in his face.

He arrived as if in a hallucinatory nightmare. Staggering, he pulled himself out of the Daewoo and stumbled to the edge of the canal. He blinked. Were his eyes deceiving him? Or was he already asleep and dreaming? The pole that indicated the level of the water—normally almost completely submerged—was at least half visible. The canal was practically dry. There was no way it would swallow up their car.

A terrible scream made Mr. Li shrink in on himself, until he realized that it was he who had cried out in agonized fear. He slapped himself on both cheeks.

Stay awake! Do not give up! Not at this final moment….

With great difficulty, he turned. The wind buffeted his arms and legs. Back to the Daewoo. Back to Huong. They had to go together. He should never have allowed himself to be distracted by that call from their daughter. He had said everything there was to say in his letter.

Li shrieked in frustration, but his voice was eaten by the wind, which by now had become very fierce.

Somehow he made it back to the car. There would be deeper water farther up the road. He managed to crawl into the driver's seat. His eyes closed. He rested his head against the wheel, just for a moment, and tried with all his might to open his eyes. It was not easy, but he succeeded. Like a drunkard, he reached for the key, which he had left in the ignition. There was no strength left in his muscles. His arms were clumsy appendages that defied his will. At last the engine caught, or at least he thought it did. Perhaps the rumbling he felt was the trembling of his body.

He raised his head to see if anyone was nearby, but there was nothing but sheets of rain. He could feel motion. Was it the car? Or something else?

He reached for the steering wheel, but it was gone. Or perhaps his arms were no longer functioning. Li was able to turn toward Huong, who still sat quietly beside him. He tried to speak to her, but his tongue was frozen. Clouds of white mist circled around her, almost concealing her from sight.

Mr. Li faded into darkness, surrounded by images from his past. He saw Huong as a young girl, strolling beside the river.

Blushing, she took his hand. A feeling of inexpressible joy overwhelmed him.

Bao Li, 64, was discovered asleep in his vehicle by a passerby, parked beside a shipping canal. His wife was on the passenger seat beside him, her throat cut. Based on the extenuating circumstances presented by his attorney, Li was given three years' incarceration. The judge pronounced this sentence with tears in his eyes. As he spoke, the courtroom was completely silent. The prosecutor, however, insisted that this had been a brutal and carefully planned murder, and appealed to a higher court. With dry eyes, the appeals judge sentenced Li to twenty-five years.

11

———————

SOUL MATES

BY CHRISTINE OTTEN

They were on our doorstep at ten after six this morning. I know the exact time because a fraction of a second before the bell rang—one short, two longs—I woke up and looked at my iPhone. Six ten. It was just getting light. I knew it was the cops. I mean, you just *know*. I heard Mom's bedroom door creak, her footsteps on the stairs, the murmur of voices. So I splashed some water on my face, sprayed my pits with Axe, and got dressed. I was calm. At times like this, my emotions just sort of freeze. I grabbed the Prada jacket Miriam gave me, slipped my bare feet into my Pumas, and went down. I'm a good boy, I am. I tried to ignore Mom's expression; if there's one thing I can't stand, it's that exhausted, disappointed look she gets in her eyes: *Can't I ever have a moment's peace?* Instead, I focused on the crew-cut heads of the two detectives standing in the doorway, their hands deep in the pockets of their ugly cheap H&M jackets, and said, cheerfully as I could manage, "Good morning, gentlemen, and what can we do for you today?"

You could see them thinking *this is one polite Algerian.* You always gotta stay a step ahead of them. Be the strongest, the smartest, don't let them figure you out, and most important: keep your anger under control. I learned that at kickboxing. Not too long ago, I got pulled over on my moped on the Meteorenweg because I was supposedly driving too fast. I was heading to the Mandarijnenstraat to deliver six frikandels, three croquettes, a deep-fried bami slice, a couple of kebabs, and fifteen euros worth of French fries with mayo. I guess they were having a party. So, anyway, I was in a hurry, nobody wants soggy fries and lukewarm frikandels. I don't understand how anyone can stomach that disgusting *haram* shit in the first place, but whatever, ours not to reason why. The point is, I got pulled over. Must of been the cop's first week on the job. "Sir, you're driving much too fast." We both knew it was bullshit, I wasn't doing more than twenty kilometers an hour, twenty five tops, we both know the only reason he flagged me down is I look like a Moroccan—a Marrow Khan in Tuindorp Oostzaan, I'm a poet and I don't know it!—but whatever. He whips out his little citation book to write me up, and I say, "I'm terribly sorry, officer, but my gramma is sick, she's in really bad shape, and I don't want her to be alone, that's why I was in a rush."

When he hears me talking in complete sentences without a hint of an accent, his eyes practically pop out of his head. "Oh?" he says.

"She lives right around the corner here, on the Zonneplein." Which is one hundred percent true: Mom's mother lives on the Zonneplein, upstairs from a Turkish grocery.

So the cop waves me on, and that's the end of it. Which is why I say: you have to stay a step ahead of them. Don't give 'em the chance to fuck with you.

· · ·

Anyway, I had a good idea why the detectives were at our door. See, the Chink's been missing for five days now, and the Mercury's been shuttered, although the old gook normally opens up at noon so's he don't miss a chance to cash in on the lunch trade. He didn't tell me he was gonna be gone: no email, no text, nothing.

When I showed up for work five days ago and he wasn't there, I tried his doorbell—he lives upstairs from his snackbar-slash-Chinese-takeaway, see. I was only inside his apartment one time, and the stink of grease made me want to hurl. He really needs to do something about his ventilation.

So I got no response when I rang, and there wasn't any lights on I could see. Pissed me off, because it was payday, and man does not live by tips alone. For the last couple months, the old guy and me have had a little side deal. "Call it hush money" is the way he put it. I never asked for nothing extra. Didn't need to. The old guy read in my eyes I knew the score. I mean, I'm not *stupid*. He never should of asked me to fetch that box of croquettes from the freezer, the fool.

All those bricks of brown and white powder hidden in among the frozen snacks and fries! Street value? I have no idea. Jesus, I mean, you want to play gangster, at least you could be a little careful about it. Fine, well, anyway, the way I saw it we had us what you call a win/win situation there. And I could use the extra cash. Him, too, apparently. The Mercury Snackbar on the Mercuriusplein ain't exactly a gold mine, if you catch my drift. Until he gets the windows washed and loses those disgusting orange plastic stools and the greasy Formica countertop and does something about the ventilation, he pretty much *needs* a little side-line if he wants to stay afloat, you see what I'm saying?

I understand the Chink. He's gotta think about his future. He's not gonna wind up some old geezer wasting away in that pitiful apartment on the Mercuriusplein, not when he could live out his golden years in Malaysia or Hong Kong or Singapore or wherever the hell he comes from, amirite? So I figured he emptied out his bank accounts and was having himself a roll in the hay with some Chinese hottie in a massage parlor off in Whereverland. I was actually kind of proud of him. I wasn't worried about our deal, or about the cops implicating me in his drug trade, because there was absolutely no paper trail or anything else pointing my way. I'm the delivery boy for the Mercury Snackbar, and that is *all* I am.

Except, with those two cops standing there awkwardly at the door, I began to feel just a wee bit sweaty.

The older of the two—you could already see the male pattern baldness making inroads on his temples—cleared his throat. "We're sorry to bother you so early, but I'm afraid we have bad news. May we come in?"

No way, I thought. But Mom automatically took a step back. I could see fear in the slump of her shoulders inside her pink robe. She grabbed my face and started whining like a wounded animal. "Where did I go wrong, Armin? You were always such a sweet little boy!" I was afraid she was about to keel over, so I slung an arm around her to keep her on her feet. I mean, I *am* the man of the house. But I guess I can't blame her for projecting her shit onto me.

"Calm down, Ma," I said. "Don't worry. Let's hear what the officers have to say."

To make a long story short, the Chink was dead. At least the detectives *thought* it was the Chink they'd found hacked to bits and the bits deep fried, "considering how close the dumpster in the Maanstraat is to the Mercury Snackbar and his contacts in the Chinese tongs." The only thing they could say for sure at this point was that what they had found was definitely human remains, though they were in such a state they weren't sure it would ever be possible to positively identify the victim. Somebody from the neighborhood had called it in. His little Staffordshire Terrier had started barking and howling when they came in sight of the dumpster. The smell was pretty ripe, they said.

The older detective must of seen the dismay in Mom's eyes, 'cause all of a sudden he put a hand on her shoulder and said they were ninety-nine percent sure it was the Chink, and they hoped the techs would come up with like a molecule of DNA that would lock in that last one percent. No such thing as a perfect crime, he said, puffing out his chest, "even though there's usually a loose end or two, we know that from experience," looking like he was starring in an episode of *CSI*, like he was some kind of big shot. "We don't want you folks to worry, now, ma'am, do we? Tuindorp Oostzaan's such a quiet little neighborhood, where nothing ever happens." I could hear the contempt in his voice. On the downtown side of the IJ, they think we're all hicks up here in Amsterdam-North.

So I told you I sort of freeze at times like this, right? My friends don't call me Ice for nothing—after the old rapper-slash-actor with the pigtail from *Law & Order*, you know? Maybe the story was a little too crazy to believe. Even Mom just stood there crying silently instead of busting out screaming. But I realized pretty quick that the cops weren't out to tie me to whatever had gone down. When you're in their headlights, you *know* it. They were pretty chill about the whole thing. Just said they'd appreciate whatever I could tell them about the Chink, seeing how I was the Mercury's scooter boy and all—I wanted to correct them and say *moped* boy, but I didn't think I ought to interrupt—and I saw the old guy pretty much every day, so maybe I could help them with their enquiries. I told them I thought the Chink was out of town for a couple days, he said something about needing a break, checking out the tulips at the Keukenhof, yadda yadda yadda, and running a Chinese takeout-slash-snackbar in Tuindorp Oostzaan ain't exactly what you call a sinecure, right? Meanwhile, the little gears in my head are spinning overtime, you know what I mean?

See, something told me maybe the deep-fried dead guy was *not* the Chink.

Maybe I watch too many cop shows. On TV, nothing ever turns out the way you think it will, right?

But there was something else. Which is why I'm writing all this down, not as evidence but as a sort of testimony, in case something happens to me. For Mom's sake, you with me? Ain't nobody I love more than her, not even Miriam.

I don't know if I can call Miriam my girlfriend, exactly, since she's married and all that. She and her husband and their two little girls live in one of those villas on the Kometensingel, a fancy place next door to the house where our family doctor used to live. Once upon a time, Mom was the cleaning lady there. So one night they order a double portion of chow mein from the Mercury. I deliver it, Miriam answers the door, and the rest is history.

Trust me, Miriam is not just some ordinary chick. She is what I'd call a perfect ten. From our very first date, though, she told me she was never ever gonna divorce her husband, 'cause her own parents split when she was fifteen and she wasn't gonna put *her* girls through that kind of trauma. That's class, amirite?

Her husband's a lung doctor in some hospital up north. His name's Ed. He's forty-four. (Just so you know: I'm twenty-four.) I only know him from Miriam's stories and his Facebook page. Soon as the detectives left, I went online: his most recent photo was posted yesterday, from a bar, right after the Ajax-Sparta game. He was grinning into the lens with this smug doctor expression on his face and a glass of beer in his hand. Ajax scarf around his neck. *See how normal I am?* You could almost hear André Hazes singing in the background. That's why he bought that house in Tuindorp Oostzaan, to prove what an ordinary guy he is. Miriam told me his whole bio. Ed's dad worked in the metal foundry on the Distelweg, the five of them lived in this dreary little bungalow on the Pomonastraat. Ed was a nerd, so after high school they told him he could go to college, and he grabbed the chance. Props to him and his family, I gotta give them respect. If my loser of a father had half the guts Ed's dad had, I could've… nah, never mind, I don't want to go throwing stones.

Anyway, when Miriam met Ed, he was a member of like a fraternity, you know what I mean, a group of students who were ashamed of their origins and put on high-class accents like they were part of the Royal Family. At first, she said, she thought it was kind of cute, that Ed was trying so hard to fit in. She told me she saw right through his act and decided she could help him "grow into himself." I mean, bullshit, right—and she knew it was bullshit even at the time. But a woman like Miriam's gotta have a project. Sometimes I think maybe I'm her newest project, but at the same time I think *what the fuck?* I'll tell you what: she's *my* project. I love her.

Miriam and me come from two different worlds. Her mother was something high up at the university, and her father was a bigwig at Nestlé. When she was growing up, they moved to a new country every couple of years: Egypt, Canada, Nigeria, South Africa, Russia, Morocco. I mean, she's a woman of the world. Sometimes she tells me, "Ed's a real Tuindorper, totally white bread. But you, you've got that Algerian blood." She has this tone when she says it, like, *this is heavy, man.* And the look in her eye, yowza. I don't know exactly what it all means, but so what? The bottom line is it's pretty great with us between the sheets, if you follow me.

But I digress.

I love Miriam, you with me? And I know she's stuck between a rock and a hard place. Hey, put yourself in her position: your hubby's cheating on you with some pretty young intern while you sit home and look after a couple of kids. That'd make you nuts, amirite?

So, okay, this is where the story really begins.

From the first time we ever did it—Ed works irregular shifts and I'm pretty flexible, so she texts me when it's okay to come over—she's spilled her guts to me. I'm not so dumb I believe in love at first sight, but *something* just clicked between Miriam and me. *Soul mates*, she calls us. That's such a Miriam thing to say. "We're both outsiders," she tells me. "We understand each other." It don't bother me she's fifteen years older. Just the opposite: I think older women are sexy, they know exactly what they want in bed.

Shit, I'm getting off track again. Focus, Armin!

So Ed's fucking this intern, and Miriam finds out about it. She confronts him. He goes all guilty, all pitiful, all *I'm sorry, you're the one I love, it don't mean nothing*, and he begs her to forgive him. And she *does*, the dope.

Okay, fine, I know what you're thinking: *she's* cheating on *him*, too. To which I say: *Well, who started it?* Miriam was lonely. Can you blame her for taking comfort from a guy like me? A guy who at least *listens* to her?

As my Mom's only son, trust me, I have learned how to listen.

So Miriam forgives Ed. But meanwhile, Ed goes right on nailing this intern every chance he gets. They're snorting coke—possibly coke they get from the Chink, what do I know?—and Ed don't realize right away the woman he's boinking is the devil in disguise. But then, see, the bitch commences to blackmail him. *If you don't leave your wife and kids, I'll tell the hospital adminis-*

trator what you been up to. I'll say you forced me into it. Abuse of power, shit like that. So you got a doctor riding the coke train and banging an intern: Ed would definitely lose his job and probably his medical license or whatever you call it. I got all this from Miriam.

So once again, Ed fesses up, only this time Miriam plays it smart. She "forgives" him, she says, only this time she has a plan.

"You're my sweet revenge," she tells me, this one time after we do it. We're smoking cigarettes in bed. Ed's working a double shift, and the girls are at his parents'. "You're my secret weapon."

Tell you the truth, that comment shook me up a little. It wasn't so much *what* she said but the *way* she said it, the bitterness in her voice, and the way she looked... like I wasn't even there, like I wasn't lying right beside her in the bed.

Anyway, Miriam don't trust Ed no more, but she don't want to leave him because of the kids. So she goes all detective on his ass: when he's in the shower, she checks his email and his texts. And that's when the shit really hits the fan:

I'll kill Miriam if you don't divorce her.

You'd better get rid of your daughters. My patience is running out.

You're mine!!!

I hate Miriam.

Miriam's a cunt and has to die.

And then there are Ed's wimpy responses:

Calm down, sweetheart.

I need more time.

I love you.

This is all pretty recent, by the way. I was with Miriam just last night, and she brought me up to speed.

So now I gotta be careful what I write. I don't want to screw anybody over until I'm a hundred percent sure. I know what it's like to be blamed for shit I didn't do. I mean, how many times have we had the cops at the door because So and So made a crack and everybody's all *it must've been Armin who done it.*

How am I supposed to prove I *didn't*, right?

I mean, come on!

Look, I figure *you'd* probably freak if you found out *your* husband's lover wanted *you* dead, right? So I told Miriam maybe she ought to report it. Which by the way was really weird coming out of *my* mouth. Report it? Like the cop on the corner is your friend, right? But I just didn't trust the situation. I was worried about Miriam.

"This is private," she said. "I don't want the girls to hear anything about it. I'll deal with it." And then she climbed on top of me and drove me out of my gourd with her tongue. We fucked like we never fucked before, like... well, like wild animals. It was like Miriam squeezed herself *inside* of me. She bit me, licked me, raked my back with her long sharp nails, sucked my balls, Jesus, I thought I was about to black out, and meanwhile she whispered all this shit I figured was meant to stir me up and make our coming even more explosive, words and sentences I didn't really absorb, you know what I mean, we all say weird stuff when we're excited, I mean, I get it that Miriam wished the bitch was dead, and I'm not a baby, I've got a pretty rich imagination myself, if you get my drift, I've downloaded some illegal videos, you know, where Somebody A really *hurts* Somebody B, hits her, beats her with whips, cuts her with razors, tortures her, snuff films, I mean, that shit's fucked up.

Anyway, I didn't think much about the fairy tale she told me last night until those cops showed up this morning, but since then I can't get it out of my mind.

And I can totally see it happening.

Miriam waiting outside the hospital for her husband's chippie.

Inviting her for a cup of coffee so they can "talk things out." Driving in Miriam's mint-green Mini Cooper convertible from North Holland down to Tuindorp Oostzaan, the wind in their hair, it's actually much too cold to be driving with the top down but Miriam wants to teach the bitch a lesson, *she's* wearing a leather jacket and a cap, she's prepared, she snuck the Mercury Snackbar's keys out of my pants pocket the day before, when I slipped out of bed to take a dump. Miriam parking the car somewhere on the Meteorenweg, and the two of them strolling to the snackbar, Ed's cunt grossed out when she sees the Mercury's grimy windows, *this is where you want to go for coffee?* The Chink's already long gone, Miriam knows that because I told her. Fine, so she holds the door open for the bitch, gives her a little wink, they're in this together, they understand each other, they both know Ed's a piece of shit and they'll figure a way to get through this, but the second Miriam locks the door behind them the nightmare begins, Miriam's thought of everything, the ropes, the bread knife, the chain saw, she switched on the fryer before she headed north so it would be nice and hot by the time they got back, she don't leave nothing to chance, and meanwhile the cunt's all shitting bricks and begging Miriam to let her go, but Miriam's got her chained to the meat hook that's attached to the kitchen ceiling by then, like a dead pig, like a dog—the Chinks eat dog, don't they? —her mouth duct-taped, and while the bitch shivers from the cold and the terror Miriam goes to town, one finger at a time, one toe at a time, the blood dripping into an old-fashioned iron bucket, the cunt turning yellow then gray then finally white and blue and she's not dead yet, her left shoulder jerks when Miriam slices a chunk of meat from her leg and tosses it into the boiling oil in the fryer, can you imagine watching this happen to *you*, you know you're gonna die and there isn't a fucking thing you can do about it, just hope you'll pass out soon, but Miriam goes at it for hours, big pieces, torso, thighs, arms, she trims them to size with the chain saw and one by one the hunks of meat and bone and hair and guts and everything all disappear in the boiling oil.

You understand I see the situation in a different light, now the cops have been and gone.

You are my sweet revenge. You are my secret weapon.

See, Miriam's always been sort of a mystery to me. A woman like that, a woman of the world, so... *smart*, so well spoken, and beautiful, too, even though she's already past forty, I never met nobody like her in my life. We might of come from different planets. You see where I'm going with this?

Is it possible the detectives showed up at *her* door before they came to mine? Like maybe yesterday, so she already knew about the mess in the dumpster before we got together last night? She lives practically right around the corner from the Mercury, she's a steady customer, I drop off an order of chow mein like two, three times a week. The detectives must know that if they're halfway decent at their jobs.

They go around the neighborhood, door to door, asking questions, don't they?

Meanwhile, I never once noticed my key to the Mercury was missing, so maybe Miriam made the whole thing up. I mean, maybe she's gotta fantasize shit like that to keep her frustration from driving her nuts, what do I know? Her husband's rich, but money don't make nobody happy. Status, neither. I know that much by now. And her whole story could of come straight out of a bad episode of *Midsomer Murders*. Mom watches that show every Wednesday night.

I get it, Miriam wanted the bitch out of her life, but even if she *did* decide to waste her, even then, she would of just run her down with her Mini, wouldn't she, or got a gun and blew her brains out. Wouldn't she? I mean, I just don't see Miriam going to town with a fucking chain saw. I don't think she'd know how something like that even *works*.

I know what you're thinking: Why don't I just go *ask* her? Ask her what's the real deal and, boom, case closed. But see, here's the thing: we don't have that kind of a relationship. I never ask her *nothing*. I just *listen*.

I mean—and I'm not talking about my relationship with the Chink, here, that was pretty clear-cut, no surprises, I mean, it sucks the old guy got chopped into mincemeat and all, but that's the chance you take when you get in with the tongs, he knew the risk—but the idea that I dumped myself into this rich-people's soap opera, what does that say about me?

I love Miriam and all, but what about my self-respect? What about my pride?

Maybe this whole thing's some kind of a sign. Whatever really happened, my job at the Mercury Snackbar is gone. I am now foot-loose and fancy-free. I could just hang out for a while, see which way the wind blows. Nothing's stopping me from trying something completely new, stepping out on my own. Maybe computers? Or I could take over the Mercury and run it myself. Get rid of those shitty plastic stools, put in some decent ventilation, turn it into a hip new takeout place. Snackbar Armin, something like that, everything one hundred percent *halal*. I bet there's a market for that in Tuindorp Oostzaan, especially if I hire a couple of kids with scooters to make deliveries all over Amsterdam-North. Why not?

I got all that hush money from the Chink saved up. Plus the tips Miriam always gave me—not just for the chow mein, but after we screwed, too, now I think of it.

Every cloud has a silver lining, right?

Amirite?

On the other hand, there's no way I'll ever hook up with a woman like Miriam again, that's for sure.

And what we have, that *has* to be love. I mean, the sex, the way she trusts me....

We're soul mates, aren't we?

I mean, *aren't* we?

12

———————————

A NORMAL LIFE

BY MARION PAUW

You always hated it, Anandi, when people stared at me. When there was an event at school, you *begged* me to wear "normal" clothes, so I'd look like the other mothers. And when you finally realized I had no intention of fitting in, you tore up the invitations to your parents' evenings, assemblies, plays and concerts. I'd find the shredded announcements at the bottom of your book bag, mixed in with candy-bar wrappers and other litter.

Perhaps I should have taken you more seriously, thought less of myself and my so-called ideals and acted more like the mother you wanted me to be. But I believed I had the right to be who I *am* —in the same way I always allowed you to be who *you* are.

Was I really such a terrible parent? I always wished you'd bring kids from your class home to play, so they'd see how pleasant our living situation was, but you never did. You just sat alone in your room, waiting for your childhood to end, so you could surround yourself with "normal" people living "normal" lives in their "normal" houses.

These days, by the way, I dress the way you always wanted me to, so you'll never have to be ashamed of me again. Ironic, isn't it?

Now that I think about it, I suppose I derived a certain *power* from all those staring eyes. I don't think anyone meant to be unfriendly—I certainly never experienced it that way. Most people have been programmed to look askance at anything that deviates from the norm. They don't know any better.

My life is different now—I'm sure you understand that. These days, people look at me as if they want to burn me at the stake. And another thing that's changed: I don't just *see* their reactions. Now I can *hear* them.

That's Melissa van der Sluis! Look, it's Melissa van der Sluis!

I've never really liked my name, but now I can barely tolerate all those hissing esses. I've begun to understand what makes a person grab an automatic weapon and start shooting. I've even almost begun to understand *you*. And that says quite a lot, doesn't it?

I have turned into the sort of woman who'd rather just stay at home. I wait until the fridge is empty—no canned goods, no packaged food, not a crumb left in the house—before I'll even step out to the market. When I *do* go, I wait until shortly before closing time. And even then I have to concentrate on my breathing and talk myself through it, the way I'd comfort a terrified house pet.

Head high, back straight, shoulders firm. Don't let them see that you're afraid, that would only encourage them.

Of course I've tried disguises. Hats, dark glasses, wigs. But there's always some news junkie who recognizes me, one of those people who pride themselves on scouring the paper from first page to last and never miss a true-crime program on cable. Being unmasked feels even worse than just being spotted without my camouflage. As if, over and above all my other supposed sins, I'm also a hypocrite.

Sooner or later, I tell myself, *they'll lose interest. Someday. Someday I'll be able to show myself in public again.*

Someday, I want to be as "normal" as you always wanted me to be.

I have a friend, Anandi. Her name is Nettie. I'm well aware that the only reason she wants to *be* my friend is so that, at the birthday parties and barbecues she attends, she can dish out the sort of gossip that never appears in the newspapers. I see right through her selfish motives, but I'm grateful to her all the same. I've known her since high school. After the—what should I call it? the drama? the *incident?*—after the story broke, she reached out to me. Why did I let her into my life? Because there wasn't anyone else, and sometimes even the sound of my own breath frightened me.

Today is Wednesday, and that means lunch with Nettie. She decided it would be good for me to train myself to handle social situations. Otherwise, she predicted, I'd spend the rest of my life as a hermit.

I don't want to go out for lunch, but I know Nettie gets a kick from being seen with me in public. So once I week I force myself out of bed at eleven, take a shower, and put on something unremarkable. Nettie says the sooner I start behaving normally, the sooner others will *see* me as normal. She reads a lot of self-help books and takes a meditation class. She wants to know if I ever really *did* feel "enlightened." Oh, and also if it's true that we practiced free love in the commune....

I drag myself to the restaurant in the shopping street closest to home, head bowed so I don't have to see the way the passersby look at me. It's harder to block out the hissing.

Melissa van der Sluis, Melissa van der Sluis, isn't that Melissa van der Sluis?

Nettie's already seated, and of course she chose a table by the window. She's wearing a bright-orange blouse, almost the same shade I used to wear, with a coquettish little skirt and a pair of knee-high boots.

"Lis!" she says, much too loudly. She's called me "Lis" from Day One, to show the world what a special connection we have. "Hi, hon, you okay?"

She throws her arms around me theatrically. I accept her air kisses on both cheeks as if I'm ten years old and she's my grandmother.

When I sit, she resumes her own seat and shakes her head. "You don't eat enough," she says. "Every time I see you, you look thinner."

"I have no appetite," I say.

She leans in closer, allowing me a glimpse of her wrinkled *décolleté*. "Have you heard anything from Anandi?"

It annoys me that she starts in on you so immediately. Usually, we devote a quarter of an hour to the weather and the latest summer fashions, until I run out of things to say and she concludes that it's okay to turn the conversation in your direction.

"No," I say, and that's the truth. "She doesn't want to have anything to do with me. I've told you that."

"But she's getting out in two weeks. Where's she going to *go*?"

"Have you decided?" asks the server, who has appeared beside our table. She's a little older than you, I think, Anandi. From the way she avoids looking at me, I know she knows who I am.

"I'll have the tomato soup," I say.

Nettie reacts as if I'm an infant. "You should have something more *filling*, hon." And when I don't respond, she tells the girl, "Bring her a hamburger, too." For herself, she orders the carpaccio, hold the cheese and bread. She's always dieting, because she eats way too much chocolate.

"Of course she's only eighteen," says Nettie. "And when you

think about what that child has *been* through. I really hope you'll make the first move, Lis. After all, you *are* her mother."

"I told you, she doesn't want anything to do with me. So what am I supposed to do?" The words tumble out so loudly, the people at the tables around us fall silent.

"Don't be angry, sweetheart," says Nettie. She pats the back of my hand. "I know how hard this must be for you."

As a sort of protest, I don't eat a bite of my burger and barely touch my soup. I see Nettie watching me, but she doesn't dare say another word. When I glance away, she sneaks a fry from my plate.

Why does everyone seem to believe that children are malleable? As if there's a recipe for raising them: a pinch of this, a dash of that, stir thoroughly or they'll be spoiled. If a kid doesn't turn out right, well, the mother must not have followed the instructions properly.

I know *you* blame me for everything that happened. You're not the only one. Everybody thinks it was all my fault. I mean, I'm the mother, I *must* have known there was something wrong with you. I should have intervened. But how?

There are so many depressed teens in the world. Does every one of them have to be seen as potentially dangerous?

Tell me, Anandi, when should I have stepped in, and what should I have done?

Of course, you could have taken *some* responsibility for your actions, but no, you managed to convince the judge that your childhood was one continuous trauma. I had to sit there and listen to the most *awful* stories about myself. I never really cared about you. Sometimes, I sent you to school without your breakfast. I dressed you in ridiculous clothes, and the other children laughed at you. You felt unsafe amongst all us grownups. I made you—and this is what cast me in the *worst* possible light—made you watch what went on in my bedroom.

All right, for God's sake, let's talk about Guillaume. I actually *never* discuss him, did you know that? Nettie *begs* me, but I can't even bring myself to say his name out loud. It's the same with Leonard's, Cecile's, Majetska's, Ravi's, Reginald's, and Butter's names.

Do you ever think about them? If you do, how do you remember them? A group of chanting loons in orange robes? A pile of bodies, dead on the ground? Or do you ever remember that Cecile wrote little stories for you, and Leonard painted a mural of dolphins on your bedroom wall? Because those happy times were part of your history, too, though you seem to have forgotten them.

Are *you* able to speak their names? And if you do, how do you feel? Proud of yourself? Justified?

Or are you sorry, Anandi, for what you did?

You used to ask me how come you didn't have a mother *and* a father, like "normal" kids do. You said the word "normal" as if normality was life's Holy Grail.

Maybe I *should* have tried to figure out who your father was— there were four possibilities—just to make you happy, but to me your having a father seemed like it would have been more of a limitation than an enrichment. Osho says we spend our lives attempting to escape the imprinting inflicted upon us by our parents. Okay, maybe I paid too much attention to all that Osho stuff, that's entirely possible. If so, I am truly sorry.

But then Guillaume came along. From the first moment I saw him, I was absolutely certain that the two of us belonged together.

I hope that you—despite everything that's happened—will someday meet *your* soul mate, someone whose very heartbeat is an echo of yours.

Of course you despised Guillaume. I think you realized that we were made for each other, which left *you* on the outside looking in. But I assumed you were just going through a phase. If I allowed you to feel your feelings, I figured, eventually you would come to accept him.

There was that one night, though. I was lying in his arms, exhausted, overwhelmed by the caramel scent of his hair and the surprising softness of his skin. And then I saw him staring at the doorway.

The door was open, and you were standing there. Lord knows how long you'd been there. I searched for words... and for a sheet to cover our nakedness, but I was too late. With all the disdain you could summon at your tender age, you said, "You... are... *disgusting*."

And you weren't the only one who resented my relationship with Guillaume. The other members of the commune all complained. We were supposed to be a single unit, all of us, and it was wrong for any two of us to form a separate couple. So Guillaume and I decided to move out. And take you with us, of course.

Guillaume wondered if we ought to wait a while before moving in together, since you had by then given up pretending he didn't exist and had substituted outright rudeness.

"She'll come around," I told him. "She's at a difficult age. But look at it this way: she's always wanted to leave the commune. So actually we're giving her what she wants."

And I still think you *would* have come around, sooner rather than later, if you'd only had the chance. We could have been happy, the three of us. I hope you realize that, lying there on your thin mattress in your empty cell.

You told the judge that you acted out of despair. You couldn't handle it any longer, saw no other way to rid yourself of your "tormentors." And he believed you. He even sympathized with you. Were you pleased when you read the headlines?

After Years of Neglect, Cult Girl (14) Strikes Back
Anandi Acted in Self-Defense, Judge Rules

But, really, what had Leonard, Cecile, Majetska, Ravi, Reginald, and Butter done that they deserved to die? Was I missing something? Could I have been *so* blind?

I don't deny that it must have been confusing for you to grow up in an environment that was so different from the outside world. We had no rules, no set routines. Yes, we sometimes used mind-altering drugs, convinced they would bring us closer to some Universal Truth. And yes, it's true, sometimes I forgot to put you to bed at a reasonable hour, and you'd fall asleep on a pile of cushions in the living room. I never thought you saw any of that as *harmful*, though, because you were so totally *loved*. Your name means "happiness," and that's what you brought to the commune, to all of us. Or don't you remember that?

Facing the facts is hard for me, Anandi. Sometimes I wish something terrible *had* happened to you, so I could understand what you did. But other than a few missed meals, a mother you were ashamed of, and a circle of adults around you who spent a lot of their time high and babbling—nonsensically, I realize now, when I look back at us—about Universal Love, I can't think of anything.

Do you want me to apologize? To say that I ought to have given up on my beliefs and ideals in order to provide you with the "normal" life you craved?

I can't do that.

All I can say is that I *never* meant to cause you the least bit of pain.

Still, you wanted to punish me, and you certainly have been successful. I've relived that night not once but a thousand times—the mind has the unpleasant tendency to turn negative experiences inside out and dissect them down to their smallest details.

What I find most striking is how carefully you thought the whole thing through. It wasn't just some spur-of-the-moment decision—your level of premeditation boggles my mind. How long did you brood before you took action, Anandi? How many times did you run the film of your grievances inside your head? How often did you think your way step by step through your plan?

"You can find everything on the Internet, Your Honor," you told the judge, with just a hint of a laugh.

So you gathered wild cherries and belladonna from someone's garden. I can *see* you, in my mind's eye: your bike leaned carelessly against a tree, you with a brown paper bag full of poison in your hands. What were you *thinking,* Anandi? Did you have any doubts? Did the Internet tell you how *gruesome* a death those berries would cause?

That night, you came into the meditation room. You knew we'd all be there for our evening session, and you knew the windows were too small for any of us to climb through. You'd made smoothies for us, you announced, a combination of forest berries and ginger. When you said the word "ginger," you looked at me meaningfully. I remember feeling hurt, because you *knew* I can't stand the taste of ginger. And since when, by the way, do forest berries and ginger go together? I told myself to look at the positive side of it: for once, you'd done something *nice* for the group. I was just imagining that you were sending me some sort of hidden message. *Not everything's about you, Melissa,* I told myself.

I had no idea.

You gave everyone except me a glass and filled them to the brim. Leonard raised his to his lips before you were done, but you told him—forcefully, I remember—to wait for a toast. And everyone waited obediently until all the glasses were full, surprised but delighted by your unexpected gesture.

"Sorry, Mom," you said, as the rest of them clinked their glasses. You had a strange expression on your face as you spoke those two words.

"It's all right," I said, and I forced a smile.

"I'll make you one without the ginger, okay?"

That sentence, that one sentence. I thought it hinted at reconciliation, and I loved you so much in that moment that I could have exploded with joy. Mothers are like Labradors: you can ignore us for days on end, deprive us of food and water, let us lie in our own shit... and we'll still jump up and frolic the instant you walk through the door.

You left the room. I don't recall whether or not I heard the key turn in the lock, but in my nightmares that one sound drowns out everything else. I turned to Guillaume. His glass was almost empty. We shared a smile. I know that, right then, we both believed everything was going to work out just fine.

A little later, Leonard said, "My throat feels funny."

"Mine, too," said Butter.

After my lunch with Nettie, I decide for the umpteenth time to make an end of it all, but I haven't the strength. It's not until almost eleven, when I'm home and exhausted from weeping, that I think to check my email. (Nettie has offered to screen my messages for me, but I refuse to grant her that pleasure.)

When I've deleted the usual assortment of death threats, I move on to the requests for interviews. I've never yet spoken to the press, and I have no intention of doing so. Nettie says it would be good for me to tell my side of the story, but who am I to rain on the reading public's parade?

And then I see a message from the juvenile detention center where you've spent the last three years. Some woman tells me she's your social worker, and you want to see me! About the future, she says. The sight of that phrase—"the future"—makes my stomach clench.

Given all the letters I've sent you, you probably think I can't wait to enfold you in my arms. And there's a part of me that wants exactly that. Imagine: I still want you in my life. And yet my fingers hover apathetically above my keyboard.

What is it you see happening in "the future," Anandi? You and I going shopping together, like any "normal" mother and daughter? You joining Nettie and me for our Wednesday lunches? The two of us in the kitchen, baking a cake, like we used to?

I still have my orange robe—I've kept it stashed away in a box in my apartment—although it now smells of musty cardboard and mouse droppings instead of the Krishna Leela incense I used to burn. I put it on and examine myself in the mirror. My face is very pale against the orange, and I have dark circles under my eyes.

I find a pair of scissors and cut off my hair. How long it's grown! It's not that I like it long. I simply haven't been able to make myself go out to a salon. What would I say to a beautician? *Please, miss, make me beautiful?*

I cut it as short as I can with the scissors and then plug in the electric clippers. I bought them in the early days, just for this purpose, and I've kept them, too, in the same box with the robe. Their buzzing so close to my ears is almost unbearable, but I persevere.

When I'm done, I look much more like the me I remember.

. . .

In the living room, I sit on a cushion, my legs folded into the lotus position. I concentrate on my breathing. On the ball of fury in my belly, the bitter taste in my mouth, the chill in my groin. I sit and sit and sit, until I feel—somewhere deep inside me—a piece of my true self begin to blossom.

When I go out into the street and am surrounded by faces—angry faces, shocked faces—I focus on my heart, which bravely pulses, never missing a single beat.

In the train, on the tram, on the bus—the journey is long and complicated—there are more faces, and all of them clearly show their owners' opinions of me.

One woman, as she gets off at her stop, snarls, "You don't deserve to live."

I have no answer for that.

There are more surprised and shocked and disapproving faces at the detention center, shooting curious looks my way like arrows. I feel them hit, and every one of them stings.

I am led to a small visiting room, furnished with a bench that's meant to be comfortable and two wooden chairs on either side of a wooden table. There's a succulent in a clay pot in the middle of the table.

I have no idea what to say to you. I'm not sure I'll even be able to look you in the eye. I stare at the calendar on the wall, aware of the cardboard-box smell that clings to my robe.

I hear your footsteps approach. You still have the same walk, Anandi. If I'd been a "normal" mother, I would have taught you to pick up your feet, since shuffling wears out the soles of your shoes faster.

My heart continues to beat. I take a deep breath.

You come into the room. I'd almost forgotten how beautiful you are, with your pale-blue eyes and blond hair. You've grown a bit, not much but enough to notice.

You stand there, waiting. Perhaps you expect me to try to hug you, but you ought to know that's not going to happen.

You sit on one of the wooden chairs. Your social worker shakes my hand and pronounces a name I immediately forget.

You and I look at each other.

"So," the social worker says, her voice cheerful, "Anandi has told me that she'd like to work on re-establishing contact with you. She understands that it will take time, but we're glad you've agreed to take this first step."

You and I look at each other.

What now, Anandi? What comes next for us?

13

EIGHT DAYS A WEEK
BY NICOLET STEEMERS

The square was almost deserted. Paul and Birgit walked side by side in silence, heading for the bus stop. In the puddles at their feet, the light from the streetlamps danced with the reflected neon glow of the shop windows.

Birgit took Paul's hand. "I'm sorry," she said. "I had no idea Mark would leave the conference early. He wasn't supposed to be home till tomorrow." They passed the skate park and the graffiti wall. The rain had laid a veil of tiny pearls over her hair and face.

"You could call him," said Paul. "Tell him you're staying with a girlfriend. The two of you decided to spend the weekend walking in the Veluwe."

She shook her head. "I'm not going to lie to him." When he didn't react, she said, "You don't know him."

"I don't want to know him," Paul said, smiling. "We'll still see each other Tuesday, right?"

"Of course we'll see each other Tuesday. At the faculty meeting, ten o'clock."

He squeezed her hand. "I mean later. We're both done after sixth period."

"Hey, jackass." A broad-shouldered shadow—hard to tell if it was a man or a boy—appeared from behind the skate park's concrete halfpipe, three others in dark clothing in his wake.

Paul automatically stepped in front of Birgit. "You guys have a problem?"

"Do *we* have a problem?" He was a teenager, Paul saw now, as the boy jabbed a bony index finger at the wall. "You see that, man? You see that name?"

"I see it." Paul considered the odds. There were four of them, all in black leather jackets and low-rider jeans, baseball caps turned backwards, tough-guy style, over long greasy hair, their ears and eyebrows pierced, chains draped around their necks—but no weapons, at least none visible. Maybe their best bet was just to take off. With a little luck, they could outrun them.

"Say it out loud, loser," the kid demanded.

Loser? Paul straightened his back and folded his arms across his chest. "My name's Paul," he said. He read out the name painted on the wall: "Deadly J. Now you want to let us pass?"

A heavy hand dropped onto his shoulder. There was a grin on the face beneath the ball cap. "It's Deadly G."

"That's what I said."

"You said it *wrong,* man. It's English. But I'm not gonna make a big deal about it."

"Good," said Paul. "Especially since the right way to say it in English is Jay, not Gee."

"Oh, yeah?" Deadly J's face was so close Paul could see his pupils were dilated, so wide they almost swallowed his irises.

One of the other gangbangers took a step forward. "He oughta know, Deadly," he said, his weak face pinched in a hard expression. "He may be a schmuck, but he's a teacher. Teaches fuckin' English."

Paul jerked around to look at the kid. "Do I know you?" he asked.

"I know *you*, schmuck. That's enough."

A memory flickered in the back of Paul's head, but it blinked out again when Deadly J punched him in the face. He staggered and fell, banging his shoulder on the concrete halfpipe. Birgit screamed. The tough guy bent over him, a nasty smile twisting his lips. Paul curled up as if he was terrified, but when the Neanderthal came close enough, he hauled out and planted a fist hard on the kid's nose. The other three threw themselves at him, cursing wildly, and the fight would have ended very differently if a car hadn't pulled out of the parking garage at that moment, its headlights illuminating the scene. The driver slammed on the gas and, tires squealing on the wet pavement, raced toward them. As Deadly J and his buddies scattered, the boy who'd recognized Paul as a teacher yelled "I know where you live, loser!" over his shoulder.

The driver's window opened. A middle-aged woman, her only companion a fluffy orange weepul hanging from her rearview mirror, leaned out and said, "What's going on here?"

Paul came awake with a start. In his dream, he was being sucked irresistibly closer to a thundering waterfall. Eyes wide, he sat up in bed, and the landscape morphed from wild mountains to the dim outline of his night table. He waited for the roar of the falls to fade away into the land of nightmares, but it didn't happen. Smoke billowed into his bedroom through the crack between the door and the hardwood floor. He kicked off his blankets, jumped out of bed, and threw open the door. The flames reached to his shoulders, licked hungrily at his face. He slammed the door and raced around the room, snatching up his clothing, his shoes, whatever he could grab. The smoke blinded him, and he lost his grip on most of it. When he finally jumped out the window, all he had was his cell phone and a pair of jeans, his wallet and keys in the pockets. The Christmas tree he hadn't gotten around to dragging out to the curb broke his fall, and he wound up with nothing worse than a fractured arm and a twisted ankle to add to the bruises he'd collected during the fight earlier that evening.

"I was walking a friend to the bus," Paul said. "And then these four guys came out of nowhere." He'd already told the story twice, and now the two detectives—a man and a woman—were guiding him through it yet again.

"You said one of them seemed to know you. Do you have any idea who he was?"

"No," Paul sighed, but the moment he said it the memory returned. A weak face, a hard expression. Thinner—still a child, really—but it was definitely him, and suddenly he remembered the boy's name. "Jeffrey Weeme," he said.

The male detective made a note. "Excellent. What can you tell us about him?"

"Nothing. He was in my class three or four years ago."

"We'll check him out," the officer said, and, to his colleague, "You want to pass this on to Jos?"

The woman nodded, took a tablet from her shoulder bag and began typing.

"You live alone?" the man asked.

"Yes."

"And the friend you were walking to the bus—?"

"—lives across town."

"You had—you have a big house. Are you divorced?"

"Widower. My wife died three years ago." He shivered and glanced at the clock on the interrogation-room wall. It was a quarter past three in the morning. Despite the heavy sweater he'd borrowed from his neighbor across the street, he was cold.

The woman detective read an incoming text on her phone. "Good news," she said. "The fire's out. It'll take five or six hours for it to cool down, and then we can go in and see what we can find."

"Is there anything left?" asked Paul, preparing himself for the worst.

"I don't know. We'll have to wait till we can get inside." She brushed a strand of hair behind her ear. "You've been through a lot," she said, her voice friendly. "You ought to try to get some sleep. Later today, we'll want to talk with your friend, so we'll need to have her phone number. That can wait a while, though."

Paul's face reddened. His agreement with Birgit was that he would never call her, never email her or text her. Outside of school, she was always the one who made the first move. Was this going to mean the end of their affair?

"Of course," he said.

The hotel looked out onto a garden, its centerpiece a tall sculpture that seemed to be made of a pile of rusted bicycles. He'd been there now for two days, and though concerned friends and family members had practically begged him to stay with them, he couldn't bring himself to leave his room. Several times he'd picked up his cell with the intention of calling Birgit, but each time he'd set the phone down, her number undialed. He'd also managed to resist the urge to go look at the ruins of his house. He was lying on the bed, paging listlessly through a magazine, seeing nothing, when there was a knock at the door.

"Come in," he said, sitting up.

The two detectives filed into the room. "Arson," the male half of the team said, before they'd even seated themselves. "Our colleagues went in with accelerant-detection dogs, and they found the flashpoint almost immediately: the doormat. Looks like the perpetrator poured gasoline through your mail slot and then tossed in a lit match. One of the dogs found a jerry-can lid in your yard. There were a few drops of gas still in the lid, and our forensics lab is comparing that sample with the gas that was found inside your house."

Paul's eyebrows arched.

"I understand your surprise," the detective went on. "Most people don't know that traces of an accelerant can be identified at the scene of a fire, but there's always something we can find, even if it's just a fraction of a microliter. And these days the arson dogs make it a lot easier. Used to be we had to go through the house with a sniffer, a special machine, and it could take days, a week, before we came up with anything useful. But the dogs can smell an accelerant practically before they step over the threshold."

"Even so," said Paul, "say you can establish that the gasoline used to set the fire came from the jerry can. How does that help? Do you know where the jerry can came from?"

"Not the jerry can, no. But no two gas pumps deliver the exact same mixture. And whenever a gasoline truck fills a station's underground tanks, the new mixture that comes out of the pump will be different than what was in there before. If we can match the drops we found in the jerry-can lid and the ruins of your house to a particular station, that'll put us a step closer to identifying the person who bought the gas."

"Meanwhile," the woman said, "we found Jeffrey Weeme and questioned him. He claims he has an alibi for the night of the fire. We're checking his story now. And we still need to talk with this

Deadly J and the other two kids who attacked you. So far, Weeme refuses to tell us their names. But don't worry, it's just a question of—"

Her cell phone rang. She answered it and listened attentively. A broad smile blossomed on her face. "We've got a match," she said, after she broke the connection. "The gas in the jerry-can lid matches the accelerant that was used to torch your house. And we've pinpointed the Q8 station in the Bekenweg as the source. Luckily for us, it turns out they put in surveillance cameras about six months ago. If you'll give your friend a call, the four of us can take a look at the tapes. If we can spot one of the creeps who assaulted you filling a jerry can with gas, we've got him."

Birgit was just getting into a groove on the indoor rowing machine in the basement when her cell rang. It was sitting on the floor beside the machine, and she glanced at the screen without breaking her rhythm and frowned. Paul. Mark was upstairs, painting the garage, so she picked up. "Hey, we agreed you—"

"I know," he told her, "but I need you to do something for me."

She listened in utter shock as he explained about the fire and the investigation.

"Why didn't you call me right away?" she demanded, when he had finished.

"Well, our agreement...."

"Jesus, Paul, this was an emergency. Those bastards. Did you lose everything?"

"Probably. I haven't gone back to look." He was silent for a moment, and then he said, "Can you meet me at the Q8 station in the Bekenweg, right away?"

She changed out of her workout clothes and, two minutes later, was in the garage. Her husband was balanced precariously on a stepladder, his back to her, painting one of the roof beams. His boom box was blaring: "Ooh, I need your love, babe, guess you know it's true."

"Mark!" she called, but she couldn't compete with the Fab Four.

"Hope you need my love, babe, just like I need you," John Lennon sang, and Birgit tugged on Mark's sleeve to get his attention. He dialed down the volume and grinned apologetically.

"Too loud?" he said.

"No, it's fine. I have to go out for a bit. I completely forgot to pick up snacks for the class party tomorrow. I won't be long."

"No hurry," he said. "This'll take another hour, at least." He came down two steps and kissed her. She returned the kiss, careful to avoid the smear of paint on the dimple on his right cheek.

Then she got in the car. As she backed out of the garage, Mark cranked the volume back up, and she drove off to the accompaniment of the Beatles wailing, "Ain't got nothing but love, babe, eight days a week!"

"Three people filled jerry cans with gas on the evening of the fire," the detective said. "I want you to look closely at the tapes. The images aren't always as clear as they could be, so it might be an item of clothing or the way one of them moves or some other detail you recognize, rather than the face. But there are definitely two of them who fit the description you gave us." He nodded to his partner. "Go ahead."

Birgit and Paul stared intently at the monitor. The first figure they saw was an old man. Paul shook his head, and the detective fast-forwarded the tape until a younger man with dark curly hair came into the frame. "Okay, look closely at this one. Could he be one of the kids who attacked you? He's not wearing a ball cap here, but maybe there's some other feature you might—"

"No," said Paul. "It's not him."

Birgit was also shaking her head. That meant that two of the three suspects were eliminated. So it had to be the third one, who'd walked up to the pump with a jerry can about an hour after Paul had finally seen Birgit onto her bus. Under the table, she laid a hand on his leg and felt the muscles in his thigh tighten.

The third man entered the frame, and Birgit's breath caught in her throat.

He was wearing a hooded jacket she didn't recognize, the hood up and concealing most of his face. There was a loud buzzing in her ears, and she forced herself to stare at the screen without blinking.

Paul's voice came from far off. "No," he said, and he slumped back in his chair, disappointed. "Not him."

"Take a good look," the detective insisted. "It's hard to see, with the hood up like that. Try to imagine him in a leather jacket."

Paul shook his head. "No, I'm sure. He's too old. He must be at least thirty."

The detective turned toward Birgit. "What about you, Mrs. de Jong? Are you sure this isn't one of the guys who jumped you?"

She swallowed, staring at the image frozen on the screen. The dimple on his right cheek was absolutely unmistakable.

Digging her nails into the palm of her hand, she said, "Positive. I've never seen him before in my life."

14

PROMISES TO KEEP

BY GERT-JAN VAN DEN BEMD

"What can I do for you, young lady?"

The voice that comes from the little speaker above the four doorbells anonymously labeled 4A, 4B, 4C, and 4D is soft, overly formal. Apparently its owner can see me, though I don't spot a camera in the small foyer between the unlocked street door and the locked inner door, a checkerboard of alternating clear and frosted panes of glass.

"I'm here about the—"

"Ah, Mrs. van Tilt, I'll be right down."

A moment later, a silhouette appears behind the glass, and the door swings open. The man reminds me of the farmer in that famous American painting, not just because of his white shirt and black suit jacket but also thanks to his high domed forehead and wire-rimmed spectacles and close-cropped gray hair.

"The buzzer that unlocks the door is broken," he explains.

He leads me up a flight of granite steps. His apartment door stands open. His slippers whisper across the hallway's laminate floor, my sneakers squeak with every step. He shows me into a compact living room. The ceiling, the wooden paneling, the floor, the furniture, everything is in shades of brown. One lonely photograph hangs on the wall: a man and a woman in seventies hairstyles standing before a white wooden house. More "American Gothic." No, that's not true. These two are better looking than the farm couple.

"Sit down, please, and I'll go and get it."

He nods at a caramel-colored love seat. The cracked leather pillows at each end might have been left out in the sun for years. There are no plants in the room. A glass vase on an end table is lined with lime rings suggestive of long-ago bouquets.

The man comes back with a cardboard shoebox. I can read the label: black pumps, size thirty-six. He sits opposite me in an armchair exactly the right size to hold him, as if it has been molded to the precise measurements of his body.

He deposits the box on a low coffee table and lifts the lid. "Here it is," he says solemnly, "the 1139."

We look down at a model locomotive, lovingly built of gray and yellow plastic and lying like a dead wagtail on a bed of shredded crinkle-cut packing paper.

The man waits patiently for my reaction, but for a moment I'm at a loss for words.

"What did we say?" he finally asks. "Fifty euros?"

I clear my throat. "Yes," I say, "but—"

"But?"

"But what about the other item?"

"The other item?" He glances at the locomotive. "There's just the 1139. Everything else is gone." His smile turns melancholic, and I realize that the train car is perhaps the last remaining piece of what has been for him a beloved hobby.

"I mean the gun."

"Excuse me?"

"The gun. The Luger."

The smile vanishes from his face. "I don't know what you're talking about."

"Your other ad. It was only online for a moment, but I happened to see it. Someone must have reported it to the webmaster, and they deleted it. I suppose selling firearms over the internet isn't permitted."

The man looks at me, and I can't tell if his confusion is real or feigned. "I don't have a gun," he says. "I've never had a gun."

I force an understanding smile. "You don't have to worry, I'm not a police officer. I want to buy the Luger. The ad said one hundred euros."

He gets to his feet. Without a word, he fits the lid back onto the shoebox and leaves the room. I can hear him rummaging around in what I assume must be a spare room used for storage. An ironing board, a mountain of laundry, a toolbox, cartons of accumulated knickknacks, piles of yellowing newspapers and magazines. Somewhere amidst all of that is another cardboard box, or perhaps he has it wrapped in a square of canvas. I can almost smell it, oil and metal. *Let's go,* I think. *You want to be rid of it.*

The man returns. His hands are empty.

"A hundred and fifty for the gun," I say, but he walks past me in silence and opens the door to the entry hall.

"Good evening, Mrs. van Tilt," he says, turning my name into an insult.

He doesn't accompany me down the hall to the apartment door. The lock is tricky, and he brushes past me with a sigh. I smell soap and something woodsy. I step back to give him room, but now I'm further inside the apartment than he is, which stirs a feeling of discomfort.

Behind me, someone coughs.

A woman—dyed blond hair, eyeglasses with pink lenses—is

looking at me. In her hands is a small carton, smaller than the shoebox.

"Come with me," she says.

The man swallows an oath and relocks the apartment door.

The woman and I sit side by side on the love seat. The man remains standing. The little box is on the coffee table, its lid removed. Inside is a Pistole Parabellum P08, commonly referred to by the last name of its designer, Georg Luger.

"He promised me." She nods at the photograph on the wall. "That was taken on the day of our engagement, forty-three years ago. We promised each other that, if one of us ever wanted to die, the other would arrange it. We bought that thing"—she waves a hand at the gun—"and agreed that it was what we would use. Pills are so uncertain. And now I'm ready, but he turns out to be a coward."

The man closes his eyes.

"Six years ago," his wife says, "I was diagnosed with cancer. They had to remove my left breast. They took the right one, too, though it was perfectly healthy. 'Just to be safe,' the doctor said. *Safe.*"

She rests her small right hand for a moment on the curve of her knitted sweater. "He offered to 'recreate my femininity,' was how he put it, and gave me a choice between silicone or saline implants. I was so thin he couldn't use my own tissue for the reconstruction. Thin as a rail, even then." She laughs ruefully. "I chose silicone, because I thought it looked more natural. Within a year, one of them began to leak. They had to remove it, but it was too late: the poison had already spread through my body. It infiltrated my nervous system. Sometimes the pain is absolutely unbearable."

"Would you like something to drink?" the man says, but the offer comes across as a diversionary tactic, an attempt to distract his wife from her story. "Coffee? Tea?"

"I've known for a week now that it's time." She taps an index finger against the side of her head. "It's here, now, too. I can't go on any longer, it's more than I can live with. Can you understand that?"

I nod.

"But he won't do it."

"I love her too much," the man says hoarsely.

"Nonsense! You loved me more when you made your promise than you love me now. When we were in bed, you kissed my feet, you touched me in places you won't even *look* at now. I repulse you."

"That's not *true*, Kathy. I love you as much as I ever did. It's just... I couldn't go on without you."

"If you don't do what you promised, Yves, that won't keep me with you. It'll only make the loss harder and sadder."

She reaches into the box and grabs the pistol by its barrel. "Here! Do it!"

I jump up and stand between the man and the gun, my thigh brushing for a moment against the black metal.

"Was it you who advertised the gun for sale?" I ask the woman.

She nods hopelessly, her anger spent, and lays the pistol on her lap.

"I hoped someone without such high moral standards might see it and come." A smile flickers across her face. "Perhaps a professional. *I* would have paid *him*—I have some money saved." She raised her chin to indicate her husband. "He saw the ad and deleted it. But not before *you* saw it, and connected it with the other one he'd placed, the one for his bloody trains."

"I'm not the professional you hoped for."

"You can't always get what you want," she says wryly.

For a full minute, the three of us stare wordlessly at the gun.

How soundproof is this room, I wonder. All I can hear is the woman's slow breathing, which synchronizes with her index finger as it strokes the Luger's dull barrel.

"We'll do it together, you and me," I tell her husband, and then add to Kathy, "if that's all right with you."

She nods. "Oh, yes," she says, and turns to him. "It's what I want, Yves. Please."

He looks at me, ashamed of his weakness, grateful for my courage.

"I'll get everything ready," he says.

Kathy lies on top of the comforter that decorates their double bed. She's freshened her makeup, brushed her hair, put on a hint of perfume, changed into a black dress, nylons, and pumps, as if she's off to a party. Her husband has put on a tie and patent leather shoes. I feel like a slob in my T-shirt and jeans.

Yves sits on his side of the bed. The surface of the nightstand beside him is bare, except for a simple lamp. The matching night-stand on her side, where I'm sitting, is littered with blister packs and plastic bottles of medications and painkillers.

He hands her a square pillow embroidered with the image of a sad-eyed faun.

"Should I give you two some privacy?" I ask—but I know that, if I leave the bedroom, I'll never find the nerve to return.

"No, stay," she says. "You're part of the family now."

The man nods his agreement. He leans down and kisses her on the lips, then on the forehead. He gently moves her hands, so the pillow is against the side of her head.

"Not there," she says, and lays the pillow on her chest.

I pick up the Luger. Despite its slim shape, it's heavy in my hand, much heavier than I would have expected, as if all the mass in the room has drained into it, and the bed, the nightstands, the three of us have become weightless.

I touch the end of the barrel to the pillow, right between the faun's sad eyes. Yves's hand is rough and hot. Mine encircles the grip, but I leave room for his finger on the trigger, and then Kathy's hands wrap around ours, her palms and fingers in the shape of a heart. Now only the barrel remains visible, a little black finger pointing at the woman lying on the bed.

She looks at me—in politeness or gratitude, I don't know which —but I will her to turn away, back to her husband, where her gaze belongs. He kisses her again, and for a moment lays his head against her bottle-blond hair.

She whispers something in his ear and closes her eyes.

The pillow muffles the report, and a lone feather floats into the air.

We descend the granite steps together and reach for the lobby door at the same time. Our fingers touch. His flesh is cold now, even colder than mine.

"You'll be okay?" I ask.

"Yes," he says. "I'll tell the police I heard a shot and went in and found her dead."

"They'll suspect you. They always suspect the spouse."

"I'll be fine," he assures me. "Whatever happens."

He makes a half-hearted attempt to hug me and opens the door. Despite the warmth of the evening, a chill runs down my spine.

"You don't have to answer this," he says, nodding at the cardboard shoebox in my hands. "You told me you wanted the locomotive for your husband. Did you want the gun for him, too?"

"No," I say, "the gun was for me. I thought my life had lost its meaning. I was wrong."

I step out into the moonlight, and, smiling, he swings the door shut behind me.

15

BENEATH THE SURFACE
BY MARJOLEIN VAN DER GAAG

The air, heavy and humid, wraps around Dorien like a clammy blanket. It's almost unbearable, worse than a sauna. She climbs into the bleachers in bare feet and pulls off her sweater. Even in just a T-shirt, she's perspiring, moisture pooling at the small of her back. Judging only by the temperature, you'd think you were in some subtropical swimming hole, but that's the only similarity. This indoor pool, where her daughter Isabel takes a lesson every Friday afternoon, is bare and basic. No diving board, no slide, none of that. Just a pool, twenty-five meters long, barely big enough for the children to meet the requirements for their official swimming certificate.

Dorien brushes a strand of curly brown hair from her forehead and drops onto a wooden plank, sandwiched between other parents who are just as overheated as she is. A stout, ruddy-faced mother with droplets of sweat pearling her upper lip offers an encouraging smile. How does the old saying go? *Shared pain is less pain.*

She looks jealously at the kids sitting on the edge of the pool.

Her Isabel chatters with another girl, their feet kicking happily in the clear water. When the lifeguard blows his whistle to indicate that break time is over, Isabel turns in her blue swimsuit and waves. Dorien smiles and gives her a thumbs up.

This is Parents Day, a chance for moms and dads to observe their children's progress. Dorien is pleased simply to see her daughter come to class without protest. That right there represents quite a *bit* of progress, she thinks.

In the water, the kids practice the backstroke—with mixed success. Isabel bumps against one of the boys in her group and giggles. Dorien smiles absently, her thoughts drifting back to that fraught first lesson, a year ago.

The image of Isabel's panic-stricken face is burned into her memory. Weeping, the girl stood beside the pool, glued to Dorien's side as if she would never let go, hysterically screaming Christian's name again and again.

Dorien picked her up and hushed her and took her home. That was the first time she and Remco really understood the terrible impact the last day of their Italian vacation must have had on the girl. Isabel had never spoken about it, and Dorien and Remco hoped she'd been too young to understand what had happened. But apparently not.

Today, though, a year later, Isabel seems comfortable in the water. When the lesson ends, she runs to Dorien, beaming. The lifeguard strolling behind her throws the parents in the bleachers a cheerful salute.

"I made it to the next level!" sings Isabel proudly.

Dorien holds out her arms, hoists her daughter into the air, and spins in a victory pirouette. Isabel's cool wet body and the drops of water that sprinkle from her blond ponytail feel lovely against Dorien's hot skin. "I knew you would!" she says. "You were wonderful! I'm so proud of you! This calls for ice cream, don't you think?"

She is delighted to see that swim lessons have evolved for Isabel into playtime, as they are for most children. There are moments when Dorien thinks she sees something dark in the depths of Isabel's eyes and wonders what's going on inside that little head, but she doesn't ask any questions. Let sleeping dogs lie. And of course Remco doesn't want to hear a word about any of it. According to him, life goes on, and it benefits no one to dwell on the past.

There are surely psychologists who would disagree, but just the *word* "psychologist" sets Remco off. All that crap about *feelings*, that's not for him. These days, he says, it seems like *everyone* needs some level of counseling. In his opinion, people should just pull on their grownup pants and *deal* with the slings and arrows of outrageous fortune. Maybe he's right. Things do seem to be going much better with Isabel, and—so long as that remains the case—Dorien is willing to keep her mouth shut, if that's what it takes to keep the home fires burning peacefully.

"Get your shoes and jacket on," she says, "and we'll go pick up Grandma and Jelte. I bet they'd like some ice cream, too."

Since she retired from her career as an EMT, Dorien's mother looks after two-year-old Jelte on Friday afternoons. That way, Dorien can work a half-day and take Isabel to her swim lesson in the afternoon.

Dorien has already slipped into her sneakers. She stuffs Isabel's socks, wet from the locker-room floor, into her jacket pocket. Her mother probably has a dry pair the girl can wear.

Outside, it's sunny for a change. The sports center's grubby parking lot seems noticeably friendlier than it was when they arrived. A gull scurries about on the asphalt near her car, in search of something to eat. Although it's officially spring, you wouldn't know it—thanks, rain showers!—but yesterday's storm has fortunately moved on.

With Isabel buckled into the passenger seat of her silver-gray VW Passat, Dorien turns the key in the ignition, and Bruno Mars' up-tempo voice fills the car. "When I see your face," she sings along, "there's not a thing that I would change." She grins at her daughter, who croons her own incomprehensible version of the song, and strokes her hair fondly. "'Cause you're amazing, just the way you are."

It's not far from the sports center to the house on the Velperweg where Dorien grew up, the house where her mother still lives. The single-family home, built sometime in the thirties, is much too big for a woman alone. Ever since the unexpected death of their father, Dorien and her sister Katinka have tried repeatedly to convince their mother to downsize, but Isabel's stubborn grandmother has vetoed each attempt.

"If you think you're going to force me into one of those little apartments for *old* people," she snapped, two years ago, when Dorien tried yet again to broach the subject, "you might as well start planning my funeral."

Dorien's cell phone rings as she turns into the driveway and parks behind her mother's dark-blue Skoda. It's Anton, who owns the realty office where Dorien has worked for the past five years. She hesitates to pick up, but Anton rarely calls on her afternoon off. There must be a good reason for him to bother her now.

Five minutes later, she regrets having taken the call. She takes her key from the ignition and leans back against the headrest. She never works on Saturdays, but Anton has roped her into doing a showing tomorrow. Debby's in quarantine because her son has tested positive for COVID, Bart's on vacation, Anton himself has a funeral to attend—under the circumstances, she couldn't bring herself to say no. Especially when she heard it was that old wreck of a house on the Vosdijk. The place dates back to 1880 and is on a nice lot, but it's been empty for three years. Hardly anyone has even viewed it—understandable, given the property's gruesome history.

"I don't think this couple knows what happened there," Anton told her. "Let's keep it that way, shall we?"

"Does it have to be tomorrow? Can't they come another day?"

"They're driving down from Groningen, and tomorrow's the only time they can make it. And by the way, the woman asked for you by name. Apparently you know them? The Jansens?"

Sitting behind the wheel of her car, Dorien rolled her eyes. The Jansens. The name meant nothing to her.

"Well, you'll meet them tomorrow," Anton said. "Thanks for doing this."

Dorien notes the appointment in her agenda: ten thirty, Vosdijk. This means she's going to have to ask her mother to babysit again, since Remco's playing in a tennis tournament. She really ought to pick up some flowers as a thank you.

As Dorien replaces her phone in her brown leather shoulder bag, Isabel—who got out of the car at the beginning of the conversation with Anton—returns. She pulls the passenger door open, an indignant expression on her little face.

"Grandma's not here."

Dorien frowns and unbuckles her seat belt. "She must be, Goofy. Maybe she's in the attic."

Isabel shakes her head with determination. She takes Dorien's hand and pulls her around to their usual entrance, the back door. Dorien has a key to the front door, but during the day, when her mother is home, the back is never locked. Dorien finds this practice unsafe, but it's yet another taboo subject.

They walk through the kitchen—where all the ingredients for a lasagna have been laid out on the countertop—to the living room. Indeed, both rooms are unoccupied. On the coffee table sits a teapot, a half-empty teacup, and the same Verkade cookie tin Dorien remembers from her childhood. Jelte's sippy cup lies on its side on the hardwood floor.

Dorien goes out to the foyer and calls "Mom?" up the stairs. Jelte still wears a diaper, and perhaps her mother is changing him.

There is no response to her shout.

"I *told* you," Isabel says, the little smarty-pants. "And I already *looked* upstairs." She marches back up the steps, and Dorien tries again: "Mom?"

Again, no answer. How strange! She follows her daughter to the second floor and checks the spare bedroom at the front of the house. No one there—no one in any of the upstairs rooms.

"Maybe they're playing hide and seek," Isabel suggests. "I'll look in the basement."

Dorien shakes her head thoughtfully and watches Isabel jump downstairs, step by step. She goes in the opposite direction, up to the attic. There is no one there.

Back on the ground floor, she looks in the laundry room. There's a basket of wet clothing on top of the washing machine. This is very weird. Her mother would *never* leave the house without hanging the wash on the line in the back yard or putting it in the dryer.

When she returns to the living room, she finds Isabel in the "playground," a corner her mother has arranged especially for her granddaughter's visits, holding an animated conversation with Sammi, her favorite Barbie.

"Where's Grandma?" she asks. "She's not in the basement."

Dorien shrugs. She has no *idea* where her mother and Jelte could possibly be.

Her eyes return to the coffee table and the half-empty teacup. Her mother must have left the house in a hurry. But where to? And *why?* Did something happen to Jelte? Did he hurt himself, and her mother had to take him to the doctor? But surely she would have *called.* Anyway, her car is in the driveway, and Jelte's stroller is in the front hall, and the back door was unlocked.

Dorien fishes her cell from her bag and speed-dials her mother's number. There's a buzzing sound in the kitchen, and she goes there and sees the phone vibrating in the middle of the breakfast table.

She drops onto a kitchen chair and stares out into the big backyard, where she and Katinka spent many happy hours as children, where Isabel and Jelte play when the weather permits. Her mother always sees that the yard is well taken care of.

Though she knows there's no reason to do so, she steps out the kitchen door. "Mom?" she calls.

But of course there's no one there. Why would there be? Did she really expect to find her mother—as Isabel suggested—playing hide and seek?

In the living room, Isabel is changing her Barbie's clothes. Dorien isn't sure what to do. Wait for her mother and Jelte to reappear? There's probably a simple explanation for their absence. But the situation feels *wrong.* Her mother *knows* they always come back from Isabel's lesson around this time, and she's always here, waiting for them.

Calm down, she chides herself. *No reason to panic. They'll be home any minute.*

She returns to the kitchen and pages automatically through a magazine, paying no attention to the pictures or text. Restless, she closes the magazine and paces back and forth across the tiled floor.

The cuckoo clock hanging beside the refrigerator tells her that she and Isabel have been waiting for half an hour.

Should she call Remco? It couldn't hurt. Maybe he'll have a less frazzled take on the situation. He always says she jumps to the worst possible conclusions.

But his phone goes to voicemail, and she curses beneath her breath and breaks the connection. He's always in one damn meeting or another!

Well, she has to do *something*—the waiting is driving her up the wall.

She looks through the living-room window at the neighbor's house next door. Perhaps her mother and son are *there*. That seems perfectly reasonable. They *have* to be nearby, since the car and Jelte's stroller are here.

She spots Jelte's light-blue jacket lying in the stroller and frowns. It's not warm enough for the child to be out without his jacket—and her mother constantly harps on the importance of making sure that children are properly dressed for the weather. She checks the coatrack in the front hall and sees that her mother's gray parka is also still in the house. So they *can't* have gone any further than the neighbors'.

The Arends family has lived for thirty years or more next door to Dorien's mother, in a stately home with tall stained-glass windows, and Joanna Arends is certainly entitled to think of herself as a friend. The two ladies drink coffee together at least once a week.

Her hand tightly holding onto Isabel—who in turn clasps Sammi under her free arm—Dorien marches up the gravel path to the Arends' front door. But this house, too, is at least for now unoccupied. Though she knows it's pointless, she rings the bell a second time, but there is no response.

Tears well up in Dorien's eyes, and there's a lump in her throat. *What on Earth is going on?* Perhaps it's foolish to feel such panic—but she is by now absolutely *positive* that something must be wrong.

"They're not home, either," Isabel says cheerfully. "Can we go for ice cream just the two of us?"

Dorien puts on a brave smile. Her daughter clearly has no clue how worried she is. "That's a great idea—but first let's see if the neighbors on the other side of Grandma's house are home."

They aren't.

"Come on, Mommy, let's *go!*"

Isabel's warm hand slips into hers. Head bowed, Dorien walks back to her mother's house.

"Hey, look! It's Nijntje!"

Isabel pulls free and races across the yard to the bushes. And now Dorien sees it, too, Jelte's stuffed rabbit, which he carries with him everywhere he goes.

"And you have no idea where your mother might have taken your son?"

Dorien understands that the blond policewoman sitting across the kitchen table from her—who arrived with an older male partner five minutes ago in response to her call—is just doing her job, but still the rhetorical question annoys her. If she *knew* where they might *be,* the two officers wouldn't be here, and she wouldn't feel so desperate.

Remco gives her shoulder a gentle squeeze. By the time she finally got through to him, she was out of her mind with worry. She caught him partway home, and he was stunned by the story she told him.

"Try not to worry," he said. "They must be *somewhere* in the neighborhood. Your mother's probably just lost track of time."

"What about Nijntje?" she challenged him. "You know Jelte goes ballistic if he loses sight of his bunny for half a second."

"Yeah, that's disturbing. Look, I'll be there in an hour. If they turn up, call me, and I'll go straight home, instead."

She ended the call with a sinking sensation in her chest. Remco obviously didn't see how serious this was. She found her mother's address book and picked up the landline.

Her first call was to Aunt Annie, who hadn't spoken with her younger sister in several days. Annie was in the middle of preparing dinner, and she soon excused herself and broke the connection.

Margot, her mother's closest friend, was equally unhelpful.

"Mom, I'm *hungry*." Isabel was on the verge of a meltdown. "When are we going *home*?"

Her daughter's mournful expression opened the floodgates of Dorien's own tears. She pulled Isabel onto her lap and kissed her hair. "Sweetheart, this is hard for me, too. But we can't just leave. We have to find Grandma and Jelte."

She searched the kitchen cabinets for something to eat. The lasagna her mother had apparently intended to make would require more work than she felt able to handle. Instead, she opened a can of tomato soup and emptied it into a saucepan. That and some bread would have to do.

It wasn't long afterwards that Remco arrived, frowning. Dorien shook her head, and the bewilderment on his face gave way to concern.

"This is crazy," he said. "They can't just have disappeared." When he returned to the kitchen after making his own tour of the house, he said, "We'd better call the police."

For just a moment, Dorien stared at him in irritation. "I said that an hour ago, but you didn't take me seriously."

Remco closed his eyes. She was right: his mind had been so busy with work that he *hadn't* taken her seriously.

This wasn't the time for an argument, but Dorien wondered if by now there was any *point* to calling the police. How long had her mother and Jelte been gone? If it was only the child who was missing, alarm bells would ring and there'd be an immediate Amber Alert. But Jelte was with his grandmother, a responsible adult, not some doddering old fool.

Remco, however, was not to be denied. He took a deep breath and drummed his fingers on the table. "Come on, Dorien, we both know something's seriously wrong." His voice trembled with emotion. "Dammit, I'm worried about our son. Who knows what might have happened. Maybe your mother fainted somewhere, and Jelte's roaming the streets on his own. We need to notify the authorities."

Dorien nodded. Of course he was right. Why, she wondered, hadn't she already called the local hospitals? What if there'd been an accident? She looked up the number of the Rijnstate Medical Center and, heart pounding, asked for the emergency room. She was transferred several times and finally learned that neither her mother nor her son had been admitted.

The blond policewoman eyes her seriously. Dorien thinks she must be *very* young, but she knows from experience that there's no direct relationship between age and competence. When the two officers arrived, she'd automatically assumed the older male would be in charge, but in fact the roles seem to be reversed.

"I know how hard this must be for you," the woman says, "and I understand you're impatient, but we have to keep calm and consider all possibilities."

Dorien nods. She's glad the police are here, though she can't even *guess* what they must be thinking.

"Have you looked to see if anything's missing? Something your mother would have taken with her, even though she left her phone behind? A handbag, maybe, or a wallet?"

Dorien, despondent, shakes her head. Her mother's handbag is hanging on the coat rack with her jacket.

The situation simply doesn't make any *sense*. Her mother and Jelte seem to have gone up in smoke. There's nothing to suggest they ever left the house—but they are undeniably gone.

The officer scribbles something in her notebook and looks at Dorien and Remco sympathetically. "Can you tell us more about your mother? Has she been confused recently? Depressed?"

Again Dorien shakes her head, this time with assurance. "Absolutely not. She's a strong, independent woman. Nothing throws her off her stride."

"And your father?"

"He—he passed away."

For a moment, the policewoman seems embarrassed, but Dorien smiles away the *faux pas*. "It was eight years ago. Sudden— he collapsed in the middle of a tennis match. My mother was left on her own, but she handled it really well."

The officer makes a note. "A new relationship since then?"

Of course this question was to be expected. How should she respond? She glances at Remco. The fact is, she'd rather avoid the subject. But the look her husband gives her in return makes it clear that he feels otherwise.

"Well, possibly." She can hear the uncertainty in her voice.

And now the older policeman steps in. "Was that something she didn't talk about?"

Dorien sighs. "My mother and I talk about everything—*except* that. She's never really taken my sister and me into her confidence about—her private life."

The questioning expressions on the faces of both officers encourage her to go on.

"She *did* have a relationship with a man we disapproved of, years ago. We told her so, and it turned into a—an uncomfortable situation. You'd be better off asking Margot, Mom's best friend."

Meanwhile, Dorien's thoughts drift back to Jacques, her *father's* best friend. Or at least that's what she'd always thought. When she and Katinka were little, Jacques and Ellen and their son Robert often visited the house on the Velperweg. The two families even vacationed together. Jacques and her father had known each other since high school. When he and Ellen divorced, he poured out his heart to his closest friends: her parents. From then on, it was almost as if Jacques had moved in with them.

That was almost ten years before her father's death. Dorien remembers Jacques as a constant presence in those days. But she and Katinka were stunned when, just a few months after her father's passing, the relationship between Jacques and her mother seemed to turn romantic. Where had *that* come from? Had Jacques been *waiting* for her father to die? Had he had his eye on her mother all this time? And—a terrible thought—could the two of them have become involved *before* her father's death?

Dorien was furious about that possibility, more so as she began to put the puzzle pieces together. "Uncle Jacques," as they called him, had come to the house often, not only when her father was home, but even—maybe *mostly*—when he wasn't. Why would he come by when he *knew* her father was at the gym or had a late meeting at work? And why did Jacques and her mother seem so comfortable together?

Although her mother always denied that there'd been anything between herself and Jacques while her father was still alive,

Dorien never quite believed her. She refused to attend a Christmas dinner to which they invited her and considered the man a vulture, preying on her mother's kindness.

The atmosphere within the family became so poisonous that finally, after two years, her mother agreed to end her relationship with Jacques. No reason was ever given, but Dorien didn't care. What mattered was that it was over.

But apparently it was *not* over, after all. Six months ago, Dorien saw the two of them together, sitting side by side at a table outside the White Villa in Sonsbeek Park. Dorien was livid. She'd thought Jacques had moved away, and not just to the suburbs but all the way up to Alkmaar, where his son Robert now lived.

Her instinct was to confront them, to demand an explanation, but Remco held her back. The next day, when she reported to her mother that she'd been seen with Jacques, she denied that the two of them were back together. He was in Arnhem for the weekend, and they'd met for lunch as old friends. Her mother had in fact mirrored Dorien's anger. Who did she think she *was*? She wasn't owed an explanation.

Her eyes full of tears, Dorien tries to focus on her cell phone's screen. The Amber Alert—with its photos of her mother and a laughing Jelte—turn this bad dream into a hard reality. Jelte and her mother are missing.

The police officers have taken the situation seriously, since all the evidence points to an abrupt and unplanned departure. In addition to the Amber Alert, a team of patrolmen and patrolwomen are conducting a door-to-door canvas of the neighborhood.

The antique wall clock in her mother's living room tells her it's ten thirty. This late, the unavoidable conclusion is that something is *very* wrong. Dorien has spent the last hour on the phone, calling her mother's friends, family, and acquaintances—to no avail. No one has any idea where the missing grandmother and grandson might be. She's also texted her sister, asking her to call as soon as she can. Katinka and her boyfriend are spending two months traveling across Asia. Dorien doesn't like the idea of upsetting Katinka—what could she possibly do from faraway Malaysia?—but she can't just leave her mother's other daughter in the dark.

The only person she's been unable to contact is Jacques. She's texted him, urged him to call, and she hopes to hear from him, but she knows Jacques isn't any fonder of her than she is of him.

She turns to Remco, who has dropped onto the sofa, despondent. His thinning blond hair is mussed, his eyes dull. He's just come back downstairs after, with much trouble, managing to get Isabel tucked into bed. The girl was exhausted, but the stressful events of the day kept her head awhirl. It took quite a while, but at last, whimpering softly, she fell asleep.

Dorien's throat is dry. The uncertainty is driving her mad. Her phone buzzes for the umpteenth time: her many phone calls have led to an avalanche of text messages from shocked friends and family members who express their support and want to know if there's anything they can do to help. All well intended, but Dorien is in no shape to respond.

This latest message, however, comes from a blocked number. As she reads it, she can feel the blood drain from her face:

Your little one is missing. Chilling, right? Well, things like this happen. It's a big responsibility, looking after a child. Not everyone can handle it. Of course, you know exactly what I mean....

"Dorien?" Remco's voice brings her back to the present moment. "You look like you've seen a ghost."

Shaking violently, she shows him the text.

His eyes go wide.

She chews at her lip, and her thoughts return to Lake Garda, eighteen months ago.

It was warm in northern Italy—actually, it was bloody *hot*. Armed with a cooler and an umbrella, they'd stretched out for the fourth consecutive day at what they'd already come to think of as "their" section of the beach. The heat made any other plan for the day seem impossible.

The same Dutch family as yesterday and the day before arranged themselves beside them. Remco and Dorien chatted pleasantly with Wouter and Mireille, while Isabel played with their son, who was a year younger.

Maybe things had gotten *too* pleasant. She can still hear Mireille—perhaps half an hour before it happened—saying, "No, thanks, no more for me. I have to keep an eye on Christian."

But Dorien had waved away her hesitation. "One more glass won't hurt you. We might as well kill the bottle."

The men were off picking up a pizza. Giggling, Dorien was showing Mireille an article about sex toys in a women's magazine she'd brought from home when Isabel came running up to them, out of breath. Christian, she gasped, was gone.

The next hours unfold in Dorien's memory like scenes from a movie. Mireille's anxiety—and her own—soon turned to panic. Which turned out to be justified. She will never forget the sight of Christian's lifeless body being pulled from the water. A doctor who happened to be sunning on the beach did everything in his power to bring the boy back to consciousness. In the end, an ambulance rushed him to the nearest hospital, siren wailing. But it was too late.

Dorien thinks of Christian every week, and her thoughts are awash with guilt. She is certain that Mireille blames her for what happened. It was she, after all, who had provided the bottle of wine. It was her fault that Mireille hadn't kept a close enough watch on her child.

Of course, no one *forced* Mireille to drink so much wine, but Dorien agrees that she bears some responsibility for Christian's death. Why hadn't they *both* paid more attention to their children? Yes, it was Christian who died, but it might just as easily have been Isabel.

Remco and Dorien returned to The Netherlands early for the funeral. They would gladly have stood by Mireille and Wouter through that awful time, but Mireille slammed the door against any further contact.

Horrified, Dorien stares at her husband, sees in his eyes that he has reached the same conclusion she's come to. This hateful text is from Mireille.

"How could she *send* this? I mean, when you think about what *she* went through...."

Remco, nodding thoughtfully, sinks back on the couch. Then his face clouds with confusion. "How does she know Jelte's gone?" he says. "They didn't list our last name in the Amber Alert."

Dorien swallows, and her pulse quickens. Remco is right. How could Mireille know what's happened?

And then she remembers something Mireille said to her on the phone, a week after the funeral, their last conversation: "Sooner or later, you'll get yours."

At the time, she wrote the comment off—Mireille was overwhelmed by grief and not thinking clearly—but now she realizes that it might have been not just a cruel prediction but a threat.

Could *Mireille* have had something to do with Jelte's and her mother's disappearance?

"We have to tell the police about this," says Remco, and Dorien nods her agreement. Yes, of course they do.

But before they can make the call, there is another text:

Have you figured it out yet? No police, Dorien. Come alone, now! I don't want to wait for the showing tomorrow. You know where. I'll give you ten minutes.

Remco's brow furrows. "What does she mean, 'the showing tomorrow'?"

Dorien washes a hand across her mouth. "It's a vacant house, been empty for years. Someone called the office, said they were interested. I'm supposed to show it tomorrow."

She looks at the clock. It's a quarter to eleven. She'll have to hurry. She snatches her jacket from the coatrack and digs in her pocket for her keys.

"Just a second." Remco grabs her elbow. "We have no idea what she might do. You can't go by yourself."

Dorien shakes her head. "You're right: we don't know what she might be planning. That's why I *have* to go alone, like she said."

But Remco doesn't step out of her way. "What's the address? I'll call it in."

Dorien's mind races. Mireille's text says *not* to notify the police. She can't take the chance. What if the madwoman does something to Jelte? She comes to a decision.

"You know it. That old place on the Amsterdamseweg, the one with the nice gables. We drove by it the other day."

Remco nods.

"You make the call," says Dorien. "I'd better go."

She pulls free of her husband's grip, races out of her childhood home, gets into her car, and zips backward out of the driveway. In her rearview mirror, she sees two officers—who are standing at a neighbor's front door and questioning the occupant—reach for their radios.

Her heart pounding, she heads for the Vosdijk. It's only a two-minute drive. Have Jelte and her mother been so close, all this time? Desperate, she wonders what she will find at the supposedly empty house. And why did Mireille choose it for her hideout?

The moment she considers that question, she has the answer. The Vosdijk house is well known—not just here in the city but nationally. The gruesome drama that was enacted in its backyard pond was on every newscast: a mother drowned her young twins, then took her own life. Surely Mireille didn't pick the location randomly.

What should she do? Even though Mireille chose the spot, she doesn't feel right pulling into the driveway. Instead, she parks a hundred meters farther up the road and runs hunched over back to the house, hidden from sight by the hedge that fronts the neighboring homes.

There is very little light. She proceeds slowly up the long curving driveway, her heart in her throat, her breathing ragged. What does Mireille *want*, and is she in this alone, or is Wouter here with her?

The sight of the old red Jaguar parked beside the house takes her completely by surprise. What on earth is *Jacques'* car doing here? She doesn't understand this at all. It can't *possibly* be a coincidence.

She peers into the darkness. Where should she go? No light shows from inside the house. Ringing the doorbell seems absurd. Is Mireille even *in* there? How could she have gotten inside? Of course, a kidnaper wouldn't hesitate at a bit of breaking and entering.

Dorien heads for the ramshackle wooden gate that leads into the large backyard. It seems better to take this route. She pushes the gate, and it gives—but only slightly. She pushes harder and feels resistance, as if something heavy is lying against it. With all her strength, she shoves the wood with her shoulder, and it moves enough for her to squeeze through the opening—where she trips in the darkness over the obstacle that has impeded her. Her palms scrape on the gravel path and her legs become entangled in what seems to be another pair of legs, human legs. She screams, and scrambles away in panic.

The body is lying face down on the path, but she recognizes him at once, even in the darkness: Jacques. She cups her hands over her mouth to stifle another scream. What in the *world* is going on?

Dorien hears footsteps and freezes. A bright light shines in her eyes, forcing her to turn away. And then she hears the familiar voice.

"So you see, Dorien, I don't intend to let *anyone* fuck with me. Poor guy turned up at your mother's house at exactly the wrong moment. Convenient, though: I forced him to drive us here, and I sat in the back seat with your brat and watched the family drama play out between him and your mommy up front. I never dreamed I'd get that lucky."

Dorien's mouth is very dry, and she attempts to swallow. What is Mireille saying? She wishes she could see the woman's face. But the bright light from what seems to be her cell phone's flash makes that impossible.

"What do you want, Mireille? Where's my son? Where's my mother?"

A scornful laugh echoes in the night.

"What do I *want*? I want something you can't give me. I want my child back. I want my family back." Mireille sounds on the edge of hysterics. "I want everything you destroyed."

So she *does* blame Dorien for what happened. As if she herself wasn't even there at the time.

Dorien takes a deep breath. "Mireille, what you're doing won't bring Christian back. You're just making things worse for yourself."

Her words hang emptily in the air.

"Shut up! How *dare* you preach at me! I don't care anymore, I just want you to feel as horrible as I do. I want you to know what it's like to hold a dead child in your arms. Bas, come here."

Her flash swings to illuminate the dilapidated shed in the backyard.

"No, let him go!" It's her mother's voice, and it is followed by a scream that is unmistakably Jelte's.

"Quiet, you dumb bitch," a deep male voice orders, and then come the sounds of a slap and a thud, as if someone has fallen against the wall of the shed. Has her mother been knocked to the ground?

A bald man Dorien has never seen before drags her son into the light. Jelte is dressed only in jeans and a red sweater. No jacket, no shoes or socks. His weeping rips a hole in her heart.

"Jelte!"

The stranger and Jelte are perhaps thirty meters away, and Dorien takes off running toward them.

Before she has halved the distance, the flashlight swings her way, and Mireille barks, "Stop!"

The woman's icy tone brings Dorien to a halt. The light moves to the back of the yard, to the pond. She can make out Mireille standing beside an iron bench close to the water—which, in the glare of the flash, glitters ominously.

"Come here," Mireille orders.

Dorien approaches the bench slowly. She recognizes Mireille's long blond hair and slim figure.

"Sit."

Dorien does as she's told. Her mind is racing. What should she do? How much time does she have? How could she have been so stupid as to send Remco and the police to the wrong house? Will they figure out where she *really* is? She has to keep the woman talking as long as possible, buy as much time as she can.

"Mireille, you're mixed up. This isn't the woman I knew in Italy. She was a dear, sweet person. You don't have to do this. Is it really what Christian would want?"

"I told you to shut *up*," Mireille spits. "If you mention my son's name again, your little boy goes straight into the pond." The flashlight swings back to Jelte and the man named Bas. "Bring him here and tie her up."

The bald man delivers the weeping child as instructed. By now, Dorien's head is clear. The sight of Mireille and Jelte together has shocked her back to herself.

"Don't get any ideas," Mireille snaps, as if she has read Dorien's mind. She turns her phone to illuminate her waistband, and the gun she carries there is impossible to miss.

"Arms behind your back," Bas grunts.

Who is he? If Mireille won't listen to her, maybe he will. "Why are you doing this?" she whispers. "What does it have to do with you? My son is *two years old*. What did he ever do to you?"

She hopes Mireille can't hear her. But the man shows no reaction. In the light from the flash, she can see how huge his pupils are. Dorien doesn't know much about drugs, but she realizes that the man must be *some* kind of a user.

"Shut your mouth, Dorien!" Mireille's voice is as sharp as a knife. "You think you can get anywhere with Bas? Forget it! He's not like Wouter—he'll do anything for me. He knows what I need to make the pain go away. Tie her up! We have to finish this before the police get here."

Dorien's arms are roughly pulled behind her back. The man Bas is much stronger than she is. He ropes her wrists tightly to the back of the bench, then returns to the shed.

Mireille laughs. "Let's not keep any secrets from your mother. We'll make this a cozy family get-together, shall we?"

Dorien sees Bas shove her mother—face bruised, clothing filthy, unsteady on her feet—into the light of the flash.

"Sit over there, with your daughter."

Mireille yanks Jelte to the edge of the pond, and her laughter rises maniacally. Is she also on some kind of drug?

Dorien is cold. She holds her breath but can't take her eyes off her sobbing little boy.

"Enough tears," Mireille snarls. "Sorry, Dorien, but I don't have time for anymore chitchat. You know what they say: shared pain is less pain."

"Mama!" Jelte's cry tears Dorien to shreds. Mireille flings the boy into the water without the slightest hint of compassion, and Dorien is unable to do anything to stop it from happening.

"Jelte, no!" She tugs with all her strength at the rope that binds her, and takes in only fragments of the conversation that follows between Mireille and Bas:

"Get the body... we have to make it look like...."

"... gone."

"Gone? How can it be gone, you idiot?"

No answer. Only, somewhere in the night, a muffled thud.

"Bas?" And now there is hesitation in Mireille's voice. "Bas?"

Mireille starts toward the house.

"Mom," Dorien whispers urgently. "*Mom!*"

Her mother slumps against her. Is she conscious?

"Mom, Jelte's in the pond. Untie me!"

The terror in her voice brings her mother to her senses. She fumbles with the rope behind Dorien's back.

"Hurry!" cries Dorien. "Every second counts!"

As her mother works on the knots, Dorien twists her wrists in an attempt to help—and suddenly she is free. She bolts for the pond and jumps into the ice-cold water, which comes only to her waist. She gropes frantically beneath the surface. Where is he? A step to the right—and she has him!

Her heart leaps. She raises his limp little body from the water. Panting, her jeans sodden and heavy and reluctant to allow her to escape, she wades back to shore and lays Jelte on the grass.

She hears a shot, much too close, and sees Mireille racing toward her, gun in hand.

"No!" Mireille screams. "You can't take *this* from me!"

Pinned motionless in horror, Dorien sees Mireille stumble, tripped by Dorien's mother, whose outstretched leg catapults the madwoman into the pond.

Dorien doesn't hesitate for a moment. She grabs Mireille's long blond hair and plunges her head beneath the surface of the water, shouting, "Mom, Jelte, please!"

She sees her mother kneel by the boy's side, position his head, clamp his nostrils between the thumb and forefinger of her right hand, and breathe into his mouth. "Jelte," the child's grandmother pleads between breaths, "wake up, baby!"

Mireille kicks Dorien's leg, knocks her off balance. Dorien is taller and stronger, but her terror causes her to loosen her grip. Mireille breaks the surface of the water, coughing, gasping for breath.

And at that moment, Dorien sees a sign of life from her son: his body spasms, and water gurgles from his mouth. A feeling of ecstasy wells up within her—but then something cracks into the side of her head, and she is pushed down into the pond. She fights back, kicks and claws at Mireille's face—until finally she regains control of the situation. Filling her lungs with air, she stares into those empty eyes and shoves the hateful face downward.

"Dorien, stop! Let her go!"

It is, miraculously, Jacques' voice, and it shocks her to her senses.

"She's not worth it. Let her up."

He wades out into the pond and wrestles Mireille, who no longer fights back, to shore. Blood leaks from a wound in his shoulder.

From far off comes the wail of approaching sirens.

"Mama."

That one precious word, barely above a whisper.

Sobbing, Dorien helps her son to sit upright. "Jelte," she says. "My dear, sweet boy."

She holds the shivering child close, hugs him tightly, kisses his wet head. She'll have to let him go eventually, she thinks, but not now. Not yet.

Through her tears, she sees her mother and Jacques approach, their arms around each other. Dorien closes her eyes. Perhaps it's time to let go of her judgments.

Jelte turns in her arms and points.

"Grandpa!" he says.

16

———————

THE LIGHTHOUSE

BY HILDE VANDERMEEREN

Paul Casteur watched the motorboat putter back out to sea. The north wind tore at his hair and made him shiver. Threatening clouds loomed overhead. Angry waves dashed onto the island's rocky shoreline, chewed at it like rats ravaging a dead body.

The lighthouse door was open a crack, and from inside came the sound of Monique opening and shutting kitchen cabinets. He supposed she was putting away the provisions they'd brought, each item in its proper place, canned goods and bottles with their labels facing forward, precisely spaced so that no two items touched. When she was finished, she'd climb the stairs and organize the bathroom, make certain the tub was ring-free, no hair left behind, then continue to the third floor and plump the pillows on the bed. Perhaps, if she had time, she'd fix them an aperitif and carry it up to the lantern room, from which—according to the motorboat's pilot—they'd enjoy the magnificent view.

The magnificent view of *what*, Paul wondered. The island was miniscule, the lighthouse its only structure. "A unique tourist attraction," Monique had promised him.

The motorboat disappeared into the distance. It would be back to pick them up in three days. Or was it four? Paul swept his gaze from left to right, tracing the horizon. He listened to the pounding of the waves and had the odd sense that the island had grown even smaller.

The first raindrops began to fall. They traced a chilly trail down his cheeks and dripped from his beard to the dirt path that led from the shoreline to the lighthouse door. He turned away from the rain and went inside. His muscles ached with every step. Perhaps he should have stayed a few more days in the hospital. A younger body would have healed more quickly from the trauma of the accident.

But Dr. Francke had given him permission to make this journey, and Monique had pressed him to agree. Paul had overheard the two of them discussing his condition in the corridor outside his room. At first, the doctor had thought it was too soon for him to travel, but Monique had managed to convince him.

He pulled the door shut. Right in front of him, blocking his view of the living room and kitchen, a steep flight of stairs climbed to the upper floors. He wondered why Monique hadn't suggested a one-level bed-and-breakfast somewhere on the mainland.

In the tiny living room, he dropped onto a well-worn sofa by the wood stove. It would take a while before the fire melted the ice from his bones. His hands shivered.

He was thirsty.

Where was Monique? He struggled to his feet and stepped into the kitchenette, opened the small refrigerator and then, one by one, each of the cabinets. He found bottled water, milk, and orange juice, but nothing to take off the chill. He closed the last cabinet door. Behind him, he heard Monique coming down the stairs.

"No whiskey?" he asked.

She shook her head.

"Beer? Wine?"

She shook off each of his questions. Sometimes he asked himself what had drawn him to Monique in the first place. They'd been together for so long, he couldn't remember exactly how it had begun between them. He looked at her. She had short brown hair. For a woman of her age, she was still quite attractive. She could thank her ascetic lifestyle for that: she was uninclined to take in alcohol or give out either money or sex. He wasn't sure which of those characteristics annoyed him the most. Was it her reluctance to grant him a glass of good wine at the end of a hard day at the store? Or the fact that she insisted on their driving the same old car, year after year? Or the depressing reality that their bedroom had long since become the coldest room in the house?

"Hungry?" she asked.

He nodded. This was a lie. He was thirsty, not hungry. She poured him a glass of water and handed him three magazines she slid from a plastic shopping bag. He examined them. One was devoted to gardening, one to soccer, and the third was aimed at active seniors.

He dropped them onto the coffee table. Monique paid no attention. She was opening a can of white beans in tomato sauce. *What the hell*, Paul thought, *is she up to?* He didn't like white beans in tomato sauce, she knew that. Soccer bored him, the jewelry shop had kept him far too busy to spare time for gardening —and, although the accident had left him weakened, he was still a long way from turning sixty-five.

Outside, the rain beat against the lighthouse's small round windows. He sank onto the sofa and reached for *Senior Life*.

Pretending to page through it, he kept an eye on Monique. The fussy way she measured out a pat of butter and placed it exactly in the center of the frying pan stoked his irritation.

He stopped at a photograph of an older couple and their four grandchildren, all of them on bicycles in some anonymous forest. He wanted to tear it out of the magazine and shred it. He felt like Monique was rubbing his face in a future they would never be able to enjoy. They had had no children, so no one would ever call them grandpa and grandma.

There was a caption beneath the photo, but the print was too small for him to read.

"Have you seen my glasses?" he asked her.

"On the table just inside the front door," she said, not looking up from her work. "You put them there when you came in."

He got up. He couldn't have left his glasses on a table. He wore them on a little chain around his neck. He'd begun doing that when he first took over the management of the jewelry store and retained the habit even after he'd sold the business last year.

His glasses were on the table just inside the front door. No chain. He put them on and returned to the living room.

Monique had her back to him. Silent as always. The butter in the pan began to sizzle. He looked out the window. The waves were breaking closer to the lighthouse now, making the little island even smaller.

Maybe it all had something to do with the store. Monique had been acting strangely ever since he sold it. The phone calls that ended abruptly the moment he came into the room. The envelopes that arrived in the mail but disappeared before he had a chance to open them. The arguments over what they should do with the money he'd gotten for the store and its stock.

He wanted to travel, lay in a cellar of fine wine, keep an eye out for a summer home somewhere down south.

She had rejected each of his proposals out of hand.

And then there'd been the accident. A semi had run him off the highway. When he regained consciousness in the hospital, the police told him that the truck driver had fallen asleep behind the wheel.

Monique emptied the can of beans and red sauce into the pan. He shuddered.

Perhaps this was her way of telling him she didn't love him anymore. Easier to serve him food he didn't like than serve the truth straight to his face.

"I'm going to the bathroom," he said.

She asked if he needed her help, but he waved the offer away.

Step by step, he struggled up the stairs. His forehead was beaded with sweat by the time he reached the second floor. Monique had misinformed him—whether mistakenly or on purpose, he had no idea. The bathroom was on the *third* floor, the bedroom on the second. He would have to climb another flight. He was dizzy and paused to catch his breath. He dropped onto the edge of the bed. Monique had left her purse on the floor. Without thinking, he reached for it and unclasped it. Her cell phone was powered down—there was no point leaving it on, there would be no signal this far out. He opened her wallet and found a wad of cash. That was surprising: their lodgings and the boat transfers, she'd said, had been paid in advance. He flipped through the wallet's contents. Business cards, tickets, driver's license, passport. Nothing special.

She called up from downstairs. Was he all right?

"Be right down," he shouted.

There was one last compartment in the wallet. His fingers trembled as he explored it. Inside, he found a faded snapshot.

A child, maybe four years old. A little girl, with two blond pigtails. He had no idea who she was. Why was Monique carrying a photograph of a stranger?

He heard her footsteps on the stairs. He shoved the picture back in its place, stuffed the wallet in the purse and tossed it under the bed. Just in time.

"I thought the bathroom was on this floor," he said.

She shook her head. "One flight up," she told him.

She insisted on helping him up the stairs. Her fingers squeezed his arm as she guided him. It aggravated him that she stood outside the bathroom door while he peed, more so when she zipped his fly for him, as if he were a toddler. Since the accident, he'd had trouble with zippers.

"You need to be careful," she said, on their way downstairs. "If you fall, we can't call for help."

They had dinner in silence. Outside, the storm rattled the windows in their frames.

Two more nights after this. Or was it three?

He didn't touch the beans. What Monique had said to him on the stairs, had that been a warning? He would have to keep his wits about him.

The nurse had forgotten to close the curtains. That was Paul's first thought. But when he opened his eyes, he didn't recognize the room. The windows were round, the white hospital walls a dull terracotta. He got up and went to the window and saw sunlight glittering on an endless blanket of sea.

He turned. The woman in the bed sat up. Her name was Monique. They were married. And there was something else. Something had happened the day before, and a warning light was blinking inside his head. But he couldn't remember what the light was warning him against.

"Did you sleep all right?" she asked.

He nodded. There was an open laptop on a desk against the wall. He pulled the wooden chair away from the desk and perched on it, and his fingers fitted into the curve of the laptop's keyboard with an ease that surprised him. It was as if he'd sat here before, at this very spot. At this desk, in this chair, with its view of the slate-gray sea. He jerked his hands from the keys as if they had burned his fingertips.

"Something wrong?" she said.

Her voice seemed strange. She eyed him as if she were waiting for something to happen.

"I'm thirsty," he said.

That was clearly not the response she had hoped for. He could tell by the slump of her shoulders.

"I'll make coffee," she said.

She got out of the bed, and a book fell to the floor. He scooted his chair back and reached for it, but Monique got there first. She snatched up the book, clutched it to her breast, and went downstairs.

He gazed out the window. Monique had changed since the accident. He closed his eyes. His hands gripped the steering wheel. He was driving along the highway, enveloped by the night. There was little traffic, and he swung around a semi with a foreign license plate. The high-mast light poles were beacons, guiding him homeward. He wanted to get there as quickly as he could. Monique would be expecting him. He checked the speedometer and eased up on the gas. She would never forgive him for driving unsafely. He would never forgive himself for putting the gems in the attaché case on the back seat at risk.

He would get off at the next exit, and after that it would only be fifteen more minutes to the house. He slipped a CD into the changer, and soft jazz filled the car.

The semi he had passed a minute earlier reappeared in his rearview mirror. It was gaining on him. He saw it sway across the centerline and back.

After the crash, everything was dead silent. Silent and empty, darker than night.

Paul opened his eyes. There was a laptop on the desk before him.

The lighthouse.

Those two words flickered on the screen. He was unaware of having typed them. The story he had always wanted to write when he retired blossomed in his mind. All at once, there it was.

He rubbed his eyes. Monique came into the bedroom with a tray. The smell of fresh coffee came with her. She set a cup and saucer on the desk. Black, two sugar cubes in the saucer.

"No milk?" he asked.

"You take it black, Paul."

He closed the lid of the laptop, hiding the words he had typed.

"Are you writing?" she asked.

He nodded.

She smiled. "It's all going to be okay," she said. "Would you like some toast?"

"I'm not hungry," he said.

"Shall I help you get dressed? Do you need to use the bathroom?"

"I want to write a little first."

She got clean clothes for herself from the closet and went upstairs. He waited until she was gone. Then he reopened the laptop. The sentences came more slowly than he had hoped. His fingers were shaking, and he made frequent mistakes. More than once, he found himself unable to remember a word he wanted.

He raised the cup to his lips. Black coffee. Why hadn't she put milk in it, the way he always drank it? He returned it to the saucer without tasting it, examined the dark liquid suspiciously. Could she have put something in the coffee, something that wouldn't have the desired effect if there was also milk in the cup? Something to send him back to sleep, so she could do whatever she liked without his interference? Maybe something she'd read about in that book she'd tried to hide from him?

He had to get a look at that book.

Perhaps there was something in the coffee that would give him a heart attack and leave no trace. *Died peacefully in his sleep*, the coroner would say.

He pushed the saucer away, and a black wave slopped over the rim of the cup.

She was up to something. He could feel it. The silences. The questions she asked him. They kept coming back to money. Money she didn't want him to spend.

Monique had never worked a day in her life. He'd always made enough from the jewelry store to support them. If he were out of the picture, everything would be hers.

He had to go downstairs and find that book. Was she still in the bathroom? He had no idea. Perhaps she'd slipped past the bedroom door without him noticing. He got up, grabbed the back of the chair to stop himself from falling. She'd picked the right time to act. He was still weak from the accident. That's why Dr. Francke hadn't wanted him to travel. But he was well enough to stay one step ahead of Monique.

The wooden steps creaked as he descended.

The kitchen was empty. The only sounds were the bubbling of the coffee maker and the susurrus of the sea outside. There was a cutting board on the counter, a knife, an assortment of vegetables she had begun to slice for soup. Carrots, leeks, onions, celery.

There were magazines on the coffee table in the living room. He picked one up. *Senior Life*. A page had been torn out of it. He found a trash basket against the room's curved wall. At the bottom was a balled-up piece of paper. He plucked it free and smoothed it out on the kitchen counter. It was the page that had been torn from the magazine. The article was about estate taxes. He could feel his heart race. His head began to throb.

His suspicions were confirmed. Monique was after his money. The money he'd gotten for the sale of the store his father had left him.

He heard her coming down the stairs. She was humming. He stood there shaking in his boots, his body a wreck, while she cheerfully planned to do away with him.

She was wearing a bathrobe. Her hair was wet. She stopped humming.

"What are you doing?" she asked him, staring at his hands.

He looked down. He was holding a knife. She dropped the towel she was carrying and put a hand to her throat, as if protecting herself. She took a step away from him and bumped into the wall.

"Is there something I ought to know?" he asked, holding out the crumpled magazine page in his free hand. "Something about estate taxes?"

She shook her head, mute.

He stepped closer. There was no way for her to escape. He raised the knife.

"You didn't just *happen* to pick this place, did you, Monique?"

A tear formed at the corner of her eye. "Dr. Francke said it was a bad idea," she whispered. "He was afraid it would be too much of a shock. But I thought it might help you."

"What might help me?"

"Coming here. I thought it might be good for you. I thought you might be able to write here, like before."

"Before?"

"Before the accident. You wrote the first chapters of your book here."

"What are you talking about? I never wrote a book."

"You did, Paul."

"Why are you lying to me?"

"I'm not lying. Please, put the knife down."

He tightened his grip. His hand was shaking violently.

"I'm a jeweler," he said, "not a writer." There was an urgency in his voice, almost a plea. "I wear my glasses on a chain around my neck."

She shook her head. "That was your father," she said softly. "Your father was a jeweler. You were a writer, until the accident."

He wished she would stop telling lies, but she went on talking, gently, insistently. He'd stopped writing, she said. They never had much money after the accident, because she was the only one of them able to work. And the accident had happened thirty years ago, not recently. Ever since, he'd refused to leave the house. All he did was sit at home and drink, trying to forget. It was the drinking that had destroyed his health, until at last Dr. Francke had sent him off to rehab.

"Forget what?" he demanded. "What was I trying to forget?"

Her face was white and drawn with fear.

"I want you to put the knife down, Paul."

"What was I trying to forget?" he shouted.

"Who was in the car with you when the truck hit you," said Monique.

"I was alone in the car," he spat. The point of the knife was only inches from her face.

"Our daughter," she whispered. "She had just turned four. She was spending the weekend with my parents, but she came down with something and you went to get her and bring her home."

"You're *lying*," he said. "We never had a daughter."

"Her name was Ruby," she said. "Our little gem. She was in her car seat in the back of the car. She's what you've been trying to forget, all these years."

She was trying to upset him, and it was working. His headache was much worse, he felt sick to his stomach. He screamed at her to shut her mouth.

But she kept on talking, and his vision suddenly blurred.

He awoke in a strange bed. The room was cold and empty. He had no idea where he was.

He got up slowly. His pajamas were filthy. Where was the woman who looked after him? Monique. They were married. He called her name.

No response. Outside, the wind wailed. Or perhaps it wasn't the wind. It was an odd noise, a *whooshing* sound that repeated itself, over and over.

There was a laptop on a desk against one wall of the bedroom. He stumbled across the floor to it and dropped into the chair. A sheet of paper lay next to the laptop. It looked like it had been torn out of a magazine. Something about estate taxes. On the other side of the page was an article about Korsakoff's syndrome. *Neurological disorder... retrograde amnesia... confabulation... commonly associated with alcoholism.* He didn't bother to read the rest of it. There were flecks of red on the page, they reminded him of white beans in tomato sauce, his favorite dish. He would ask Monique to make it for their supper tonight.

He crumpled the page and threw it away. His hands were trembling.

The laptop was powered down. He couldn't remember how to

turn it on. He got up and looked around the room. The walls were curved. He was trapped in a round cell with little round windows.

Or, no, not trapped. There was a door, and flights of stairs leading up and down.

He called Monique's name as he went clumsily down the steps. There was a living room and a little kitchen at the bottom. There were vegetables on a cutting board on the kitchen counter. They were shriveled and dry and appeared to have been sitting there for quite some time.

It was cold. The wood stove had gone out. He shivered.

He found a book beneath the sofa cushion, as if someone had tried to hide it.

The Lighthouse, by Paul Casteur.

On the back cover was a photograph of a man he didn't recognize. A young man, thirty years younger than himself. He dropped the book on the coffee table.

Only then did he notice the carmine splatter on the living room's terracotta walls.

His muscles protesting, he eased himself onto the couch.

In the distance, he could make out the low rumble of an approaching car over the steady background *whoosh whoosh whoosh*.

No, not a car. It sounded like the engine of a motorboat.

17

THE POET WHO LOCKED HIMSELF IN
BY ANNE VAN DOORN

Robbie Corbijn was looking haggard. There were bags beneath his eyes, and his sunken cheeks were deathly pale. I'd been working for his Leiden firm—*Research & Discover, Cold Cases Our Specialty*—for almost three months. During that time, Robbie had shared his files on a dozen unsolved cases with me, and we'd cleared up exactly none of them. This was why he was suffering.

That late-February morning, I stepped into the office we shared and found him at his desk, immersed in his work. I picked up a sheet of paper that had drifted to the carpet. It was an e-mail from a man who wanted to consult Research & Discover about his father's death. According to the police, he wrote, the old man had committed suicide, but our potential client refused to believe it. His father would never have killed himself. Would it be possible for him to talk with us?

"Did you make an appointment?" I asked, holding up the printout.

"As if I haven't got enough on my plate," muttered Robbie.

"Maybe you *should* see him. Once you've dealt with this new case, you can go back to the old ones with a fresh outlook. And if it's too much for you, *I'll* take it on."

Robbie eyed me, his eyebrows raised. "You, Lowina?" A smile flitted across his tired face. "You've barely begun your training, and you haven't got your PI license yet. But you really think you can handle a case on your own? Fine, I'll call him and make an appointment, and you can read through the file. But don't expect too much."

"What do you mean?"

"When I was still a cop, I investigated a number of apparent suicides. In almost every case, it turned out they *were* suicides, but the next-of-kin had trouble believing it. Suicide generally comes as a shock. Friends and family are left with guilt feelings and unanswerable questions. This is probably the same sort of situation. Our would-be client would be better off consulting a psychologist."

That very afternoon, we made the acquaintance of Cornelis Meijer. He was about thirty years old, stocky, with a full head of unruly brown hair. When we were all seated, he informed us that he was a carpenter and lived in Amsterdam. His father had also lived in the city, until his second marriage.

"My stepmother has a huge house in the Veluwe, a villa that must have cost at least a million euros. When they got married, my father moved in with her. That was seven years ago." The carpenter shook his head sadly. "Biggest mistake of his life."

"Why is that?" asked Robbie.

"He had no business getting married again, certainly not to her," said Cornelis Meijer. "She wasn't his type. She's upper class, with enough money to live the good life. She's got a summer house on the French Riviera, what else do you need to know? He was nothing more than a companion for her, someone to take her arm and parade around the village, accompany her to museums. But my father wasn't that kind of man. He had only one great love in his life: poetry."

This last word was pronounced matter-of-factly. The carpenter's voice revealed no hint of pride in his father's passion.

"He made a living writing poems?" asked Robbie.

Cornelis Meijer shook his head again. "Which is why he remarried after my mother's death. She was the one who made the money and the one who raised me. When my father found himself alone, nine years ago, he was able to survive for a while on what she left him. When the money ran out, he married Rosalinde, my stepmother."

They met, Meijer told us, at a poetry reading in Amsterdam. Rosalinde was enchanted by one of his father's poems and especially by the way he read it. They married before really getting to know each other. And things soon turned sour between them.

"My father was an irascible man, which is why he preferred to be alone, so as to avoid any possible conflict. Rosalinde is the complete opposite. She thrives on being surrounded by a circle of like-minded girlfriends, all of them just as high-class and vain as herself. She resented never having children of her own to show off and thought she could make up for it by taking a poet for a spouse. They had company every day, received a hundred phone calls a week. The situation got a little better five years ago, when my father built himself a retreat—a writer's shed—in the woods. That's where he died, but it was almost four months before his body was discovered."

"Four months?"

Cornelis Meijer nodded. "In the middle of October, my stepmother left to spend the winter in her house in the south of

France. My father stayed behind in The Netherlands. The police aren't sure exactly when he died, but it had to have been late October or early November. By the time they found him, his body was badly decomposed."

"How horrible," I said.

The carpenter gazed at me. "It was the worst news I ever received," he agreed, his expression sorrowful. "I blame myself. We didn't talk much after his second marriage, partly because I'm busy with work and have a family of my own. To tell the truth, our only contact was the Christmas cards we exchanged every year—plus the occasional Facebook post."

"And you believe your father was murdered?" asked Robbie.

"He had to have been. When I didn't get the usual card in December, I should have checked in on him. Then we would have found his body sooner."

"Why didn't you?"

"I thought he was with *her*, with Rosalinde, on the Riviera. She'd spend five or six months there, every fall and winter, and he'd generally join her for a couple of weeks in December and January. Last September, she went to France as usual, and she claims she had no contact with him for all those months. She called, she said, several times, but he never picked up. I think she knew full well he was dead. I think she had something to do with it —if not directly then indirectly."

"Her motive?"

"Pure necessity," said Cornelis Meijer. "She couldn't divorce him. Thanks to Holland's community-property laws, she would have had to give up half her wealth. And her money was the only reason they stayed together for all those years. My father was financially dependent on her. She deposited a monthly allowance into his bank account, and that's what he lived on. It wouldn't have surprised me if *he* divorced *her* as soon as he was eligible for Social Security, since their relationship had long since gone sour."

"How did your father die?"

"He was shot."

"In his shed?"

Our visitor nodded. "I think he was at his desk, working, when someone came in, overpowered him, pressed the barrel of his hunting rifle beneath his chin and pulled the trigger. But too much time went by for there to be any evidence. If I'd only tried to contact him—I can't stop blaming myself!"

"The hunting rifle belonged to your father?"

"He used it to scare away varmints," Cornelis Meijer explained, "so he wouldn't be disturbed at his work. Rosalinde's property extends back into the woods, there's no fence or other barrier. So he always kept the rifle handy."

"Did you ever visit your father in the Veluwe?" asked Robbie.

"Once, three years ago. Rosalinde was in France, otherwise I wouldn't have gone. I still remember our goodbye. The last I saw of him, he was walking up the narrow path that led out to the shed. He went in and closed the door. That was the last time I ever saw him. Three years later, he died behind that same door." Meijer sighed deeply. "If only he'd never married that stuck-up woman!"

He handed over a thin file folder and left with Robbie Corbijn's promise that we would go to the Veluwe the next day. The folder contained no photographs of the scene of Meijer's father's death and no forensic report. Apparently such evidence hadn't been thought necessary. The old man's death was so simple, such an obvious suicide, that I couldn't see any possibility of satisfying our client. Would this indeed turn out to be one of those cases where a survivor can't live with the thought that his loved one has killed himself?

The police report stated that they had been contacted on

Saturday, February 13, by Albert Meijer's elderly neighbor. She had herself received a telephone call from Rosalinde Meijer-van Henegouwen, who had made several unsuccessful attempts to reach her husband by phone from the Riviera. Although the elderly lady was not on good terms with the eccentric Albert Meijer, she agreed to check in on him, to make sure that all was well.

When she arrived at the villa, the front door was locked, but the back door stood open. She followed the path out into the woods and found the shed, whose door was closed and locked. She was certain that something must be terribly wrong, since an awful smell hung in the air. She knocked on the door and called Meijer's name. There was no response. Peering through the only window, she made a gruesome discovery: Meijer's decomposing body lay stretched out on the shed's concrete floor.

Looking through the same window, the officers who responded to the neighbor's call could see why the shed door wouldn't open: it was barred shut from the inside. The window was also locked, so they forced the door. The medical examiner determined that the cause of death was wounds inflicted by a load of buckshot. The weapon, a double-barreled shotgun, lay beside the corpse, and the dead man's index finger still rested on the trigger. The gun held one live shell in firing position and one expended but unejected cartridge. The coroner found gunpowder residue on the remains of Meijer's hand. The conclusion was inevitable: the poet had fired the fatal shot himself.

There was no doubt that it was suicide. The officers made two discoveries in the shed that underlined this conclusion: a postcard and a bank statement, both thumbtacked to the wall. The postcard had come from France and was signed by Rosalinde Meijer. On it, she had told her husband that she no longer loved him, and there was no reason for him to join her in France. The bank statement was for Meijer's account, and it showed a negative balance. Each of these items provided evidence of a motive for suicide.

The case, therefore, had been closed.

In my mind, however, there were two noteworthy points left unexplained.

First was the date of the apparent suicide. The investigating officers had found advertising circulars in the mailbox outside the villa. The oldest of these had been delivered on October 29. This led the officers to conclude that Meijer had killed himself on that date, or shortly before it. But this conclusion was contradicted by the statement given by the elderly neighbor. She stubbornly insisted that Meijer was alive at least through the end of the first week of November. She acknowledged that she couldn't actually *see* him from her property, but she had *heard* him cutting wood with his chainsaw, as he did every autumn. The reason she was so certain of the date was that November 5 was her birthday, and she had been annoyed by the noise of the saw, which had continued over the next several days. At the end of October, a storm had caused considerable damage in the woods, and Meijer was apparently cutting up the many fallen trees for firewood. But why, then, hadn't he emptied his mailbox after October 29? The neighbor had answered that question by pointing out that Albert Meijer was a bit of a hermit, uninterested in the world beyond his domain.

The second noteworthy point was contained in the statement Rosalinde Meijer-van Henegouwen had given to the police. She had reacted with surprise when the investigating detective told her that her husband had barred his shed's only door. As far as she knew, there *was* no bar on that door.

When I finished paging through the file, Robbie asked me what conclusion I had drawn.

"Suicide," I said.

"Are you sure?"

"What else could it be?" I said, shrugging. "I don't think there's any reason for us to go to the Veluwe tomorrow." I explained about the barred door and the gunpowder residue on the dead man's hand. "Albert Meijer shot himself. His son can't accept that reality, which is why he came to us. Perhaps it's partly because he blames himself for not taking more of an interest in his father."

"Guilt feelings, then." Robbie smiled. "I wonder...."

"Well, what do *you* think?"

"I think he's feeling angry, not guilty. He didn't get along with his stepmother. And Rosalinde didn't call *him* when she couldn't get a response from her husband—that speaks volumes about their relationship. Rosalinde doesn't have children of her own. Cornelis Meijer hoped he'd eventually become the sole heir to the villa in the Veluwe and the second house on the Riviera. Thanks to his father's suicide, though, Rosalinde can now remarry, and he can forget any prospect of an inheritance. The person who profits most from a verdict of suicide would be Rosalinde. So I wonder...."

"Yes?"

"Why did she wait so long before asking the neighbor to take a look? Was their marriage *that* damaged? Imagine for a moment that she *did* have something to do with his death. In that case, she *knew* he was lying there in his writer's shed. It would have been in her interest to make sure his decomposing body was found before she returned from France, so she wouldn't have to 'discover' it herself. That would have underlined her complete innocence. If we go to the Veluwe tomorrow, I'll be especially interested in that barred door, which you find so conclusive."

The next day, the sun peeked hesitantly through the clouds as we drove east along the A1 to the Veluwe. Until his death, Albert Meijer had lived on the eastern edge of this vast forested region, a little outside the village of Epe. After an hour and a half in the car, we turned into the lonely road he had called home. Villas, widely separated from each other, were set far back from the street, almost hidden amongst the greenery. I had the impression that garden sheds were popular in Epe.

I noticed that the grass verge beside the road was torn up, and there was sand on the asphalt. When I pointed this out to him, Robbie Corbijn grinned.

"Wild boar," he said. "They've had a lot of trouble with them in this part of the country. Lawns dug up, angry citizens in arms against the animal-rights activists who protest those who want to hunt them."

We drove on in silence until we spotted a mailbox with the house number we were looking for painted on it. A driveway, paved with a layer of gravel, meandered between tall rhododendrons to an expansive villa with a thatched roof. As prearranged, a uniformed policeman stood waiting for us at the front door. He was one of the pair who had responded to the original call.

"The son hired you?" he greeted us.

"We're acting in his interest," Robbie acknowledged. "But at this point we have no reason to doubt the official conclusion drawn by the investigating detectives. We've read the file. It seems to be an open-and-shut case."

The officer sighed, visibly relieved. "So you're aware that Meijer locked himself in," he said. "You'll see there's no other explanation." Suddenly he laughed. "If there is, I need to find a new line of work!"

"Is it correct that no forensics team was called out?"

"That seemed totally unnecessary."

The policeman offered to take us to the shed, but Robbie demurred. He wanted to see the inside of the villa first. We walked around back, past a carefully stacked pile of dark firewood, protected from the elements beneath a thatched overhang. The officer unlocked the villa's rear door and let us in. Robbie headed straight for the kitchen. He opened the refrigerator and took out a bulging milk carton. There was a bit of curdled milk in it, discolored and moldy. The use-by date was printed on the carton's blue cap: November 3. Robbie examined the other items in the refrigerator. He nodded, satisfied, and closed the door.

"Now the shed," he said.

Behind the house, an unpaved garden path led into the woods. We could see the shed in the distance, between the trees. It stood in a clearing, perhaps sixty feet in diameter, surrounded by tall beeches and a scattering of birches. The ground was carpeted with a thick layer of fallen leaves. The shed was weather-beaten, a compact cube beneath a gabled roof. Its sole window—four dusty panes in a simple muntin frame—faced the villa. The door, set into the shed's right-hand wall, stood open a crack.

"I'm not going in there," the officer said, wrinkling his nose in distaste.

Robbie Corbijn swung the door wide. A stench of decay assaulted our nostrils, but Robbie seemed unaffected. By the window stood a desk and a simple wooden chair. This was where the poet worked, with a view of the villa. Robbie found a pad, pens, and a box of shotgun shells in one of the desk's drawers. Everything was as described in the police report. There was a dark stain on the concrete floor, where the corpse had lain for months and decomposed.

Robbie gave considerable attention to the stainless-steel bar brackets screwed on either side of the door. Unlike the rest of the shed, the brackets were new. The copper screws that attached them to the wooden interior wall gleamed. Opposite the hinges, the screws had been torn free when the officers had forced the door.

"It would have been impossible to bar the door from the outside," the policeman said, standing well back from the doorway. "And a murderer would have *had* to do so. The barred door proves that it had to have been suicide."

"An open-and-shut case," Robbie concluded.

"Exactly."

"Where were the postcard and the bank statement?"

"To the right of the window."

Robbie Corbijn nodded. He stepped outside and looked around, taking in the bare branches of the trees that encircled the clearing.

"Those trees must have had at least some of their leaves on the day Albert Meijer killed himself."

"Correct," said the policeman, "even after the storm at the end of October. Most of the leaves fell around the middle of November."

"So the scene doesn't look now the way it looked at the time. I'd like to know what's beneath that blanket of leaves. I have a hunch it might be important."

The officer offered to fetch a leaf blower from the neighbor's house. He was only gone for five minutes. Robbie began to blast the leaves out of the clearing. Thousands of them, plus the occasional snow-white feather, flew back into the trees, and the ground beneath them came slowly into view. It was indeed a revelation. It appeared that a herd of wild boars had made themselves at home here. The ground around the shed, once carpeted with grass, had been thoroughly ravished. Thick clumps of sod were strewn here and there. Amongst the acorns and beech nuts lay dozens of red shotgun shells, all empty.

But if Robbie had hoped to find footprints, he was disappointed. The hard winter storms had blown all such traces away. The only prints to be seen were those of the investigators who had responded to the elderly neighbor lady's call. Robbie sat on the broad stump of an oak and gazed thoughtfully at the clearing and the shed. He took some pictures with his smart phone, then got to his feet.

"I've seen enough."

We thanked the officer for showing us the scene and took our leave. Robbie drove us to a café in the village for lunch. He seemed to have lost interest in the case, which did indeed seem to be open-and-shut. As we waited for our food, he paged attentively through a couple of newspapers left behind on the bar. After ten minutes, he pushed them away, bored, and fished his phone from his jacket pocket.

"So it *was* suicide," I remarked.

Robbie's fingers flew across the little screen. He smiled.

"I'm afraid that policeman *does* need to find a new line of work," he said.

"Are you serious? Was it murder, after all?"

Our server brought us sandwiches and coffee. When she had laid out our lunch and disappeared back into the kitchen, Robbie set down his phone and turned his attention to me.

"I'm fairly certain it wasn't suicide. Now I need to collect the evidence." He picked up his phone again. "While you eat your sandwich, I'll tie up the last loose ends."

"You're bluffing!"

Robbie merely smiled.

"Who did it, then? The widow?"

"No."

"Then *who?*"

"I have no idea." He grinned. "I think it must have been someone Albert Meijer didn't know, or at least not well. But with a little luck I'll be able to identify our mystery man within the next few minutes. Don't feel badly that you haven't figured it out; I attribute that to your lack of experience."

"But how," I demanded, frustrated, "could it be anything *other* than suicide? I saw everything you saw. The door was barred on the inside, and the window couldn't have been opened. It's the simplest case imaginable!"

"Ah, yes, the conclusive barring of the door. That's the key to this masterpiece. The criminal was extraordinarily clever. Had the door not been barred, then *anyone* could have entered or left the shed, but the door *was* barred, and how could that possibly be explained? Consider that the brackets that held the bar in place were recently installed—I find that most significant. Why would Albert Meijer have done such a thing, when no one visited the shed except for his wife, who had been on the French Riviera for months?"

"Because he was an unusual man, we know that!"

Robbie shook his head. "I believe it was the murderer who installed the bar. With the bar in place, the logical conclusion was suicide, but without it the possibility of murder would remain on the table. We know that *someone* was there during the first week of November, based on the neighbor's testimony. She heard the chain saw on November 5 and on each of the next several days. And yet it's noteworthy that Meijer failed to empty his mailbox. And he didn't do any shopping: he was almost out of milk, and on November 5 the milk remaining in his refrigerator was two days past its expiry date."

"What are you trying to suggest?"

"You should be able to figure it out, Lowina."

"You mean," I said skeptically, "that the neighbor lady heard someone *else* sawing firewood?"

Robbie Corbijn nodded enthusiastically.

"Do you really think," I went on, "that someone murdered

Albert Meijer, and then spent the next several days working in his yard?"

"That's exactly what I think, yes."

"But that's absurd! What killer would do such a thing?"

"Yet *this* killer did, as I'll soon demonstrate. He did it to eliminate his tracks, which required pruning some of the surrounding trees. I'll try to sketch out the circumstances for you. Once you understand what must have happened, Lowina, you'll agree that it's all quite simple. So, focus your attention! Try to see the scene before you. Think of the torn-up ground around the shed, which suggests the presence of a herd of wild boars in search of food. And yet there were acorns beneath the fallen leaves, and acorns are one of a boar's favorite snacks. No, I believe the local boars specifically *avoided* that clearing, for fear of being shot. Remember all those empty shotgun shells."

"Then what caused the damage to the ground?"

"You have no idea?"

"None."

"What about the storm in late October?"

"I don't see how—"

Robbie interrupted me. "Think back to what Cornelis Meijer told us. He only visited his father's shed once, three years ago. What did he say about the last time he saw him?"

"His father was walking up the path to the shed. He opened the door and—"

I fell silent. Robbie took a sip of his coffee.

"You see it now?" he asked, grinning.

"My God, you're right," I said, goosebumps rippling up my arms.

In my mind's eye, I saw the unpaved path stretched out before me, the view through the trees to the shed. I saw the sole window with its grimy panes, through which the policeman had made his macabre discovery.

"It's strange," I said. "The door is on the side of the shed, not in the front, facing the villa, but Meijer said he was standing at the *back* of the villa when he watched his father go in the door. His only view of the shed was up the path, and all he could have seen would have been the front. He says he watched his father go inside and pull the shed door shut, but he can't possibly have seen that from the back of the villa. Couldn't it just be a case of faulty memory, though? He *says* he remembers seeing his father pull the door closed behind him. But perhaps, after three years, he's just misremembering."

"If there weren't any other indications, I'd call that a satisfactory explanation," Robbie acknowledged. "But then there's the torn-up ground around the shed. Do you remember the trees that encircle the clearing?"

"Yes."

"What kinds of trees are they?"

"Beeches," I said. "And birches."

"And an oak?"

"No."

"And yet there were acorns on the ground. What were they doing there?"

"Now that you mention it, that's odd. There must have been an oak, after all."

"I sat on a stump and thought about it, and it took quite a while before I realized I was sitting on the answer. Quite literally, since my seat was the stump of an old oak tree! All at once, I realized what must have happened. The oak went down in the storm at the end of October, snapped off like a wooden match. It fell onto the shed and destroyed it. Some of its thicker branches must have drilled holes in the ground. When Albert Meijer began to deal with the mess, he pulled up the fallen branches, which left the grass looking as if it had been trampled by boars. He was killed while he was busy cleaning up after the storm."

"By whom?"

"By someone who built an identical shed to hide what he'd done. Cornelis Meijer is in fact a carpenter, but it wasn't him. The killer was someone who didn't know Albert Meijer, which is why he didn't know where the door and the window were supposed to be. All that was left of the shed was its concrete floor; everything else was a ruin. The second shed wasn't new—had it been, the police would have smelled a rat. So the murderer must have had access to a second shed, not a new one, the exact same size as Meijer's."

"But why would he go to all that trouble?"

Robbie shrugged. "I suggest that someone in the neighborhood must have seen him drive or walk onto Meijer's property in an angry frame of mind. Now, remember, *no one* visited Albert Meijer, so this would have been memorable. If, later, Meijer's body was found, everyone would suspect that he'd been murdered. The witness would have reported what he'd seen, and the killer would have instantly become the chief suspect in a homicide investigation. No, he had to make Meijer's death look like a suicide, to devise an ingenious ruse to camouflage the truth. First, the killer had to dispose of the remains of the fallen tree, which is why he used the chain saw—which the neighbor lady heard. He cleaned up the sawdust and the wood, probably drove it off the property late at night so no one would notice. Meanwhile, he found that card from Rosalinde and the bank statement in the villa."

Robbie cleared his throat and continued. "I spotted a garden center's advertisement in the local paper, offering build-it-yourself shed kits. You see those sheds all over this region, all of them identical in size. But those are new sheds he couldn't have used, or everyone would have seen right through his deception. What he needed was an *old* shed. So I consulted older online editions of the same paper, looking for classified ads offering items for sale." He held up his smart phone. "And here it is: someone's selling a second-hand garden shed: 'Can be taken apart for transport and reconstructed elsewhere.' The ad appeared at the end of last October. Could this be it?"

Robbie made a note. Elbows resting on the table, he returned his attention to his phone, his fingers flying across the screen.

"A week later, the ad is gone," Robbie said, glancing up. "Had the shed been sold by then? Let's dig a little deeper. Ah, here, the *next* week, here's a classified ad offering firewood for sale. Oak, it says, and here's the name and address of the seller. The same street poor Albert lived on. So this *could* be our killer."

"Explain that."

"You saw the stump of the fallen oak. That tree must have produced quite a bit of wood, but did you see it stacked up at the villa? I didn't. All I saw was a small woodpile, dark with age, left over from the previous season. No, the perpetrator had to get rid of all that oak somehow." Robbie smiled. "He could have just stacked it up behind the villa. But he was greedy and saw a way to turn a profit, and that's what's betrayed him."

Not moving from his seat, Robbie did a brief Internet search, made a few calls, and came up with some additional information. He reminded me of the snow-white feathers he'd blown back into the woods along with the autumn leaves. Nibbling at his sandwich, he began to construct a theory aloud. He sketched out a gruesomely realistic picture of a tragic confrontation between two men: Albert Meijer with his shotgun, the other figure angry at some unjust action of Meijer's. They wrestle for the weapon, and it goes off.

Not murder but an accident—yet it looked worse than it was. It was a terrible sight: a dead body, its head torn apart by buckshot. The other man, horrified by what he had done, sought desperately for a way to cover up his involvement. He came up with a plan. He found a second-hand shed for sale and bought it. He arranged Meijer's body on the concrete floor, his finger on the shotgun's trigger, and reconstructed the shed around him, everything except the roof. He closed the door from the inside, screwed the bar brackets into the wall on either side of the door, set the bar in place, climbed out over the wall—and then at last rebuilt the roof, leaving behind the appearance of a classic locked-room mystery... thus an obvious suicide.

"If we were to examine the shed more closely," Robbie said, "I think we'd be able to see that the roof was added on from the outside, not the inside. But no one stopped to think that the shed had been replaced, since there'd been exactly such a shed on that exact spot for the last five years."

By the time we were on our way back to Leiden late that afternoon, Robbie had been proven right on every point. The man responsible for Meijer's death was a pigeon fancier, a member of the local racing-pigeon club. Every day, he launched his flock of birds for an hour's flight. One day, his very best pigeon—which had won several prizes and gotten him considerable acclaim—failed to return at its usual time and in fact never did come home. Several days later, another pigeon disappeared, and this time he heard a gunshot in the distance. He set off in the direction of the sound and found his bird lying dead next to Albert Meijer's writing shed. Meijer acknowledged having shot both pigeons, whose cooing had annoyed him.

When at Robbie's suggestion the police brought him in for

questioning, the man immediately confessed his part in Meijer's death.

"It was a simple case, after all," my employer said airily, passing a slow-moving semi on the A1, "a nice break from our routine. Of course, the evidence was fresher than I'm used to."

But I saw a new Robbie beside me, noticeably changed from yesterday morning. His cheeks had their color back, and he spoke animatedly about his pile of unsolved cases. He seemed once again to believe that resolutions might be possible.

18

CHECKMATE IN CHIMBOTE
BY BOB VAN LAERHOVEN

1

A man and a woman can be evil by nature yet still believe in a love suffused with trust and chivalry.

It works out that way more often than you'd think.

It's a law of nature that villainy longs for purity.

2

Marina, *mi corazón*, what should I do?

Wait for you, or run for Chile?

Trust in the love you promised me, or decide that you were only using me?

Has this become a chess game between us, Marina? And, if it has, whose move is it?

I've registered at the El Presidente Hotel in Chimbote.

Not at La Canción, as we agreed.

This is what they call waiting to see which way the wind blows.

Fate will decide whether or not you'll find me in this paradise for cockroaches on the Peruvian coast.

I had a good reason for not checking into the hotel we agreed on: after the long drive across the desert from Lima, I pulled into Chimbote exhausted, and what the hell did I see parked in front of La Canción's entrance?

Two police cars, their side panels gray with desert sand, their windshields filthy.

Coincidence?

Those cars had come a long way, same as me.

I peered through the hotel's plate-glass window.

Two uniformed cops stood at the reception desk. They were talking with the desk clerk. They looked like twins in their matching reflective sunglasses.

I continued up the street. You don't know this yet, Marina, but with my beard gone and my hair trimmed short, I look quite different. More Indian, like my dad.

My altered appearance has one disadvantage: I no longer resemble the photo in my Belgian passport. That could cause problems when it comes time to cross the border into Chile.

It's not easy being a jewel thief, eh, Marina?

You've got so much to watch out for.

3

As I walked through the dusty streets of Chimbote, I knew I had to watch out for Fernandez and Luis, who might have followed me from Lima or had me followed.

I focused my gaze straight ahead, though, like a man on a mission.

A *turista* would attract too much attention. The local *granujas callejeros* would ambush an innocent abroad and clean him out before he could cry for help.

So watch out, Willi.

Not to mention the possibility that every truck driver I'd seen in my rearview mirror all the way from Lima to Chimbote might have been one of Fernandez and Luis' henchmen.

That's why I stopped at one of the roadside cafés, where the drivers take a time out for a quick line of coke to keep themselves awake, and trimmed my hair and cut off my beard. I abandoned my rental car there and thumbed a ride the rest of the way.

It would be ironic if the taciturn trucker who brought me to Chimbote was himself an accomplice of Fernandez and Luis, but I calculated that as less of a risk than sticking with my rental.

Anyway, I did what I could, and here I am, roaming the streets of Chimbote, thinking and thinking and thinking....

High above the fisherman's smokehouses, ospreys and vultures dance across the sky.

I make a decision: tomorrow I'll hang unobtrusively around La Canción and watch for you. Meanwhile, I'll book a flight that'll take us to the border.

Us, or just me.

That all depends on you, Marina.

Am I just another pawn in this game we're playing—or am I indeed your king?

4

The El Presidente is close to the fish-meal factories.

At night, the red glow from the factories illuminates the desert behind the town. The sight reminds me of the Gates of Hell as my father described them to me when I was a boy. Sailors love telling tall tales, and my dad was no exception.

The man could lie so convincingly that he believed his own stories. He was a Quechua Indian from Chile, and Indians don't believe in reality. To them, the world is a misty forest concealing many secret chambers.

In 1973, when I was twelve, my father said he was going to spend six months working for his brother, who owned a tin mine in Chile. He would be a rich man when he returned to Belgium.

My last image of him: the hull of a ship as tall as a church spire, dad high above me, looking no bigger than an ant, leaning against the railing, waving at us. My right hand clasped tightly in the hand of my silent mother, who did not wave back.

Because it was thirty years ago, I can't remember his face. But I remember his voice: I still hear it when I'm in my cups.

Memories are little slivers of the soul: that photo he showed me shortly before he left for Chile is still a part of me. Dad was sitting at the kitchen table in our gloomy flat in Antwerp. I perched beside him, doing my math homework. He was looking for something in his wallet, and a picture slipped out and fell to the ground. Happy to help him, I snapped it up. The faded sepia print showed a woman with a small face and expressive eyes. In my youthful imagination, she looked like a statue of an Indian goddess. Her fine features seemed carved out of yellow ivory. She wasn't smiling, yet she didn't seem somber, either.

Dad snatched the photo from my hands. I asked who the lady was. He looked down at her and gently rubbed his thumb across her face before he returned the bit of old paper to his wallet.

"Who is it, pa?" I insisted.

"*Mi hermana*, son, my sister. Now make sure you get those

numbers right, so you don't wind up a dockworker like your old man."

A Quechua's lies can become other people's lives.

That's why my father lived on in the stories told by my mother, who was born in Brussels but wound up in Antwerp during the Second World War. Even after he'd abandoned her, he remained her favorite redskin. During the war, he too had found himself transplanted to Antwerp, when his captain—afraid of the threat of an attack by German U-boats—had given up trying to deliver a shipload of cargo to Norway.

When I was sixteen, my mother finally told me, her eyes averted, that there was no uncle with a tin mine in Chile and never had been. Before my father wound up in Antwerp, he was already married back in South America, and he'd deserted us to go back to his first wife, the bastard.

That was the first time I ever heard her use that kind of language.

She soon relented, though, and my father resumed his previous role in her stories: a charming man, a wonderful dancer.

He could never sleep with the windows closed, she sighed. It was sad that he'd died at such an early age.

5

I can't sleep with the windows closed, either.

That's why, last night, the fish smell soaked into my skin. When I looked at myself in the mirror this morning, I had the eyes of a dead swordfish.

Even a dead swordfish, my father once told me, looks invincible.

Will today be the day you get here, Marina? It's a twelve-hour drive over pitted desert roads—not to mention the sandstorms, and the trucks that rocket toward you and swerve out of your path at the last second, like drugged mastodons.

The drivers smoke native herbs and wear the expressions of invincible swordfish. I've been feeling that way myself since I pulled off my robbery back in Lima.

Only you have the power to defeat me, Marina.

I really *have* to leave for Chile today—but I can't, even though I don't trust you.

The loot is safely hidden, yet my heart pounds so loudly it feels like it's about to burst free of my body. I hear its echo all around me: *I need you, need you, you....*

That's what my memories of your face do to me, your face carved from yellow ivory.

6

Today I bought a straw hat to protect me from the sun. The long hours I spent outside La Canción yesterday, watching the reception desk through the plate-glass window, boiled me like an egg.

I got drunk on sunshine.

The door to La Canción is a portal to a whole other world. If I step through that portal, I'll stick out like a sore thumb. Outside in the street, though, I blend right in. I've taken on the listless appearance of the citizens of Chimbote. They walk as if they haven't yet regained their land legs after a long sea voyage.

If you don't arrive today, Marina, I'm off.

I worry about you.

Would Fernandez and Luis actually hurt you, as they threatened?

I don't know. But despite my mistrust, I still long for you.

My fear grows by the hour. By now, it's almost as massive as my love—which cartwheels across the sky like the ospreys, like the vultures.

7

I lie in my rancid hotel bed, sweating.

The windows are open, the curtains closed.

My chessboard lies beside me, the pieces scattered.

Outside, the colors leapfrog against the clouds, far above the weathered buildings blackened by industrial pollutants.

The smell of fish makes me sleepy.

You didn't turn up today.

My thoughts are shriveled by sun and booze.

If you're not here by noon tomorrow, then it's my move.

Today I had a local photographer take some new passport pictures. He had an old-style flash, and the photos turned out grayish, which is exactly what I wanted.

I replaced the picture on my press pass. That took a steady hand. Of course, a sound technician's hands are well trained—even a sound technician who's been drinking more than he should.

If anyone at the Chilean border says anything about the photo in my passport, I will humbly acknowledge that it needs to be updated, but *señor,* look, here's my Belgian press pass, too, and *that* picture looks just like me, doesn't it?

My boom microphone and sound equipment will placate the immigration authorities. I'm obviously a television sound tech, sent by the Belgian VRT network first to Peru and then to Chile on assignment. My Chilean accent—my father's legacy—will further convince them.

These last days, my father seems to have blossomed within me, as if my meeting Marina awakened him from his long sleep in the prison of my soul. Only here and now have I remembered how he used to call me his "Inca boy," so proud he was of his ancestors.

I left my Belgian half behind in the salsa tents of Antwerp, where today immigrants from South America whisper amongst themselves, "Willi never said no to a mojito, in fact he never said much of anything to anyone, but, *ay*, could that man dance! Pity he was such a *perdido*; by now he's probably drunk himself to death."

Back in Lima, the rest of the crew must be frantically calling the VRT to report my disappearance.

I'll make the evening news: "In the chaotic capital city of Peru, where human life is cheap, the sound man for a VRT camera crew has gone missing."

Or will someone already have connected the dots and recognized that my absence must have something to do with the theft of the diamonds?

That would explain those two police cars—but how could they have known to look for me in Chimbote, unless you, *mi corazón*, have betrayed me?

I can't wait any longer.

If only I knew which piece you are, Marina, my white queen or the black one....

8

When a man is in love, he begins to dream of heroic deeds.

Not that that's easy in the El Presidente.

In the room next door, the same dance number has been playing for hours:

La puta que yo conozco
No es de la China ni del Japon
Porque la puta viene del Ponce
Viene del barrio de San Anton.

Are you *una puta*, Marina, nothing but a common whore like Fernandez and Luis said? That would make me the village idiot, a fool who'll promise you whatever your heart desires.

A sound engineer lives in the space between his headphones and the voices of other people. His ear is sensitive to the inner static we all have to endure.

A heart that hears voices is easy to steal.

I was like my microphone: I received but could not send.

You were the sender, Marina.

The first time I saw you, in the kitchen of Eduardo Barbosa and Silvia Stern's estate, it was as if even your shadow radiated a dazzling heat.

You looked eerily like that photo of my father's "sister," which for reasons only the subconscious knows is etched so sharply in my memory.

I'd been drinking, so I was probably radiating my own heat. The other members of the crew had no idea. Over the years, I've learned to keep my alcoholism hidden. Even badly hung over, I can still get the job done.

Evelien, our archaeologist, was busy tagging the best items in the Barbosa family's legendary art and precious-stone collection, famed as one of the most valuable in South America.

You'd been working in their kitchen for three years. You'd grown accustomed to the top-of-the-line cars, the swimming pools, the private guards, the security cameras, the Dobermans. And you knew everything there was to know about the room in which the gems were displayed under watchful electronic eyes.

Eduardo Barbosa, in his sixties and easy to look at, had granted the VRT permission to film on the premises for five days. The Peruvian arms dealer had extended every courtesy to the Belgian television crew, proud as he was of his collection of art and diamonds.

From that very first moment, Marina, you were like a loaded revolver pressed tight against my temple.

As we chatted, your energy was a flash point aimed straight at my heart. You asked about my Chilean accent, and in fifteen minutes I told you the story of my life.

Except for the booze. I held that back.

You asked me to explain the purpose of the cultural documentary we were making. Now, looking back, I think you already knew that the alarms would be turned off while our crew was preparing to film.

That was necessary: to set up the interviews with Eduardo Barbosa, we had to measure the lighting and the ambient sound. If the alarms were constantly going off, taking those measurements would be impossible.

Maybe you already had an end game in mind when, that second day, you offered to show me around Lima after hours.

We agreed to meet in the lobby of my hotel.

I was excited, I admit.

Accustomed to long years of loneliness, though, I knew better than to take anything for granted.

And yet I wasn't surprised when, before long, you led me into a little place where rooms could be rented by the hour.

The next morning, I turned up late for the crew's communal breakfast. Bart, the cameraman I played chess with in our free time, asked with a wink, "You lay awake all night trying to figure out how to counter my Fianchetto, Willi?"

I smiled. "My queen's stronger than your castles."

A queen—that's what you'd become to me, after only a single night.

9

Lust drives caution out of a man's thoughts.

Now I ask myself if the look in your eyes, a look I interpreted as passionate, might have been something else altogether.

A man is easily satisfied—even more easily if he's a secret drunk. The same little place, the same room, the same smells, gestures, sighs... the same noose that lust drapes around a man's neck.

You were murmuring "*mi amor*" when the door flew open, and those two apes stormed into the room. They held their knives to my face, introduced themselves as Fernandez and Luis, and demanded through gnashing teeth to know what the hell I was doing with their sister.

They didn't waste much time before they told me where this tragicomedy was leading: either I could buy them off, or they'd beat the shit out of me.

Curled up beneath a sweaty sheet, you begged them to leave me alone.

"*Puta!*" they screamed, shoving you aside.

There was no way I could get my hands on the amount of money they demanded, I said.

They would give me until morning, they told me. And if I ran, you, Marina, would pay the price of my cowardice. Your honor was destroyed. You were less than *un perro*. And you would die like a worthless dog if I didn't come up with the cash.

They left, dragging you with them and slamming the door behind them.

When I left the hotel, fifteen minutes later—after guzzling the contents of my hip flask—you were waiting for me.

Your brothers, you said, had gone off to celebrate their impending windfall. And in fear for your life, you'd slipped away and come back to find me.

You had a plan that would get us all the money we needed—enough to pay off Fernandez and Luis and enough more than that to give us a fresh start together.

You pressed up against me in the middle of the street and held me as if you were afraid the wind would carry me away.

You told me your plan.

I was floating overhead on a cloud of rum, and down below I could see myself in the street with you, a beautiful woman, your arms around me while, around us both, a world that had never given me a chance slowly circled.

"You didn't need to bring your brothers into it," I said. "You could have just asked me. The only thing I would have asked for in return is the illusion that you love me."

You hid your surprise behind a flurry of kisses.

10

Drunkards are usually passive, but sometimes they can be galvanized into action, usually by fear.

Like me, today.

It's time to go.

You promised me you'd come to Chimbote as soon as the police were clear that you had nothing to do with the robbery. You'd tell your brothers that I was waiting for you at a hiding place in Lima. You'd pretend to be dismayed when it turned out I wasn't there. That *granuja* of a *gringo*! First the bastard stole my honor, and now he's taken off with the diamonds.

We picked Chimbote because nobody who'd committed a robbery in Lima would be stupid enough to come here. He'd go to ground in a crowded city and get rid of the loot via the Germans, the world's best fences.

But I know a guy in Santiago de Chile. He's old, but he knows Santiago's underworld. He can help me to buy and sell—buy false passports and sell the diamonds.

If I'd had a liter of common sense, I would have gotten on a plane and left Chimbote the same day I arrived.

A drunk's common sense, however, rarely amounts to an entire liter. And a man in love has even less.

But there *are* limits. I can't wait any longer.

The two diamonds—with a combined value of, say, half a million dollars—are sitting right where I stashed them, in the little compartment in my boom which usually holds my spare batteries. I wrapped them in cotton wool so that, even if someone were to shake the boom, they wouldn't make a sound.

A clever customs agent might unscrew the microphone's grill to make sure I hadn't hidden anything inside, but the boom is so reassuringly sturdy it would take heavenly intervention for anyone to think to check it for hiding places.

I'll need a drink before I get to Chilean customs.

Alcohol calms me down.

In fact, I could use a drink right *now*.

I hoist my bottle and take a deep swallow. The rum goes down smoothly and does its job.

As I turn away from the makeshift bar I've set up on the hotel dresser, my gaze falls on the chessboard on the night table beside the bed.

The pieces dance blurrily before my eyes.

I want to watch *us* dance, Marina, you and me, but which pieces should I be looking at? The white king and queen? Or the black queen and the white pawn?

If only I knew.

I I

I knew no fear when I picked the diamonds from their display case in the vinegary sunlight that filtered through the room's silken curtains.

It was a perfect moment.

The alarm system stayed off during the down time between takes. You made the rounds of the crew with a tray of cold drinks. Our director played back a couple of shots on the monitor, and Eduardo and Silvia watched them with interest. On shooting days, we were all just one big happy family.

I said I heard nature calling and faked a visit to the bathroom, slipped instead into the jewel room and stashed two diamonds in the pocket of my jeans. There were electric locks on the display cases—but they were coupled to the alarm system and so also turned off.

Twenty minutes later, as we were ready to leave for the day and I watched our host press the buttons to switch the alarms and locks back on, I felt a shiver run up my spine. I'd been asking myself if there might be some pressure-sensitive mechanism in the system that would be able to tell that there were now two fewer diamonds in one of the cases.

Apparently not. I'd guessed that there wasn't such a safeguard in place—even the big museums in the US haven't gone that far yet —but I was still cringing when we got into our cars.

It seemed to take hours to drive from the house to the high walls—topped with broken glass and dotted with security cameras every ten meters—that surround the estate.

I fully expected to see a Jeep filled with armed guards come roaring after us. I sat there with my butt cheeks tightly clenched while the gate guard exchanged friendly quips with our driver. Finally, he swung the gate wide and we rolled out of the "country club," as the common man in Lima scornfully calls the city's wealthy neighborhoods, because of all the golf courses.

The mood in the car was exuberant. We'd gotten some terrific footage. But the sweat on my back didn't dry until we reached the hotel.

My bags were packed and ready. My rental car was gassed up and waiting for me in the hotel lot.

Within twenty minutes of our arrival, I was off again, this time alone.

I was heading for the impossible ninth rank, I thought, beyond what everyone else considers the far edge of the board.

12

It's time for me to slip away to Chimbote's little airstrip.

I can't wait any longer.

Soon now, I'll be able to afford women more beautiful than you, Marina.

I'll be able to buy my freedom from my addiction to you.

Silk sheets, instead of the yellow-stained mattress in our little Lima hotel.

I'm standing by the window, lost in thought, when there's a knock at the door.

I could gaze out this window forever: the rising sun paints the desert beyond the outskirts of the town with a blood-red glow.

The desert lies there like the end of the world. One step too far, and I'll fall off the edge.

I take that step.

And once you've taken the first step, the second one is automatic.

Just like, once you've downed that first shot, the second one is inevitable.

Just like, now and then, if I've had a few too many—like now—I hear the voice of my father's ghost, his words a prophecy I have to fulfill.

That's Marina at the door, my Inca boy, the voice says. *She is the love of your life, the woman you've always dreamed of.*

My father was such a liar.

"Just a minute," I call.

I reach for my boom.

I carry it into the bathroom, peer through the window at the hotel's parking lot and see what's there to be seen.

Checkmate.

For a long time, I watch myself in the cracked mirror above the sink.

Then I take our diamonds out of hiding and make my final move.

13

When I open the door, you force a laugh, Marina, but you recover quickly. You glow with happiness and press yourself against me.

I take you in my arms and say I knew you'd find me.

Your body is warm and cold at the same time. You press your lips to my neck, and I shiver.

Still shivering, I follow you down the stairs with my suitcases.

You talk a mile a minute, your voice echoing off the peeling walls. You paint our future as a cascade of cruise-ship sunsets.

You arrived in a dilapidated VW Beetle that's parked facing us. The trunk up front is open—as if the car is a desert animal, mouth wide, hungrily awaiting us.

I toss in my luggage and slam the trunk shut.

And then I see the face of the man behind the wheel.

And the knife Fernandez balances casually in his hands. The sun dances on the blade, a riot of pastel colors that melt into a yellowish hue.

"*Gringo*," Luis says from behind me. "Screwing my sister was not the stupidest thing you've ever done. Coming here, with a desert full of consequences all around you—now *that* was dumb."

I'm only half listening to him. I watch Marina. Her lips move, but she stands perfectly still beside the car, as if her body has turned to stone.

I hear my father's voice: *Willi, a Quechua's lies can become other people's lives.*

14

The sunlight has faded from yellow to ocher to lilac.

Soon it will disappear altogether.

Fernandez and Luis have emptied out my suitcases, smashed my microphone and my boom to smithereens—but of course there was nothing for them to find.

Out here in the desert, where no one can hear my screams,

they have used their knives, and they'll go right on using them to the bitter end, whether I answer their questions or not.

Only my father's ghost and I know that I flushed the diamonds down the toilet back in my room when I saw that you'd won our game, Marina.

I will remain silent because, without love, a mouth loses its ability to speak.

And ghosts only share their secrets with those they love.

19

DEVIL'S ISLAND

BY MENSJE VAN KEULEN

Amsterdam has changed so much since smoking was banned from bars, restaurants, and public spaces. Walk, bike, drive, or take the tram or bus across the city, and you'll see knots of people out on the sidewalks, clouds of smoke billowing above their heads. Cold weather, heavy wind, gloomy surroundings, the blare of traffic: nothing seems to bother them, especially not when a bunch of them are clustered together. I guess misery *does* love company, after all.

I am mildly asthmatic, so not a smoker, but after Jacob—who's one of my oldest pals—was deserted by his girlfriend for a stage director, I sometimes found myself part of such a group. See, it turned out not to be such a great idea to have Jacob over to my place to unburden himself of his woes: the walls of my apartment are thin and, the later it got, the louder he wailed... not to mention what his damn chain-smoking did to my air. Going out on the town with him wasn't an ideal solution, either, because I have to get up early for my job, but I couldn't just tell the poor schmuck to deal with it, because, I mean, he was truly hurting.

The last time he turned up at my door was three days ago. I was exhausted, and I'd just fished a package of soup out of the freezer—comfort food, right?—when the bell rang, and there he was, unshaven, face pale as a ghost. When I asked him if he'd eaten, he told me food was the last thing on his mind, and I stashed my soup back where it had come from.

"Let's go," I said, pulling on a jacket and leading him outside.

"Thirst never sleeps," he muttered.

"Hey, we're not gonna spend the whole night drinking. I've woke up with enough hangovers, thanks to you."

"Pain never sleeps, either, but you're better off with an aching head than a rat gnawing at your heart."

"You'll get over it, Jake."

"You say that every time I see you, but the rat just keeps on gnawing."

I wanted to tell him that accusing me of repeating myself was a clear case of the pot calling the kettle black, but I was afraid that'd result in more screaming about how nobody understood him, and he couldn't live without Martha, and he was so lonely, and he wished he was dead—or, as we'd been through two weeks previously, him collapsing to the ground and weeping like a little baby.

"Come on, let's find something to eat," I said, steering him by the elbow. "And a beer," I added quickly, before he could begin to protest.

We turned into the Pieter Baststraat and passed a storefront that had the name of our little neighborhood lettered on its plate-glass window.

"Devil's Island," Jacob growled. "If only. I wish the Devil really existed, I'd pay him a little visit right this second. Sure, fine, go ahead and laugh. But I mean it: I'd sell him my soul if he'd make Martha come back to me." He scoped out the storefront a second time. "What *is* this place, anyway? Another barbershop? Do we really need more barbers? How often do people have to get their hair cut?"

At that, he bent his head mournfully, but before he could start in on how Martha always used to cut his hair for him, I told him he was overdue for a hearty dinner.

"Booze," he said, and then, as we passed the cigar store on the corner—a prime location, right across from Café Loetje—"booze and a smoke."

I pushed him through the door into Loetje, which has evolved over the years from a small café with billiards to a restaurant three times its original size—despite which you sometimes have to wait an hour or more for a table. They were full up that night, not even a couple of stools at the bar, but one of the servers recognized me and said it'd only be half an hour or so before we'd hit the top of the list.

A minute later, we were back on the sidewalk, each with a glass of beer, surrounded by half a dozen smokers, mostly thirtysomethings and fortysomethings who I figured for realtors or practitioners of some other well-paid profession. Two of them were women, obviously having a girls' night out. Jacob gulped his brewski, alternating swallows with deep drags on a cigarette. Across the street, the Old Catholic Church loomed, swathed in darkness.

"Got a match?" came a voice from beside me.

I turned to say I don't smoke and realized the guy was talking to Jacob, not me. He held a cigarillo between slender fingers.

"Sure," said Jacob, reaching for his lighter. It took him three or four tries to produce a flame.

"Much obliged, friend," said the man.

That *friend* seemed a little presumptuous, but Jacob smiled.

"These things taste better when lit with a wooden match," the man said, exhaling smoke in the direction of the church. "But who carries those old-fashioned lucifers around in their pocket these days, am I right? I love the smell of them, though, that momentary blast of sulfur. Would you care to try one of mine?"

"Thanks," said Jacob, and he lit the proffered cigarillo with the stub of his cigarette.

I hadn't heard a polite word out of Jacob in quite some time—and spoken to a stranger, no less. I took a closer look at the man. He was not unattractive, with slick black hair combed back and reaching just below the collar of his obviously expensive jacket. All things considered, I would call him a rah-tha elegant fellow.

"May I pose a question?" The stranger's gaze flicked from Jacob to me to the other smokers. "Did any of you happen to know a gentleman who lived in this neighborhood, a certain Van der Meer?"

"Van der Meer," said a smoker, who had overconfidently left his jacket inside. "You mean the professor?"

"Indeed, I do."

"Don't waste your time looking for him: he's dead."

The man nodded. "A heart attack, I know. Does his widow ever patronize this establishment?"

"Yolande?" said one of the women. "No, I haven't seen her since he passed. Tell you the truth, when they used to eat here, I always looked the other way, and not just because he ordered his steak so rare the blood dripped over his chin."

"Gross," said her girlfriend.

"I took a class from him once, and he was what you call a real skirt chaser, totally annoying. I think *she* was one of his students, she was at least twenty years younger than him, maybe thirty."

The man nodded again, and this time blew a perfect smoke ring that drifted lazily skyward.

"When he was out here smoking," the woman went on, "I made sure to keep my distance. But I think he finally quit. The last times I saw them here, he stayed inside. I'll tell you, he seemed crankier about it on each occasion."

"They lived in a big house up the street, right where the Museum District begins," said one of the men, grinding out a cigarette with his shoe. "It came on the market three days ago, and somebody bought it without even looking inside. No surprise, really: this neighborhood's red hot."

Two names were called, and most of the smokers took one last puff, stubbed out their cigarettes in the standing ashtray, and headed into Loetje.

The few who remained moved closer to the door and went on talking, which left Jacob and me alone with the stranger.

"I bought that house," he said calmly. "I've been looking for a suitable home in the city for some time. I don't care for hotels. I'd much rather have a place of my own."

"Jeez," said Jacob, and I thought I heard a note of admiration in his voice.

"You bought a house without checking out the inside?" I said. "That seems a little risky."

"Oh, I know the place well. I paid a call there not long ago. It's quite lovely, and there's a marvelous art collection on the walls."

"I assume the art doesn't go with the property. Or are you some kind of dealer or collector?"

"Both," he said with a smile. "Which is why I spend so much time traveling. When I finish my business here, I'll return to my country house outside Seville. I may stop off in Paris, I have a little *pied-à-terre* on the Place Vendôme."

He exhaled a plume of smoke that came straight at me and sent me into a fit of coughing.

"Please forgive my filthy habit," he said. "I forget that others might not appreciate the bouquet of fine tobacco as much as I do. Van der Meer ultimately had a problem with it, too, which is why he had to give up smoking. Of course, that wasn't his only problem."

"You mean his wife?" asked Jacob. "Was she unfaithful to him? Did she drive him crazy?"

"In a way. She was, as you heard a few moments ago, quite a bit younger than he. At first, that was precisely what attracted Van der Meer to her, but their situation changed as he got older, and for the last few years it had all become—how shall I say it?—rather disastrous."

"What do you mean, 'their situation changed'?" asked Jacob. "She didn't stop being younger than him."

"Yes, but that was the point, you see. He began to blame her for making him feel like an old man."

"Sounds like she's better off without him."

"Well, I wouldn't say better off."

The man grinned, and—unlike Jacob, who had unbuttoned his jacket—I suddenly felt a chill.

"Explain that," I said.

"Yeah, you got *my* attention," said Jacob.

"Very well." The stranger flicked the stub of his cigarillo over a bike rack and into the darkness. "I was having a coffee in a café, and coincidentally she was sitting alone at the next table. She accidentally spilled her drink, I handed her a napkin, and—I don't know why, but I seem to attract people with a need to get things off their chests. Or perhaps *I'm* attracted to *them*. In any case, she told me her story. The bottom line was that her husband was a sadist who was making her life hell. There was no way he would agree to a divorce, and she couldn't possibly leave him, because she had nowhere else to go and she couldn't support herself on her own income. She was a French tutor, and not many children seem to select that language these days. How, she asked me, could she ever get free of him? Well, a nasty old man with a weak heart, the world certainly wouldn't be any worse off without him."

"Are you saying you offered to *murder* him?" asked Jacob eagerly.

"That's a strong word, friend. I wouldn't call it 'murder' to send a man on his way without ever laying a finger on him. I asked her about his weaknesses, and she mentioned something I thought I could use."

"And that was?"

"Religion." The man took a fresh cigarillo from his inside pocket and waved it at the church. "Van der Meer was a devout atheist who seethed at the sight or sound of anything remotely pious. I devised what seemed to me an appropriate plan, and I presented it to her. Might I trouble you again for a light, friend? And here, have another yourself."

The man laid a hand on Jacob's wrist. Neither of them paid me the slightest attention.

"That very evening, I appeared at their door. She admitted me, as prearranged. That infuriated Van der Meer, the idea that she would permit a stranger to invade his sanctum. I informed him, quite humbly, that I was there to return a book. 'A book?' he said. 'I never loan out my books.' 'I didn't borrow it,' I said, 'I found it lying beside your trash can.' I extended it to him, and he cried out in horror, 'A Bible? What makes you think that belongs to me? I've never owned a Bible in my life!' 'That's very strange,' said I, 'for your name is inscribed in it.' His face turned bright red, and he shrieked, 'Take it away! Remove that wretched volume from my sight!' I said, 'The seven plagues of Egypt will afflict you, brother, if you insult God's word in such a detestable manner.' He cursed at me and screamed, 'Get out, you vile liar! Get out!' I stood before him, opened the book, and showed him his name.

And that was the *coup de grace*. His eyes rolled up in their sockets, he shook uncontrollably and collapsed to the ground, stone dead. But let me tell you what happened next. His widow began to dance. She was now a wealthy woman, she exulted. She would sell the house, it would surely bring at least two million euros, she would travel to sunny climes, indulge herself in cruises, I can't remember the full shopping list. I began to feel pity for the corpse. After this tasteless exhibition, she telephoned for an ambulance, her voice atremble, and—without so much as a thank you—showed me the door."

"Women," sighed Jacob. "Such heartless creatures."

"You are exactly right, friend. We must beware their treachery. Well, I offered two point three million for the house, and the paperwork awaits completion. The professor left behind no power of attorney, so the widow Van der Meer is required to make an appearance at the signing. And that will be difficult."

"Is she already gone?"

"Not quite. Her ... departure still needs to be attended to. I would value some assistance, and if you're inclined to volunteer, I will reward you more than generously. You seem to be a man with a gray future before him, yourself in some need of assistance. Am I correct, friend?"

"Gray?" said Jacob. "My future's black, ebony. What can I do to help you?"

"This neighborhood is crowded with tourists, no one will notice two gentlemen strolling leisurely toward the Hobbemakade with a wheeled trunk. The canal there is surely sufficiently deep, and there are brief gaps in the traffic when the lights at the crossings turn red. She weighs sixty kilograms at most, and is perhaps a meter and seventy-five centimeters in height—or should I say that she *was* a meter seventy-five? I believe she must have been a jogger, since her long legs—once so alluring to Van der Meer's goatish eyes—were too tightly muscled for an ordinary steak knife."

"Jacob," I said, filled with revulsion, "don't listen to any more of this bullshit. Let's go inside, I'm cold."

"With the exception of a few soft spots, the rest is comprised of rather lean, tough meat. That particular part of the process is as yet incomplete, and I could certainly use your help there as well, my friend. It would be best, I think, to wait until the blood has fully coagulated. Van der Meer may well have decorated his home with the finest available artwork, but he doesn't seem to have paid much attention to the outfitting of his bathrooms. There are a number of broken tiles in the floor, and those will have to be thoroughly scrubbed."

"Jacob, seriously, don't listen to this lunatic!"

"If we can't fit all of her into the trunk, there's also a wheeled carry-on bag we can use."

My name was called and, almost gagging, I said, "Please, Jacob, let's go in."

He didn't react, his eyes and ears riveted on the stranger, who whispered, barely audibly, "It's a nice little piece, the fabric is Scottish tartan, so even if there *is* any blood, it won't show."

"Jacob, for God's sake!"

"Yeah, I, ah, I'll be right in," he murmured distractedly.

They seated me at a little table by the window. I peered over the top of my menu and saw them standing there outside, their heads close together. When a server came to take my order, I told her I was waiting for someone. She asked if I wanted a drink, and I said I'd have a glass of the house white.

When I turned my attention back to the window, they were gone. I have to admit that it was cowardice that kept me in my chair. I couldn't eat a thing, just sat there pouring glass after glass of wine down my throat. The place emptied out, the chairs were turned upside down and perched on the tables, and I just sat there with no idea what to do.

I tried repeatedly to reach Jacob over the next couple of days, but his phone went straight to voicemail, and at night his apartment windows were dark. I kept asking myself what could have happened to him and was plagued by the most gruesome images. I even walked along the Hobbemakade a couple of times, searching for something floating in the water.

So you can understand how relieved I was earlier this evening when I walked into Café Wildschut—one of my regular after-work hangouts—and spotted Jacob sitting in one of the shadowy corners in the back room. And you can understand how surprised I was to see him in the company of a woman—and not just *any* woman, no, but the one and only Martha. They looked so lovey-dovey I decided not to disturb them, and I hesitated for a second, debating whether it would be the better part of valor to take a seat at the bar or just leave the place altogether.

At that moment, Jacob glanced up and saw me and waved. Smiling broadly, the two of them stood and approached me. Martha handed Jacob her glass of wine so she could wrap me in an exuberant hug. I smelled expensive perfume and saw over her shoulder that Jacob's hair was freshly cut, and he was wearing a sharp new suit that had to have set him back more than he could possibly have afforded on his salary.

"How nice to run into you both," I managed.

"Back atcha," said Jacob. "We're gonna go out and grab a smoke. Come with, and we'll tell you about our plans."

A few seconds later, we were ranged around one of the high-tops on the terrace.

Martha squeezed my arm and said, "We're leaving tomorrow."

"Leaving?" I glanced at Jacob, who avoided my eyes. "I was afraid you were already gone."

He grinned and shook two cigarettes out of a pack. "We got fantastic job offers."

"What do you mean?"

"I mean what I say, my friend. Our worries are over. A new life awaits us."

"You'll come and visit us," said Martha.

"Absolutely," said Jacob. "Who knows, maybe there's a golden opportunity for *you* in the south of Spain, too, and you can quit your stupid job."

He put the cigarettes between his lips and struck an old-fashioned wooden lucifer. The stink of sulfur burned my eyes, and he blew a cloud of smoke right in my face. I made my excuses with a gesture and hurried home, half-choking.

And as I lie here in the dark, unable to sleep, I realize that my gesture was also a wave of goodbye, because I'm afraid—no, I'm quite certain—that I'll never see either of them again.

A LONG-CHERISHED DREAM
BY CARLA VERMAAT

The garden was a long-cherished dream. Although it wasn't as spacious as Nico had hoped, it was far better than the plastic window boxes on their last apartment's shabby balcony.

They'd argued about it for quite a while before reaching a compromise. Emma had wanted a big patio with a cozy table and chairs and lounges, but his idea was to divide the entire yard into rectangular flowerbeds separated by narrow strips of tile. In his imagination, he'd already planted the blood-red roses Emma loved and lavender bushes along the edges of the yard, so she could make sachets for their bureau drawers and to give as gifts to their friends and family. And of course plenty of cut flowers to decorate their living room for the admiration of visitors.

The complexities of moving and settling in had forced him to delay starting work on the garden, but as soon as everything indoors was arranged to Emma's satisfaction, he had tiled the area just outside the patio doors, and they'd picked out garden furniture of a rich green plastic with bright yellow sunflowers on the cushions.

After that, he'd finally been able to attack the hard ground with his spade, turning it over with enthusiasm and energy. And then at last he'd begun to bring his dream to life—until his shovel's blade unexpectedly struck something hard, something buried several inches beneath the surface.

Now he stood deathly still at the edge of the terrace, his heart heavy with anxiety. Unable to even imagine the consequences of his discovery, he just stood there shaking his head. His dream, cherished for so long, flickered like a silent film on the screen of his mind. With a certainty as stifling as a fist clamped around his throat, he knew that his dream would never become a reality. Even if he were able to finish laying out his tiled pathways and planting his flowerbeds, he wouldn't be able to enjoy them. Not now, now that he'd recognized that shape in the dirt.

With Emma only a few meters away, preparing their afternoon tea in the kitchen, he felt a sense of urgency. He took a deep breath and leaned heavily on his spade handle. He noticed that his thoughts had slowed, that he was having trouble weighing the few alternatives open to him. His head seemed wreathed in the same troubling fog that limited his ability to see clearly. His knees were weak, trembling, and he worried he might keel over at any moment.

Nothing would ever be the same again. Nothing. Never again.

The teakettle's whistle and the clatter of china brought him back to reality. At any moment, Emma would announce that their tea was ready. Then they would take their seats on the new garden furniture in the sun. She would start in on the latest neighborhood gossip, pouring out a stream of words that were so uninteresting they would flutter away into nothingness as he sat there over-whelmed by the dark thoughts that consumed him. She would notice that something was bothering him. Once he assured her that everything was fine, though, she wouldn't press him. That wasn't Emma's way. This was one of the rare occasions when he regretted her characteristic willingness to take him at his word.

Somehow, he managed to bring his emotions under control. He turned toward the kitchen, unaware that his fingers had left streaks of dirt on his face.

"I just don't understand what's wrong with Nick," Emma said into the telephone, her voice low.

Nico stood behind the half-opened door, listening, his mouth drawn. Why couldn't she just leave it alone? Since the day he'd made his awful discovery in the garden and been forced to drastically change his plans, Emma had suspected that something was up. And now she wouldn't give him a moment's peace.

"No, no, he's not sick, that's not what I mean."

He tried to figure out who she was talking to. Probably Lies, her best girlfriend. The two of them spoke for at least an hour every day, and when there was shopping that needed to be done, she'd rather go with Lies than with him.

"You don't think it's weird that, after all those months of planning, evening after evening sitting there calculating which flowers and plants and bushes and shrubs to put where, now he's suddenly let it all drop, just like that?"

He shook his head in annoyance. Without realizing it, she was rubbing salt in his wounds. She didn't know, couldn't imagine—let alone understand—what was happening inside him. He barely understood it himself. Except that he simply found it unacceptable to have policemen and reporters crawling all over his property. He could see the headlines: *Local man finds human skull in garden.* Forever after, he'd be remembered as the guy who'd spent most of his life in a cramped flat, working in a boring stationery whole-saler's office, who'd retired to a lovely ground-floor apartment with a beautiful garden... full of human remains. No, he couldn't handle that, it would turn his dreams to dust.

"Well, sure, Lies, of course I'm happy about it, since I wind up with a bigger patio than I thought I was going to get, but still, it's just all so *strange*."

He couldn't listen to any more of it. He slammed the door and stormed outside.

"That was Lies," she told him later. "I told her you'd changed your plans for the garden." She paused. "I still don't understand why you've suddenly lost interest in it, Nick."

"I don't know what you're talking about. I haven't lost interest. It's just that, if we leave it this way, there's so much less work to do."

He hesitated for a moment, then gathered his resolve and told her that he wanted to know who'd lived in the apartment before them.

"Where's *that* coming from?"

"It just seems like it'd be interesting to know. Who they were, what their lives were like."

"I never thought you much cared about history, Nick."

Embarrassed, he ran a hand through his hair. "No? Well, I've got to have *something* to keep me busy, don't I? I don't want to mope around here, getting in your way. It just seems like some-thing I could *do*."

She gestured absently towards the identical block of flats on the other side of their living-room wall. "You could talk to Mrs. Colijn."

"Mrs. Colijn?"

"The old lady next door, on the second floor. She was born in that apartment, she's lived there her entire life, she must know everything there is to know about the neighborhood."

"I had no idea."

She examined him reproachfully. "I run into her at the market sometimes, and we talk, but I never thought you'd be interested." For a moment, she was silent, and then she added, sadly, "Sometimes I feel like I hardly *know* you anymore, Nic."

He nodded without looking at her. He regretted not having called for her the moment he'd seen the bleached skull staring up at him from the earth and pulled away from it in shock. If he'd only told her about it then, he wouldn't now have to face the situation alone. When he thought back to his gruesome discovery, the horror of it made him want to vomit.

At first, he'd assumed the emotions would fade away in time, the awful images in his mind would dissipate into half-forgotten memories. But that hadn't happened. He couldn't stop thinking about it, and whenever they sat together in the garden, his gaze was drawn as if magnetically to that one terrible spot in the dirt.

He couldn't imagine ever wanting to work in the garden again, but there seemed to be no way around it. Emma nagged him about it more frequently, insisting that he had to finish what he'd started. There was just that one last bed to plant—why didn't he *do* it already?

Dizzy, he jabbed his spade into the ground. It worried him that the residents of the upper apartments could watch him from behind their drawn curtains, could look down and observe everything he did, every move he made. He hoped no one happened to be watching at the moment he exposed the skull to the light for the second time. He wiped his forehead and blinked the sweat from his eyes.

Keep going. Don't think about it. Don't think about anything.

The dull sound of metal on bone sent a shiver of horror through him. He wouldn't have believed it possible, but the hairs on the back of his neck actually stood on end.

As if his mind and body were no longer connected, he deliberately scraped away the earth and soon uncovered more bones. *Ribs*, he thought. So his suspicions were right. There was more than just a skull buried in his garden. There had to be an entire body there. All at once, he found himself unexpectedly, icily calm.

He blinked again, but this time his eyes were dry. As he stood there, wondering what to do next, his gaze fell on something that sparkled unnaturally against the dark-brown dirt.

He reached for it mechanically, picked it up, wiped away the soil that caked it, and stared, bemused, at a round bit of polished crystal, about a centimeter in diameter.

Mrs. Colijn lived next door, on the second floor. She was a tall, deeply tanned woman with a shapeless body and lightly bent shoulders. Steel-gray hair cut straight just beneath her ears was held off her face by cheap plastic barrettes.

"Why are you so interested in the past?" she asked, her tone not especially friendly, when Nico explained that he was wondering about the street's former residents.

"I'm simply curious," he said. If she thought he was perhaps a bit eccentric, that was no concern of his.

"Well, fine, would you like a cup of tea? If you really want to dig up ancient history, it'll take a while."

"Please."

"I've got an old photo album here somewhere," she said, searching through a row of aging volumes on the bottom shelf of an oak bookcase, "full of pictures of my family—and I think some of the neighbors."

He sat in a brown leather armchair and dutifully paged through the tattered black album she handed him.

When she came back with cups and saucers and a dish of chocolate squares broken from a candy bar on a tray, she peered with interest over his shoulder at the thick volume open on his lap.

"Ah, those are my in-laws. They were visiting us from Amsterdam." She tapped each of the four figures with a long, bony forefinger. "My father-in-law Ton, my mother-in-law Genevieve—she was French—my husband Claude, and that's me."

"Do you have pictures of the people who lived in *our* house?" he asked, cautiously insistent.

"Oh, I'm sure they're in there somewhere. We were all one big family in those days. Today, people keep more to themselves. It was different then, we all cared about each other in the neighborhood." She made a face, as if she wasn't quite sure that the Good Old Days were any better than the present.

Nico tapped the very edge of the frame, where a man with his hands in his trouser pockets was just visible. "Who's that?"

She unfolded a pair of spectacles from their case and bent over the image to study it. "Oh, he shouldn't even be in this picture. That's our neighbor. Wim Boersma. He and his daughter lived in your apartment."

She folded away her glasses and offered him the dish of chocolate squares. He politely took one. "So, are you two enjoying it here? You moved from a smaller flat, didn't you? Your wife told me how much she loves sitting out on your new terrace. It's looking lovely, Mr. Schuurman—it must be such a lot of work?"

"It is. But please, call me Nico."

"Nico, then. And I'm Penny." A smile flickered across her pale lips.

"It's more work than I expected, ah, Penny."

"Sugar? Milk?" She poured a splash of milk in her own tea and dropped a sugar cube into his. "My goodness, that Wim Boersma and his daughter didn't live here very long. When the girl married and moved away, her father went with her."

"And of course someone else lived there before them?"

"Yes, of course. A family with two sons and two daughters—and before them a family with six girls. Catholics, they were, from Brabant."

"One second." He raised a hand, and, surprised to be interrupted, she fell silent. "What was the name of the people between the Brabanters and the Boersmas? And when was it they lived there?"

"Gracious, why do you ask, Nico?"

"I told you, I'm curious."

She gazed at him so intently that he had the idea she was waiting for something else.

"Um, Penny, was there ever any sort of, well, *criminal* activity here in the neighborhood?"

To his surprise, her face lit up in a grin. "What do you think? We were all lower-class people. The families were large, and the menfolk were often unemployed. How were they supposed to feed their wives and children?"

"Petty thefts, you mean?"

"Yes, of course. You're not suggesting there were *major* crimes committed here, are you?"

"No," he said with a sigh, and he thanked her politely for the tea and the candy and the information.

.   .   .

He had the foolish idea that Emma might have changed her mind, that she hadn't boarded the cruise ship, after all, that she'd had her luggage offloaded and taken the bus back home. Only when the bell continued to ring did he realize that it couldn't be Emma at the door. She had her key with her, in case he was out when she returned.

He shuffled to the foyer, in his hand the teabag he'd just fished out of the box. The aroma from the toaster followed him, until he swung open the door and the fresh air from outside dispelled it.

"Mrs. Colijn!" He stared at her, and suddenly felt embarrassed to be standing there in his striped gray pajamas and bathrobe. Emma's absence had left him grouchy, and a distant memory of his youth had led him to the rebellious decision to make himself a cup of tea before he showered and dressed.

"What can I do for you, Mrs.—ah, Penny?"

She shook her head tightly and stepped across the threshold, forcing him to take a step back. Whatever the reason for her early appearance, it must be something serious. He told her that he was just making tea.

"Fine, then let's go to the kitchen," she said, her voice barely recognizable from their previous conversation.

"The kettle's on," he said, confused, wishing Emma were there, so that she could take over while he dashed upstairs to dress. He felt somehow at a disadvantage with his feet so white in scuffed old slippers.

The old woman strode into the kitchen but didn't sit at the little table. She tried the knob of the back door and, when she found it unlocked, turned the key.

"Mrs. Colijn?" For some reason, he found it hard to remember to call her Penny.

She calmly pointed to a chair. "Sit down, Nico."

It was on the tip of his tongue to protest that that was Emma's chair, but she stood blocking him from his own.

"Your wife isn't here," she said, leaning back against the sideboard, the words a statement, not a question.

"Yes, she left yesterday. She went on a cruise with a girlfriend."

The old woman nodded. "She told me she's always dreamed of being able to afford a cruise."

All at once he found himself hoping Emma's dream wouldn't come to as gruesome an ending as his own had.

"Cruises are quite expensive," his neighbor continued.

"Yes." He gestured towards the kettle as it reached the boil and made as if to get to his feet. "Are you sure you won't have a cup of tea, Mrs. Colijn—ah, Penny?"

"Shut up and answer my questions," she snarled.

He was so taken aback by the violence in her voice that he remained half-standing for several seconds. "What's the matter? Is something wrong? Is there something I can help you with?"

She didn't answer. "Your wife told me you had a bit of good luck, and that's why you could suddenly afford to send her off on a cruise."

He glanced at the teabag he still held in his hand and told her the same story he'd told Emma. "I won a nice little jackpot in the lottery."

She barked out a harsh laugh. "You expect me to believe that?"

He wanted to say that *Emma* had believed it, that Lies—who was always suspicious of him—had believed it, but something in the woman's hard stare told him that the words would fall on deaf ears. The Penny Colijn he had visited, who had offered him tea and chocolate and information about the neighborhood, suddenly seemed to have morphed into an entirely different person.

"You found them," she announced, without preamble.

"Found what?"

"The diamonds. You found them, you must have."

He knew immediately that there was no point in denying it. She must have been watching as he'd combed through the dirt, crumbling away the concealing clumps of earth with endless patience to reveal the glittering gemstones within.

"It's the only way you could possibly have afforded to pay for that cruise." Her steely gaze grew even harder. "Where were they, Nico? I searched for them for so long. I must have gone through the entire house twenty times."

"Which house?"

Then she understood. Her eyes widened, and a screeching sound that chilled him to the marrow burst out of her. "You didn't find them in the garden?"

"Ah, well, yes, I did." He was so mystified that it never occurred to him to ask how she knew all this.

She pointed through the little window in the kitchen door, half covered by a thin curtain. "Where exactly?"

He couldn't see any reason to lie about it. "In the last flower bed, the one I'm still working on."

"You mean he had them with him, all this time?" She examined him closely and then broke out in hysterical laughter. "Were they in a leather pouch?"

"No." He played absently with the corners of the teabag until the paper tore and the fine tea leaves drifted onto the tablecloth. "They must have been in his stomach."

He should have been surprised by this sudden clear insight, but her reaction gave him the chills. She laughed, loud and humorless, a high-pitched sound, and because he had never heard her laugh before, he didn't realize at first that her hysteria bordered on insanity.

"He *swallowed* them!" she cried. "The bastard! He cheated me!"

"I have no idea what you're talking about."

Her grin was broad and fanatic. He could see in her eyes that her thoughts had traveled back to a long-ago time.

"We were the Bonnie and Clyde of Holland," she said softly. "I can't remember which of us noticed the similarity of names—Penny and Claude, Bonnie and Clyde—but that's what gave us the idea in the first place. We had wings, my Claude and me. Post offices, betting parlors, jewelry stores, banks. Every caper we pulled, we got away with it. We had such incredible luck!"

It dizzied him. The idea that this old woman could have robbed banks, robbed jewelry stores, took his breath away.

"It all changed when that Boersma girl moved in next door," she went on. "Claude fell for her. And she saw it and played up to him, flirted with him every chance she got. He said—"

Nico reached into his memory for the name. "Jolanda Boersma?"

She ignored the interruption, lost in her story. "He didn't care about me anymore. The only thing I was good for was to help him with the robberies. And then he said we had to quit. Enough was enough. We'd been lucky to get away with it for so long, but our luck couldn't last forever, and he didn't want to wait for the tide to turn against us."

"Well, he might have been right about that."

"He wanted to get rid of me, that was the point. He wanted to go away with *her*. He wanted a divorce." Her voice was toneless, her gaze fixed somewhere above his head. "After everything we'd been through together, he wanted to trade me in for that worthless slut."

Without warning, she slid open a drawer and pulled out a

long, razor-sharp kitchen knife. "Then, finally, after we'd knocked over one particular jewelry store, Claude told me that was the last time." She traced the edge of the blade lightly with her thumb. "So I got a knife—just like this one—and I stuck him."

His heart stood still. "You stabbed him? To death? Your own husband?"

Her face was a crazed mask. "Of course. I couldn't let him leave me for her, could I? If I couldn't have him, *she* certainly couldn't! I rolled him up in an old sheet and dragged him down to the shed. Don't ask me how I did it—he was bigger than me, heavier—but I managed. I waited days, until the Boersmas were away for the weekend, and then I buried him in the garden, in *her* garden."

"How did you do that without anyone noticing?" he demanded, with a mixture of disbelief and respect.

She shrugged. "It was raining, a moonless night. Who was looking out their windows? No one. And the rain washed away any traces I might have left."

"But you never found the diamonds," he said.

She seemed completely lost in her thoughts. "I never even imagined he might have swallowed them," she defended herself.

Nico shifted position in his chair, wondering what would happen if he stood up. Just as he resolved to try it, she raised her head, suddenly back in the present moment.

"How many did you find?"

"Twenty-four."

She gasped. "It couldn't have taken all of them to pay for that cruise?"

He hesitated and, thinking feverishly, realized that the only way to convince her would be by answering quickly.

"Yes," he said, "it did."

She waved the knife back and forth, mere centimeters from his face. "I don't believe you. You wouldn't have thrown them away foolishly like that. You're not that stupid. You've still got most of them squirreled away somewhere. Where are they?"

He stared at the knife, trying to convince himself that she couldn't hurt him. She had to be seventy years old or more, at least ten years older than him. On the other hand, she was a head taller than he was, and a tremor of anxiety ran through him as he remembered that she'd locked the kitchen door.

The point of the knife was dangerously close. "I want them back, Nico. They're mine."

"They were *never* yours," he said, with more spirit than he would have thought he could muster. "You stole them. And I found them, so now they're mine."

She drew even closer, the knife blade almost touching his throat.

"When's your pretty little wife coming back? Not for ten days, I think? That should give me plenty of time to find them."

Emma had undoubtedly told her about the cruise. About the windfall he'd gotten from the lottery, his offer to send her off on holiday, how he'd said he wasn't interested in going himself but they could now afford to pay for her friend to accompany her. She might as well have come right out and told Mrs. Colijn exactly what he'd found....

"I'm sorry Emma's in for such a nasty shock when she gets home," the old woman muttered, half to herself, "but you don't leave me any choice, Nico."

She came closer, the knife glittering in her hand. He sat paralyzed on Emma's chair, held prisoner between the wall, the table, and the side of the hutch that was filled with their crystal glasses and good china. He began to talk, to argue, to beg, desperately trying to reason with her. And at the moment that he finally felt the knife's point press relentlessly into his flesh, he understood that she would commit a second murder without the slightest hesitation.

Emma looked wonderful. Her face was lightly bronzed, her eyes sparkled, and she admitted that she'd allowed the hairdresser aboard ship to tempt her into a modern cut and a color rinse that took years off her age. He quickly dismissed the suspicion that she'd met someone, another man. Emma wasn't that sort of woman —although he knew now how easy it was to be mistaken about someone's character.

"I'm so happy you finished the garden, Nic," she said cheerfully, setting a tray laden with tea things on the patio table. "I was really starting to worry when you just *refused* to plant that one last bed."

He took a seat and dropped a sugar cube in his cup. He gestured towards the bed where, not a week earlier, he had planted the rosebushes which would soon unfold their first blossoms. "You like it, Em? The roses? They'll be red, you know, blood-red, just what you wanted." He stirred his tea.

"I love it!" She opened the cookie tin and held it out to him. "Did you see Mrs. Colijn at all while I was gone? I brought a little something back for her. She's such a dear old soul."

Nico nibbled at a cookie. The thin layer of chocolate that coated one side of it melted beneath the warmth of his fingertips. "Not that I remember, no," he said, his mouth full.

"I rang her bell this morning, a couple of times," she said, a slight frown creasing her forehead. "Her downstairs neighbor told me he's beginning to worry about her. He hasn't seen her in a week or more."

Nico pulled a handkerchief from his back pocket and calmly wiped the melted chocolate from his fingers.

Then he gazed proudly out across his garden, his long-cherished dream, and with a little laugh he said, "I wouldn't worry too much about her, honey. Remember, a bad Penny always turns up, sooner or later. I'm sure she's around here somewhere."

THE NIGHT WATCH
BY MARLEN VISSER

I hate hospitals. Have done, ever since I was a kid. I was only five when my mother left me alone in a little white room, stretched out on a bed with curtains draped around it on three sides. A nurse eased her out to the visitor's lounge, murmuring, "It's going to be just fine, ma'am. The doctor takes out dozens of tonsils a week." I didn't understand the tear I saw trickle down mom's cheek. I was just going to have a little sleep, and then I'd get a present. Right?

Except something went wrong, and I woke up half choking on my own blood. I was flipped roughly onto my side and felt a thousand needles puncturing my throat. I tried to cry out for mama but couldn't make a sound.

"Lie still, young man," grumbled a stranger in a white jacket. "You're just making it worse." All I can remember is his thick black eyebrows.

Later, I turned down the melting popsicle they offered me and rejected the stuffed bear my mother brought that afternoon.

By then, my hatred of hospitals had taken root.

. . .

"Arjan, can I talk with you for a minute?" Lieke's blue eyes are wide, and her voice trembles.

She knows. She must have gotten my text. It's an hour before midnight, and I'm alone in my little office. My kingdom. The place from which I keep an eye on everything that goes on at the St. Antonius ZH in Woerden.

I don't say a word. I let her stew in uncertainty and just look at her. Oddly enough, it feels good.

I managed to avoid hospitals for years. I'm the kind of guy who never goes to the doctor. I always bought myself out of visiting sick friends by having flowers delivered to their bedsides. But then my mother had a heart attack and wound up in intensive care, so I no longer had a choice. When my parents divorced, I'd moved back in with mom. I mean, we were both alone, and we got along just fine. But living together meant obligations, and this time I knew I'd have to deliver the flowers myself. Plus an overnight bag with her pajamas and slippers. I knew which pjs were her favorites: the flannel ones that felt so soft when I snuggled with her. They can say what they like, but I was a good son.

I passed through the sliding doors of the imposing building and immediately felt nauseous. The smell! I have a very good memory, and the long-ago panic from that disaster with my tonsils once again took my breath away.

I only had to follow the signs to intensive care twice. The second time, mom's bed was empty. I'll never forget the looks of pity the nurses gave me, and with tears in my eyes I swore I would never set foot in a hospital again.

. . .

But now I *work* in one! Completely against my will, by the way. When, shortly after mom's death, I lost my job at the gas station, the last stable part of my life was knocked out from under me. I lay in bed for days, and no one missed me. Invisibility, I figured, had become my fate.

There came a time, though, when the unemployment office required me to retrain for a new occupation. There were lots of jobs in private security, and within half a year I'd finished the basic classes and got offered a night-watchman gig at Woerden's Antonius Hospital.

"Arjan, come on, I don't have a lot of time. Will you please listen to me?"

I swivel a full three hundred and sixty degrees in my desk chair and lean back, my hands clasped behind my neck, my feet on the rim of my trash basket.

She looks uncomfortable, but I don't invite her to sit. "Fine," I say.

She casts a nervous look down the empty corridor, steps into my little office, and swings the door shut behind her.

It took me weeks to disassociate from the oppressive hospital smell. I was fine in my office. But when I had to make my rounds, or when I spotted something off on one of the monitors and had to check it out, my breathing was ragged. Mostly I just sent my buddy. Until half a year ago, there were two of us on the night watch, but then the administration decided to cut costs and have us work alone on alternate nights. I'm happy about it now. I like being alone. I turn a switch inside my head, and the stink of disinfectant doesn't bother me anymore. I've become stronger.

· · ·

"It's not what you think," she says, leaning against the wall.

I remain silent.

"And we didn't plan on it happening."

Yeah, sure, of course not.

"Dr. Zacheo's been having some problems in his... personal life, and he took me into his confidence."

Oh, yes, I saw that on the screen.

"I'm not supposed to tell anyone, but the thing is, his marriage isn't working out. He's glad to have someone to talk with."

"That's what shrinks are for," I hear myself say. Me, who doesn't believe in all that psychology stuff.

"He can't. He knows them all. And doctors never make good patients, anyway."

But he's certainly lured you into his clutches.

"Arjan, you and I have always gotten on well together. Why did you send me that text? You could have just pretended you didn't see anything."

Her voice is softer now. Her posture, too. She leans toward me and gazes at me with those big blue Bambi eyes. She thinks she can talk me out of it.

The first time I saw Lieke, I could tell at once that she was different. She had a sparkle to her. Most of the nurses in training keep me at a distance. They're ambitious and eager to learn, and they hang on the doctors' every word. They're here with one goal in mind: to climb as quickly as possible up the medical ladder. So a night watchman doesn't have anything to offer them.

But Lieke was different. On her very first night shift, she leaned in my office door and said hello. Her smile hit me deep inside, right in the gut. With a voice like velvet, she asked me where to find Station 3H. I started sweating but managed to keep my expression calm. A security guard has to know his place. So I told her where to go and how to get there, and she thanked me with a thumbs up. Tough, but at the same time a little seductive. When she walked away, I couldn't keep my eyes off her hips, which swayed slightly beneath her tight white jacket.

"You're right, Lieke, we've always gotten on just fine."

Her eyes light up. She thinks she holds a winning hand. It's time for me to take charge of the situation.

"I thought we had something special," I say. "And I was happy to give it time. I didn't want to push too hard."

I read that phrase somewhere, *don't push too hard*, and after that first time we met, I decided it applied to Lieke and me. I used to come on too strong with girls, and that never once worked out. This time, I'd play it cool.

"Arjan." She blinks rapidly, and her voice becomes unsteady. "I think there's been some misunderstanding."

Oh, yes, it was a giant misunderstanding when she let herself be tempted by Dr. Zacheo. And in the linen closet, no less! My stomach turns, and I try to forget the sick images I saw on my monitor, but I can't. Those same thick black eyebrows I remembered so vividly, only this time no white jacket. It must have been lying on the floor, out of camera range.

It happened exactly a week ago. I'd made a habit of keeping an eye on Lieke, my girl, my everything. I knew when she was on the night shift. She always arrived at a quarter to eleven and always stopped by my office to say hi. We chatted about the events of the day, the news, the weather. Comfortable, the way you'd talk with your girlfriend after a day's work. At least that's what I thought.

That last time, she even brought me something. Beaming, she gave me a nut bread she'd baked herself, wrapped in aluminum foil. That's when I knew for sure: she wanted to make me happy. It was so sweet! And I knew what it meant: first you feed the object of your desire, and then you move on to the next stage of your conquest. I've seen it a million times on National Geographic.

Until he ruined everything.

The dirty bastard.

I followed Lieke every day on my ten little surveillance-camera screens. The images weren't top quality, yet my heart throbbed every time she crossed one of those grainy monitors. And not just my heart. The idea that I could secretly track her movements around the hospital was more exciting than any R-rated movie.

It was just a question of time.

"I like you, Arjan, I really do—but as a *colleague*, that's all." She's standing straight, her back pressed against the door. I look at her, and something strange happens inside my head. I can see her bright blue eyes, but I'm not drowning in them like I usually do. Something unsettling begins to brew in the pit of my stomach.

"Maybe... maybe we can make a deal, Arjan, you and me. You don't tell anyone what you saw, and I'll give you something. What do you want? Money?"

A shiver runs up my spine. She wants to make a *deal*? She thinks she can *buy me off*? After all the pain she's caused me? With the same man, by the way, who caused me so much pain when I was a kid?

"What do I want?" I repeat. I wasn't counting on anything like this. I have to think clearly, rely on the sober watchman inside me.

"Well?" She's recovered her confidence and nods encouragingly.

I spin my chair slowly toward her and study her from head to toe. "I have an idea," I say.

When I saw it happen—that horrible, unmentionable thing, in that closet full of bed linens—I was so shocked that I told my supervisor I was sick and went home. Stayed there for three days. After that, I knew what I had to do. I'd saved the video file to a thumb drive, which put me in control. I could protect Lieke from further mistakes.

On Day Four, I was back in my office, and I looked her number up on my computer. My text might have been a little heavy handed, but it was in service of a higher purpose. I couldn't let her slip out of my life, only to be mistreated by that hog of a doctor.

"Well, what?" she asks. Am I imagining it, or do I see a glimmer of relief wash across her face? If so, it's premature.

"I want to kiss you."

"You—what?"

"Just a kiss, Lieke, that's all. You asked me what I want, and that's it. If you kiss me, I won't tell. I don't want your money."

There's a strange grimace on her face, and I see her hesitate. She's trying to decide how much her career and Dr. Zacheo's are worth.

An old American song from the radio echoes inside my head: "One way or another, I'm gonna gitcha, gonna gitcha gitcha gitcha...."

I feel like I don't know who I *am* anymore.

She sighs. "All right, fine. When?"

"Now," I say, and I drop the blinds that cover my office

windows. She jumps at the sound, but before she can resist, I grab her by the neck, pull her head right up to mine, and press her lips apart with my tongue. She mumbles a protest, but I'm only getting started. My tongue probes deep inside her mouth and tries to capture hers. It's as if she's playing hide and seek with me. I pull her body close with my other hand, so her firm breasts press against my chest. It's horrible, and delicious, and I wish it would never end.

And then my cell phone rings. The interruption distracts me, and Lieke wrenches free of my hands. She stares at me, her big eyes welling with tears. Her hair is a mess, and her lips are bright red, though I'm positive she isn't wearing any lipstick.

"That's it, then," she says hoarsely. "This is over. I've paid my debt, and now you have to keep your promise."

I swipe away the incoming call and sit there in silence.

As she turns away and opens the door, I see a tear trickle from the corner of her eye. Without turning back, she hurries down the corridor, and her buttocks move rhythmically with her quick steps. I can't tear my gaze away from that.

"Oh, this isn't *nearly* over," I whisper. "It's just beginning."

I swivel back to my computer, open the personnel directory, and scroll down to the Z's.

ABOUT THE CONTRIBUTORS

RENÉ APPEL is the author of twenty-seven crime novels, two of which have won the Golden Noose, the annual award for the best Dutch-language crime novel of the year. He's also written more than thirty short stories, several of which have been published in English in *Ellery Queen's Mystery Magazine* and *Alfred Hitchcock's Mystery Magazine.* In 2023, Genius Book Publishing released an English translation of his novel *The Amsterdam Lawyer. amboanthos.nl/auteur/rene-appel*

MICHAEL BERG spent almost twenty-five years producing programming for Dutch Public Radio. He emigrated to France in 2004 to write crime fiction and debuted in 2008 with *Twee Zomers,* followed by nine more novels, including *Nacht in Parijs,* which won the Golden Noose in 2013. *Hôtel du Lac, Het Meisje op de Weg,* and *Broertje* were all included on the short lists for various awards, and more than half a million copies of his books have been sold. He moved back to The Netherlands in 2017 and

Terugkeer, the first volume of his *Mergellandmoorden* trilogy, was published in 2025.

DOMINIQUE BIEBAU is a Flemish author of literary crime fiction, short stories, and poetry. His four crime novels have been lavishly praised by readers and critics in Flanders and The Netherlands. His second novel, *Russisch voor Beginners* (*Russian for Beginners*), won both the Hercule Poirot Prize and the Golden Noose, the top awards for Dutch-language crime fiction.

WOUTER BOONSTRA spent fourteen years as a freelance journalist and since 2018 has served as an editor at *Binnenlands Bestuur*, the Dutch trade journal for civil servants and administrators. He's also written and recited poetry for various occasions in Amsterdam and Groningen. *wouterboonstra.nl*

THEO CAPEL is a child psychologist who began reviewing crime fiction in the 1970s and writing it himself in the '80s. His series character, Hank Stammer, runs a one-man debt-collection agency and first appeared in *Weggegooid Geld* (1981). *talesforasmile.substack.com*

HERBERT DE PAEPE is a journalist and fiction writer who lives and works in Ghent, Belgium. Between 2010 and 2019, he collaborated with Els Depuydt on five crime novels, and since then he's written two more solo. His short stories have appeared in EQMM and *In Tenebris,* a Belgian fantasy-fiction magazine. He is currently working on his eighth novel.

BRAM DEHOUCK was the first author to win the Golden Noose and the Shadow Prize—the two most important awards for Dutch-language crime fiction—for the same novel, *De Minzame*

Moordenaar (2009). *Een Zomer Zonder Slaap* (2011) made him only the second Flemish author to win a second Golden Noose; it also won the Hercule Poirot Public Prize and was nominated for *Crimezone*'s Best Thriller award.

LOES DEN HOLLANDER has been writing since the age of eight, originally poetry but later columns, short stories, and eventually crime novels. Since November 2006, she has published thirty psychological thrillers, three collections of short stories, one mainstream novel, a nonfiction book, and three novellas. In 2022, she received the MAX Gouden Vleermuis for Lifetime Achievement.

ELS DEPUYDT lives and writes in Ghent, Belgium. As half of the author duo De Paepe & Depuydt, she collaborated on five crime novels with Herbert De Paepe, each set on a different continent, and contributed two stories to EQMM, including "Garage 27." Her solo psychological novel *Mia* was published in 2017, followed in 2024 by *Alles Voor de Kunst*, a thriller. *elsdepuydt.com*

BAVO DHOOGE is the author of more than a hundred and twenty books. One of the most widely acclaimed crime writers in Belgium, he has won all the major prizes for crime fiction. His fantasy thriller *Styx* (which was published in English in 2015) was made into a miniseries for Netflix Belgium in 2024. *bavodhooge.com*

INGRID OONINCX writes psychological thrillers featuring realistic characters, surprising plots, and lots of action. She debuted in 2010 with *Nickname* and since then has added six more novels and numerous short stories. She's a member of De Moordwijven, a group of five well-known female Dutch crime writers who work on individual projects but also collaborate, most recently on the anthology *The Cocktail Party*. She lives with her family in Tilburg. *ingridooninxcx.nl*

CHRISTINE OTTEN is a Dutch writer, journalist, and performer. Her novel *De Laatste Dichters* was translated into English as *The Last Poets* and has also been adapted for the stage and translated into Arabic. Her 2020 novel *Een Van Ons* was based on her experiences as a writing coach in a Dutch prison, and her stage play *Gevangenis Monologen* is based on the lives of ex-convicts. She is the founder of *Stichting Blocknotes*, a nonprofit that empowers incarcerated people in the development of their creative-writing ability. *christineotten.nl*

MARION PAUW is a best-selling Dutch author and a two-time winner of the Golden Noose (in 2009 for *Daglicht* and 2022 for *Vogeleiland*). She is fascinated by the psychology of crime and the impact of trauma on its victims. She currently divides her time between Amsterdam and the south of Spain and between writing and hiking in the mountains.

NICOLET STEEMERS writes novels, short stories, and plays. Two of her novels have appeared in English as Storytel Original audiobooks: *Ellen Holms, Private Detective* (2023) and *The Club of the Klutzes* (2024). *nicoletsteemers.nl*

GERT-JAN VAN DEN BEMD is a Dutch writer and artist. He holds a PhD in endocrinology from Erasmus University Rotterdam and a bachelor's degree in art from Sint Joost Art School in Breda/'s-Hertogenbosch. His most recent novel, *Lex*, was one of fifteen semifinalists for the Hebban Thrillerprijs 2025, sponsored by Hebban, the most popular online platform for Dutch book lovers. *grandfoulard.com*

MARJOLEIN VAN DER GAAG won the Silver Noose for the best Dutch-language short crime story of the year in 2022; it was published the following year in EQMM and is reprinted in this volume. In 2024, her novel *Verlaat de Gevangenis Zonder Betalen* and her novella *5 voor 12* were published in The Netherlands, and *Verlaat de Gevangenis Zonder Betalen* was subsequently named one of the five finalists for the Hebban Thrillerprijs 2025. She also writes children's books. *marjoleinvandergaag.nl*

HILDE VANDERMEEREN has written more than fifty books for adults and children. Her work has been translated into several languages and won several awards. Two of her short stories have appeared in EQMM; in 2017, "The Lighthouse" was a Derringer finalist. In 2023-24, she collaborated on the scripts for the Belgian television series *Juliet*. *hildevandermeeren.com*

ANNE VAN DOORN debuted in 2004 as "M.P.O. Books" with a series of police procedurals. As "Anne van Doorn," he writes contemporary mysteries inspired by classic crime fiction from the genre's Golden Age. Two of his short stories have been published in EQMM. He is currently looking for an agent to represent his first English-language novel, *The Delft Blue Mystery*, a procedural set in New York, and working on a sequel, *The Jigsaw Puzzle Mystery*.

MENSJE VAN KEULEN debuted with the novel *Bleekers Zomer*, now considered a classic of Dutch literature. Since its publication in 1972, she has written novels, short stories, poetry, journals, and books for children. Her work often appears on long- and shortlists for literary awards, and she has won the Annie Romein, Charlotte Köhler, Constantijn Huygens, and J.M.A. Biesheuvel prizes. *mensjevankeulen.nl*

BOB VAN LAERHOVEN is a Flemish author whose work exists on the borderline between mainstream literature and the mystery/suspense genre. He has published more than fifty books and has been translated into a dozen languages, including Amharic. His English titles include the award-winning *Baudelaire's Revenge*, *Return to Hiroshima*, *Alejandro's Lie*, *The Shadow of the Mole*, and *Scars of the Heart*. *bobvanlaerhoven.be/en*

CARLA VERMAAT is an accomplished author and painter. Born in The Netherlands, she later moved to Cornwall in England, then to Vancouver in Canada, and has now returned to her native country. She writes her award-winning Tregunna Cornish Crime Novel series in English and her Barbara, Politievrouw series in Dutch. *carlavermaat.com*

MARLEN VISSER is the author of *Stem!* (nominated for the best first Dutch-language crime novel of 2015), *Meesterdeal*, *Noodlot* (nominated for the Best Thriller Hebban Prize in 2021), *Latte Macchiato* (a Storytel Original), *Verraderlijk Patroon* (a suspenseful YA novella), and *Kat in de Stad* (a feel-good book told from the first-"person" perspective of a cat). *marlenvisser.com*

A NOTE ON COPYRIGHT

These stories were all originally published in Dutch, and the Dutch versions are copyrighted by their authors. All were translated into English by Josh Pachter, who holds the copyright to the English translations, which were first published as indicated below and are reprinted here with the permission of both their original authors and the translator.

"After the Fall" by Bram Dehouck is copyright © 2015 and was originally published in English in the February 2015 issue of *Ellery Queen's Mystery Magazine*.

"Anchored" by Wouter Boonstra is copyright © 2020 and was originally published in English in the September/October 2020 issue of *Alfred Hitchcock's Mystery Magazine*.

"Beneath the Surface" by Marjolein van der Gaag is copyright © 2023 and was originally published in English in the March/April 2023 issue of *Ellery Queen's Mystery Magazine*.

"Checkmate in Chimbote" by Bob Van Laerhoven is copyright © 2014 and was originally published in English in the June 2014 issue of *Ellery Queen's Mystery Magazine*.

September/October 2019 issue of *Ellery Queen's Mystery Magazine*.

"Promises to Keep" by Gert-Jan van den Bemd is copyright © 2024 and was originally published in English in *Black Cat Mystery Magazine* #15 (August 2024).

"The Red Mercedes" by Theo Capel is copyright © 2004 and was originally published in English in the June 2004 issue of *Ellery Queen's Mystery Magazine*.

"Soul Mates" by Christine Otten is copyright © 2019 and was originally published in English in *Amsterdam Noir* (Akashic Books).

"Stinking Plaster" by Bavo Dhooge is copyright © 2011 and was originally published in English in the September/October 2011 issue of *Ellery Queen's Mystery Magazine*.

"The Stranger Inside Me" by Loes den Hollander is copyright © 2019 and was originally published in English in *Amsterdam Noir* (Akashic Books).

"What's Become of the Baby" by Dominique Biebau is copyright © 2024 and was originally published in English in *Friend of the Devil: Crime Fiction Inspired by the Songs of the Grateful Dead* (Down and Out Books).